Fiction

CW00738777

THE LOVE OF IMPOSSIBLE SUMS

Panayotis Cacoyannis

Copyright

Cover Design by Keith Voles

Acknowledgments

With thanks to Kate R and Cornerstones Literary
Consultancy for their tough but brilliant editing advice, to
Keith Voles for the excellent website and graphic design,
and most of all for another exceptional cover, and to
Michael Duerden for his limitless patience and unfailing
technical wizardry.

For All Who Are Now Absent
And For All Who Remain...

One for Sorrow

One for sorrow,
Two for joy,
Three for a girl,
Four for a boy,
Five for difference,
Six for gold,
Seven for a secret never to be told,
Eight for a wish,
Nine for a kiss
Ten a surprise you should be careful not to miss.

(Variation on a Nursery Rhyme)

ONE

Eden, my Eden. I feel your presence everywhere. It fills every absence, every vacant space, eating up a part of me, taking possession.

I am never entirely alone; I am never entirely myself; more than ever I feel incomplete.

In any meaningful sense, do I even exist?

A thought has just occurred to me: a part of me has now become your afterlife. It fails to give me comfort.

The elevator makes a funny noise as it rattles to a stop. The metal door towards the exit slides open. A mass of heavy coats slithers through – a single solid body almost uniformly black. It's as if a freezing nation is in mourning.

A shuffle of feet, invisible in the congestion: from a cauldron of damp, steamy breaths, bodies are expelled like a fart. At the barriers plastic tickets touch out, flaps swinging open, then shut.

A man into his phone: *Is it really any wonder?*

The blackness now less black in the sunshine. Dispersed, disunited. "One" broken into several, each another "one".

One plus one now equals less than one, the opposite of then. Then with you, now without you. The embodiment of paradox: now with you again, the addition results in subtraction. Every day a lessening, a step to annihilation, until the sum of one plus one becomes a vanishing.

I crave for aloneness. I crave for the end.

Forgive me,

Forgive me,

Forgive me.

"Less than one" among many as I break from the crowd, I have exited Russell Square Underground station on a cold Friday morning in early December just a few spare minutes before noon, in time for a coffee with Patrick and Claw, then poetry at 12.30. Stunned by the brightness of daylight, so acute it has crisply made the vista of architecture clench its teeth for fear its every contour might crack, I breathe the cold air out in a sigh, and momentarily the mist from my breath conjures the illusion of a smudge. As though that indistinctness is a general need, scattered men and women puff away at cigarettes to produce thicker clouds, while the sucking mouths of others, glued around industrial-sized vaping contraptions, are pumping out a more enduring mist that makes the imposter smokers look almost ethereal.

The intensity of the sun makes me squint, but my pale eyes have watered already, and instinctively I rub them both at once with my knuckles, bloodless like my fingers in the cold. My mind, already crowded, finds space for two more thoughts: that I should have worn my sunglasses today, and that I cannot quite believe I am here, on my way to - of all the most preposterous things – They Them (I have taken the ticket out of my coat pocket and am looking at it in the shade of a canopied doorway), a Poetry Reading Event promising a "rare and unforgettable performance" by a poet "like no other", according to Claudia, who likes to be called Claw, written and pronounced like the pincer of a crab.

I ask myself: *Oliver, Oliver, why are you here?*

Because three nights ago, late, just before midnight, Claw literally caught me with my pants down. The phone was on the bedside table, and when I hopped to it and saw her name light up across the screen, I kicked my trousers off and I answered.

When I met Eden, just under nine years ago (five of heaven plus almost four of hell, including the months she was sick), when I was almost thirty-two and she had just turned thirty-three, Eden had been friends with Claw since school (although Claw was two years older) and Claw was married to Sigismund, who was already forty-one. But then Sigismund ran off with a boy half his age, and emerging like a phoenix from the sidelines, not as unexpectedly as in my ignorance I had imagined at the time, Patrick soon took his place.

Eden had met Patrick through work, and the rest of us had met him through Eden. Some years later I had found out from Eden, who had known all along, that while Sigismund was still married to Claw, he had also had a fling with Patrick.

'Sigismund? Had a fling with Patrick?'

'Yes,' Eden had confirmed with a nonchalant nod. 'But it didn't last long. And Patrick was also attracted to Claw, so when the fling was over and Sigismund had moved on to William, Patrick seized the moment and invited her to dinner. He told her about Sigismund, but she still said yes, and she's been saying yes ever since.'

'Jesus!' I had always been more easily fazed.

Except for Sigismund, whose childhood and early teenage years had been stolen by Grimsby (he spoke little of his family and with enunciated hatred of *Grim*sby), the rest of us had all been born and differently bred in North London. Claw's family were wealthy and traditional, Hampstead Tories of the old school, Eden's Camden firebrands of the left, mine just about managing near Euston and mostly indifferent, Patrick's struggling in Wood Green. All five of us had been to university, where only four of us had shone: I had scraped through my Media Degree with a Third.

'Claw might grate on you at first, she takes some getting used to,' Eden had forewarned me, 'but Sigismund is lovely - smart, funny, you'll like him straight away.'

And I had, eventually; and then I had become extremely fond of Patrick, who was smarter and funnier and much more down-to-earth - Sigismund's cerebral scholarship (he was some kind of historian) and childish self-absorption had occasionally got on my nerves.

Eden's friendship with Claw was so close it had withstood even Claw's second nature, and for all her flaws and frailties, Claw had been equally devoted to Eden; right up until the end, her support had been loving and constant. And for that my debt to her would always be enormous, and my affection for her too, in spite of her many shortcomings.

When I saw her name flash on the screen of my phone, I answered immediately. Do I regret that I hadn't switched my phone off when she called? Do I regret that I answered? Am I glad I agreed to today? Remembering my absurd conversation with Claw, I am certainly amazed that I did.

Why? Why had I indulged her? Because I wanted the distraction to last longer? Because secretly I wanted my plan to be thwarted, or at least put on hold?

A poet "like no other" says who?

Sigismund, said Claw. He saw the "rare and unforgettable performance" when it previewed for one night at the Brixton Palace Hall.

This came as a surprise.

'You and Sigismund are speaking again?'

Claw stuttered a reply that kept changing.

'N-no, definitely not... Well, only very rarely... He's called once or twice out of the blue.'

To talk about poetry?

Among other things.

'Oh,' I said. 'Among *other* things.'

Humouring her, teasing her, causing the interruption to last longer, while still holding on to my plan.

'Yes, Ollie, *other* things. Seven years is a very long time. When a marriage ends after such a length of time, there are always loose ends.'

'There are?'

Not so much for her, but apparently there were for Sigismund, she said. And most recently, one week ago to be precise, Sigismund had called her specifically to talk about "the unmissable" They Them and the upcoming Poetry Reading Event at the Cutting-Edge Arts Centre just off Russell Square. For which she had secured three tickets. One for Patrick, one for her...

'And one for you, of course.'

'I don't think so, Claw. I've never been to a poetry reading in my life. If I'm honest, poetry's not really my thing, it just goes over my head. All I hear is a jumble of words with no meaning. And They Them, what's that all about?'

'Oh, Ollie, you know how hard it was to get tickets? I had to suck up to that hideous little man who runs the National, Sir Charles something-or-other, old friend of Sigismund's from Oxford, they used to wank each other off every Wednesday afternoon in the Bodleian. "My dear," he said when I met him at his club, "what an utterly unpleasant surprise!" Honestly, Ollie, I felt like such a fool.'

Typical Claw. Over the top, always with a carnal anecdote at hand. I have always wondered if this might be a front, a coping mechanism of some sort, a curtain that hides something behind it. But something like what? I have yet to find a credible answer, and so I take her at face value: invariably as a competent professional, frequently as a clown with a big heart, and sometimes as a monster.

'All the more reason not to waste your spare ticket,' I said. 'There must be someone else you can ask, someone who actually enjoys poetry readings.'

'But I want you, not someone else, because this isn't just *any* poetry reading, it's the hottest show in town, and everyone who's anyone will be there.'

'Well, happily I'm no one, so I doubt I'll be missed.'

'You're hardly no one, and you'll be sorely missed by me. And Patrick won't go unless you're coming too, so I *need* you to come. Please, Ollie. Will you do this little favour for me, *please*?'

While I listened to Claudia's imploring, I surveyed the perfectly parallel lines of six different pills (a multicoloured mix of capsules and tablets) that were already beautifully arranged on the bedside table beside the unopened bottle of vodka (ironically a gift from Claw). The plan had been to first switch my phone off, and then to ingest all the pills, quickly washing them down with as much of the vodka as I could manage before passing out, hopefully never to wake up. If my calculations were correct, within an hour, or two at most, my heart would go into a tailspin and stop. I was not entirely clear what lasting damage might be caused to any or all of my organs if, by some fluke of misfortune, my heart proved superhuman and I happened to survive, but that was such a longshot that I was almost excited about taking the risk.

The array of poisonous pills had first made their appearance on my bedside table the previous weekend, and the delay in taking them had been intentional, an integral part of my plan. It goes against my nature to act impulsively, and being aware of the finality, and fatality, of the contemplated course of action, I had decided that a daily confrontation with the physical manifestation of its method, and a correspondent driving-home of its irrevocable consequence, would confirm it as my free and certain choice. And that night, when Claudia called, while undressing I had felt such a lightness of being, such intoxicating inner peace, that I had almost sleepwalked into taking that last step. But then my telephone had come alive, causing me to almost trip, and when I saw her name flash on the screen, a sudden desire to hear Claw's voice had impelled me to answer.

I had no fear of no longer being alive – all fear had ended with Eden - and death seemed preferable to a joyless life. It was a simple weighing-up of pros and cons, and at that point, I had not yet changed my mind: that night would be my last – the pros of a permanent absence were many and the cons rather scant. But then halfway through the call, Claw's ridiculous monologue (only she could weave together such deliciously exaggerated praise for possibly gender-political poetry with the sleaziest gossip regarding Sir Charles), had somehow filled me with a mist of last-minute second thoughts. It's possible the second thoughts had been there already, and I had answered Claw's call grateful at that moment for a pause that might save me from myself and from breaking my promise to Eden. Or perhaps my desire to hear Claw's voice was unconsciously a desire to be reminded of Eden one more time.

While I continued to be mesmerised by Claw's hypnotic voice (a low purring murmur whose pitch hardly varied, no matter how outraged or angry or horny she was), the tip of my right index finger made slow rearrangements to the six lines of pills, mixing up their colours and shapes. Anyone watching might have thought I was immersed in solving some intricate puzzle whose rules were known only to me.

'You must, you simply must,' Claudia went on in her pleasantly monotonous drone, only slightly deeper when her intention was to emphasise a word. 'Now say it, go on, *please* say you will. It's been far too long since the last time we met, and I *miss* you; shutting yourself off from the world is all very well, but I'm *not* the world, Ollie, and neither is Patrick, we're your friends, and not just your friends but your *best* friends.'

'My *only* friends,' I said, mimicking her dull intonation.

'I know, but I didn't like to say in case you thought I was being mean. And I know that it's always been your choice not to have many friends, but you've become even more anti-social, practically a hermit since… But anyway, best friends, only friends, what's important is we're friends, so is it too much to want to believe that we're as special to you as you've always been to us? To both of us, yes, but *especially* to me, as you and I know and Patrick must never find out.'

Ha! I gave out a muted chuckle while my finger lightly flicked random pills out of place. This was a strategy of hints that she often employed, but whereas once it had enraged me, I had now become so accustomed to it that I actually found it amusing. Too many years had passed, and so much had happened since the incident which Claw still insisted on occasionally alluding to, that by now it struck me as either a fiction or something I bore no connection to. In the darkness of my loss, it had become, like so much else, a distant and irrelevant footnote in a past that now consisted of nothing but Eden. But I also understood that what for me was an irrelevance was for Claw a lazy shortcut she would use to affirm to herself how special our friendship was, which was probably another expression of grief. As for any implicit threat, we both knew it was just for dramatic effect: were she ever to carry it through, Claw had nothing to gain and my friendship and Patrick to lose.

Still using my finger, I scraped out two eyes and a smile in what had now become an almost perfect circle, and the six disordered columns that had first become a heap were now a tidy smiley face. Swooping down on all the colourful, pick-and-mix pills that made it up, I snatched a whole handful, and still with the phone in my ear I brought the mound of poison to my nose. How easily the torpor of palliative care could be turned into permanent sleep; what I held in my hand was the gift of a weapon, lethal and smelling of coldness. I turned my hand sideways, then funnelling the pills through a loosely clenched fist I watched as they slipped through my fingers like fruit machine nuggets, a jackpot of kindness returning to the broken circle and erasing what remained of the smile.

The heating had come off and the room was becoming too cold. I had always liked the cold, and I lay on the bed, now naked apart from my T-shirt and socks and the warmth of the sound of Claw's voice, which my silences failed to discourage from pushing ever forward after each unanswered pause.

'Listen to me, Ollie. You'll rot if you don't get out of that house… If I'm honest, I'm surprised you're still able to live there at all… I mean, I know we're not supposed to talk about what happened to Eden, but this definitely isn't what Eden would've wanted, you being stubborn and refusing to live…'

Refusing to live. The irony of it, on the night I should have died but had now decided not to – not yet. And not because of Eden or what she might have wanted but because of a ridiculous phone call - from an equally ridiculous friend whom I couldn't help being fond of. Unthinking, tactless, self-centred, quite often unwittingly cruel, a larger-than-life nincompoop, Claw was somehow also the epitome of kindness. Did Dr Claudia Ellis, respected physician and happy wife of Patrick, still make a habit of one-off seductions, I wondered. I tried to recall how long ago exactly I myself had fallen prey to inevitably having sex with her just once.

'And not only that but you live there *alone*…'

Claw stopped herself abruptly; in the uneasy lull that followed and that neither of us broke, *of course* I remembered: *three years*, plus the time between a June and a December, since being shitty to Eden and Patrick, and shittier to myself. I had calculated backwards from the number, smaller and yet infinitely larger, that could only have inadequately measured the eternity since losing Eden: three years minus sixty-three days. That number had eclipsed every other, in the same way its first signpost on the same day in that June had eclipsed my betrayal.

The *when* had been easy to determine, and the *how* had been a chance hour alone, but the *why*? *Why* had I consented to a betrayal I had not remotely yearned for? *Consented* was perhaps a misnomer, and so was *seduced*. There had been no preamble, nor any moment that had signalled a conscious decision. Sex had just happened, and for me, but most probably also for Claw, it had been a mechanical action, an exchange without emotion or even the least expectation of pleasure. It had lasted for a length of time that in my consciousness had shrunk almost as soon as it had ended into a minuscule dot: a black hole at the centre of my being. Then, 'Good!' Eden had said, and time had again become light, not yet blighted by the impenetrable darkness lying in wait not far ahead.

Claw broke my brooding on the ungraspable notion of time with a gravelly gulp. 'I'm an idiot, Ollie, I'm sorry. Never know when to stop, always go too far.' She gulped again, even more loudly, and for a moment or two I heard muffled noises, which I knew not to interrupt, then Claw cleared her throat and resumed in her normal, unflappable voice: 'Trust me, it'll be fun. And you'll be spending some quality, meaningful time with good friends who miss you. Friends who care about you very much, who've *never* stopped caring.'

'I know, Claw, and I'm grateful.'

'Oh, Ollie.'

'And if it means so much to you, of course I'll come.'

They Them, the "rare and unforgettable performance" by a poet "like no other" was three days later, on Friday at half past twelve in the afternoon at the Cutting-Edge Arts Centre just off Russell Square. Sixty-three minus three was sixty, and on one of those sixty days, whose passing would inevitably measure the eternity at three years exactly, by some means or other I would cease to exist.

'Forgive me. Forgive me. Forgive me.' I spoke the words out loud, aware that my intention amounted to a second betrayal, a breach of all my promises to Eden.

And here I am.

Fogbound in the mist of my breath, warming my hands with its moisture.

Standing in a doorway like a smoker, while around me the scattering blackness, added to continually by streams of new arrivals, moves about in hurried jerks.

I imagine the scene from above: ants, mechanically acting out our existence, hunting, gathering, occasionally mating. Vaping fruity flavours, clinging on to life in clouds of steam. A recalcitrant few, poisoning themselves with tar and nicotine.

The man into his phone: *Is it really any wonder?*

Where are they going, all these people? What mysteries await them, what wonders, what catastrophes? A thousand worlds play out all at once, lives of circumstance, coincidence and luck, in each of them a thousand different stories, unconnected to each other but also bound together by a unity that makes each world alive.

And my world?

Broken by the addition, I have now become one minus two: a subtraction - in amongst the blackened silhouettes, a hollow displacement of matter.

I seek distraction everywhere, in the glow of the sun and the blue of the sky - in all immensities that mirror my smallness. Each day a small consolation. Soon, sooner…

In the periphery of my vision, a shadow, then a voice, interrupting:

'Excuse me, do you have a light?' A woman's voice, an abstraction that has taken solid form by removing itself from the crowd.

I use both hands to pat my pockets; sometimes I still carry a lighter, a habit from my days as a smoker.

You have to give up, Eden said. I took two more puffs and I did, that same day. My last cigarette, years ago now.

'Umm,' I say, and I look at the stranger. Black hair, black coat, black scarf, black jeans, black trainers. Under the coat, black jumper too, probably. Taking her in, I suddenly feel in the grip of the strangest sensation. 'Yes, I think I do. Somewhere.'

It occurs to me I wouldn't mind a cigarette; instantly the thought becomes a craving. But the reason is not nicotine; I know it has something to do with the stranger.

Seconds later I'm caressing the old Dunhill between forefinger and thumb as I extract it from my left trouser pocket. When I flick it open, it lights up with a strong reek of petrol, reminiscent of the past. The flame is feeble and blue.

'It's an old one,' says the stranger, bending to the flame as it trembles, then standing up straight to inhale.

'Mm, thank you.' A smile, happy: two equal and beautiful curves, now bending to blow out the smoke.

And suddenly a stranger's smile reminds me of Eden.

A pinch of the brows. 'Sorry,' says the stranger, 'would you like one?'

'Yes,' I say, 'why not.'

'You're not a smoker.'

'I am. I mean I was.'

A narrowed darted glance. 'Then don't. You shouldn't.'

'No, really, I'd love one.'

'Are you sure?'

I nod. I take one. Another flick of the Dunhill and a long inhalation – first an odd sensation, then a craving, now a cigarette.

Standing in a doorway, a smoker again. With a stranger and a tall narrow case. Black, wooden, on wheels. Three shapes in bizarre shadow theatre.

'Dead body,' says the stranger, and laughs.

I stare ahead, lost inside my head, where everything reminds me of Eden.

'In the case,' the stranger explains.

I nod again as our eyes meet. The sensation becomes even stronger, still alien but suddenly not unfamiliar. A warmth, almost forgotten.

'Not really,' says the stranger.

'I know.'

'Three people actually asked me. "Is that a dead body?" Two on the train and one in the street, just a minute ago. I said, "No, can't you see, I'm taking my dog for a walk." None of them laughed. You're not laughing either.'

'Sorry.' I want to say more but I can't find the words.

'Ah, but you're smiling.'

Am I?

'I'm Alex, by the way.'

'Oliver,' I say.

We shake hands. Neither of us wears gloves. The touch makes me shiver. The first touch since Eden.

An ashtray on the wall, shiny metal with holes. We stub our cigarettes out and slip the butts through.

'I should go now,' says Alex.

'Me too,' I say. 'Meeting a couple of friends for a coffee.'

'The dog and I are off to read some poetry,' says Alex, nodding at the case. 'Care to come? Bring your friends.'

I take the ticket back out of my pocket. 'Small world,' I say, holding it up.

The man into his phone: *Is it really any wonder?*

Yes, I want to say, still in thrall to the shiver and warmth.

'Ha!' says Alex with a shrug.

'I heard everyone who's anyone will be there,' I manage to say. 'Everyone who's anyone and me.'

'I'll save you three seats in the front. Not anyone plus two.'

I watch her walk away with the black wooden case. She looks back. She smiles and we both wave.

One plus two now equals what?

I made my confession to Eden on the night of the same day it had happened – the day I had let both of us down. I loved her in a way that had always precluded deceit, beyond even the fear I might lose her: loving in fear isn't love.

We were in the bedroom, and I was sitting fully clothed on the edge of the bed, watching her getting undressed. It was June, around the middle of the month, and she was dressed very lightly, in a see-through summer blouse over a short denim skirt.

Words without descriptions came out in knotted sentences she didn't interrupt, and I knew they had been spoken but had only vaguely heard them.

'Good!'

In my despair I had expected a different reaction.

I blinked, keeping my eyes shut for more than a second, then flashing them open again, to watch as she slowly unbuttoned her blouse. When Eden was angry, or upset, her lips would always purse, the edges curling downwards asymmetrically, the right side slightly more than the left. Neither pursed nor curling, rather they were smiling, not excessively, perhaps, but smiling all the same, two equal and beautiful curves. When Eden smiled, my world became a dream, all the more so because it was real – it was as if what we felt for each other could almost be touched. It took my breath away just to be near her.

I blinked more rapidly now, still watching as her left arm disappeared behind her back to undo her bra. When Eden was angry, or upset, she invariably averted her gaze, cold as it fixed itself somewhere far beyond.

'Good,' she said again, more softly this time, still smiling and looking straight at me.

Good? What did she mean? That it was good I had cheated?

'I don't understand,' I would have said, but as though reading my mind, Eden spoke again before I could.

'Cheating is like scratching when you have an itchy back. Once you've started you can't stop. Having sex with Claw is more like having to get rid of phlegm when you've got a chesty cough. Except that when you've done it once, you know you're never doing it again.'

'But I shouldn't've done it at all. And I don't understand why I did. I'm not even attracted to her. I've never been attracted to her.'

'I know. But she's Claw, and everyone has sex with her once. I've seen it happen so many times that I knew it was only a matter of time before it also happened with you. And now it has, I'm relieved, because the first time is always the last.'

'It doesn't feel right that you're not angry,' I said. 'I'd probably feel better if you'd punched me, or shouted at me at least.'

'But I wouldn't.' She stepped out of her skirt. Broadening her smile, she cast her gaze at me flirtily. 'So, really, you're being selfish.' Naked, she walked over to where I was sitting. 'You slept with Claw and now you want *me* to make you feel better.' She bent down and started to undo the buttons on my shirt, as slowly as she had unbuttoned her blouse.

Was this forgiveness or revenge?

My shirt halfway down one arm and wrapped around the other like a sling, I felt broken. 'Stop,' I said. And looking up at her, 'I've not just been shitty to you. I've also been shitty to Patrick.'

Eden sat next to me and manoeuvred me out of my shirt. 'It's no use to anyone you feeling shitty.'

'You think I'm being selfish again.'

She took back her hands and shook her head this way and that in gentle tiny movements. 'I think you're being you,' she murmured. And then, after a sigh, her smile now more ponderous. 'I think you're trying a little too hard to be all of us.'

'I'm not sure what that means.'

'It means that people aren't all the same. Patrick is Patrick and he's happy with Claw. Claw isn't sure who she is, but she's as happy with Patrick as Patrick is with her - they did it once and they've been doing it ever since. You should stop trying to figure them out.'

'Don't you think I should tell Patrick what I did? We're supposed to be friends. And I like him.' When I tried to pull my shirt back on, Eden stopped me.

'Take your jeans off,' she said.

I wasn't sure what was happening or why, but I knew I didn't want it to stop.

'Just undo the zip and I'll pull them off for you,' Eden went on. 'But first kick off your trainers.' She slid off the bed and her breasts hardly drooped as she stood with her knees bent, leaning on her thighs. I was under her spell, and all I could think of was how beautiful she was. 'Now lift both your legs, and don't make me ask you again.'

I didn't. I lifted my legs and she pulled my jeans off.

I stretched my body out across the bed. I was naked; I was miserable and ashamed; I was happy. Lolling in the post-sex euphoria unique to making love with the woman I loved, I was everything at once.

Earlier I had made a confession. A few hours before that, something else had happened that I had felt the burning need to confess almost from the moment it had started. How *had* it started?

'Good!'

By the gasp of that single exclamation and the beauty of two equal curves, as though by a magician's sleight of hand the enormity of my lapse had all but been conjured away.

'Good!'

Unbelievable.

Eden in a nutshell.

'Only you,' I would say to her as soon as she came out of the bathroom.

My Eden. More than anyone could ever wish for, more than I deserved. In my undeserved good fortune lay my happiness, but my wretchedness too. The euphoria had not made me stupid. There had been nothing inevitable about what I had done; and I *had* done it, it hadn't just happened. Eden was wrong. The blame could not all be laid at Claw's door, as though she were a natural force that could not be resisted. I had not been assaulted, I had not been coerced, I had not even attempted to say no. It had started and then it had finished, and I had taken part.

But really, how *had* it started?

I remembered we were in her bedroom, on her bed, spread out over the bed sheets. And before that we were in the hallway of her house. 'I've made some brownies for Eden.' I was there to pick them up. 'Not too sweet, the way she likes them.' I remembered her laughing, then I remembered her tongue in my mouth. I couldn't remember undressing. I remembered using a condom, and later in the bathroom wrapping it in paper to flush it down the toilet. In the mirror my lips had looked swollen. 'What have I done?' Was I *that* kind of man?

'Good!'

Had Eden really said that?

It would have happened sooner or later; with Claw it always did. But the first time was always the last.

Had Sigismund known? Did he know now? And Patrick? Should I or shouldn't I tell him? What would be the consequences if I did?

All these thoughts were swimming together in my head while I was lying on the bed with no clothes on, waiting for Eden to come out of the bathroom. Some were in the slow lane, and some were in the fast lane, and others swam zigzags from one to the other. This last thought, of my thoughts negotiating swimming-pool lanes, made me laugh, but not loudly, almost under my breath.

Then I looked up, and when I saw Eden staring at me from the bathroom door, her nakedness as though mocking mine, I knew something was wrong.

And all my thoughts became a single thought, but it was not the right one.

'Oliver?'

I sat up and swivelled to the side of the bed, with the sheet wrapped around me. 'I know,' I said. 'I'll go, you don't have to say it.'

When Eden said nothing, I stood up and started picking up my clothes: my jeans and my boxers from the floor where Eden had dropped them after pulling them off, my shirt from the chair where I had lobbed it.

'Oliver, stop.' Eden's voice was barely a whisper.

'You don't have to feel sad. Honestly, I'll be fine.' I wouldn't be, but it wasn't Eden's fault, it was mine.

'I think something's wrong.'

I sat back on the edge of the bed clutching my clothes. 'I know,' I said again. 'I'm sorry.'

Eden stood in front of me and took my hand in hers.

'There's a lump under my arm,' she said, 'can you stand up?' And when I did, she raised her right arm and guided the tips of two of my fingers across the surface of her skin, from the side of her right breast to the area under her armpit. 'There, can you feel it?' She pressed down on my hand, making small circles.

I could feel it. But it was nothing, just a swollen gland. So why was Eden doing this? It wasn't funny, so what was it? Was it my punishment?

'I don't understand,' I said.

She moved my hand away and craned down to look under her arm. 'Oliver, look, you can actually see it.'

And then it hit me; this was not about me. Eden was worried, unnecessarily. She had not, after all, had second thoughts; she had not, after all, become enraged about what had happened – about what I had done, about how she had reacted, about how I had allowed her to react. She had not, after all, regretted having sex with me.

'Let me see,' I said, and she was right, I could see it. I ran my fingers over it again. 'Honestly, it's just a swollen gland. You're coming down with something, probably. If it was anything else, you'd've noticed it before. It's too big to miss.'

'I noticed it about a week ago,' said Eden. 'And I thought the same – just a swollen gland. But just now I also found one in my breast.' She moved my hand out of the way and we sat down side by side on the bed.

'A swollen gland and a cyst. If it was anything more serious, you'd have other symptoms.' I heard the fear in my voice, and I felt shame I couldn't hide it, more shame than I had felt when I realised how self-centred I had been to suspect that my wife might have invented a lump as a punishment, more shame than I had felt about having sex with Claw that same day. I had no right to show any fear. I had no right to *feel* any fear, and no right to doubt even for one second that, whatever this might be, we would manage to get through it together. And I realised that again I was being selfish.

Eden turned to look at me, the curves of her smile slightly skewed. 'I'm sure you're right,' she said. She leaned her head against my shoulder, our lonely naked bodies uniting.

I make my way to Marchmont Street swamped by feelings I had grown unaccustomed to: curiosity; surprise; and, dare I say it, perhaps even joy, or at least a tingle of it. And all together these fledgling sensations seem to amount to something more, to a mood not quite of wellbeing but rather of that muted warmth I had felt overcome by earlier on, and whose shiver as I arrive at the *Moonlight Café* still persists.

Claw and Patrick are sitting at a corner table at the back. They both see me and Patrick stands up, his tallness slightly stooped as he leans against the table with his fists. I wave at them. Only Claw waves back.

I shake Patrick's hand and I bend down to kiss Claw. I kiss her cheek; she kisses the air - loudly: Mm-wah!

Early middle age, or late youth as Claw would have it, sits with her well; the years have not yet discernibly marked her appearance. She is now forty-four, three years older than me. Only Patrick is still under forty; he's a boyish thirty-nine, and not the type to be perturbed by growing numbers, Claw's or his own. On the face of it impervious to fashion, what he wears somehow always seems to suit him to a tee - all of it today is brown except his coat which is black, as though he too shares in the general mourning.

'And the other,' says Claw, turning her face. An olive-skinned natural blonde, she wears little make-up, just a touch of mascara, a pale green eyeshadow, vaguely metallic, and pinkish red lipstick; all very subtle. Her expensive taste is stylish without being ostentatious, and the brightness of her tailored combinations, today an emerald two-piece, shines more vividly in the shadow of Patrick's drabness - I have always suspected collusion.

I bend down again to kiss her other cheek; she kisses the air - loudly: Mm-wah!

I remember her smell. Why do I remember her smell?

'I told you he was coming,' Patrick says, slouching back into his chair, as awkward sitting down as he is standing up. There is a military look about him that gives a false impression of stiffness; Patrick is anything but. He is ruggedly handsome and at first may appear reserved, taking time to take the measure of strangers. He does give fools short shrift, but is disarmingly soft with his friends.

I look at my watch, it's after ten past twelve. 'Sorry I'm late.'

'You're normally early,' says Claw.

'I felt like a cigarette.'

'I could smell it in your breath that you've been smoking,' says Claw. 'I thought you'd given up.'

'I gave up years ago.'

'You've got time for a quick coffee if you'd like one,' says Patrick. 'Might help to keep you awake, for this "rare and unforgettable performance" that we've apparently got Sigismund to thank for. Did you know he and Claw are on speaking terms again?'

Claw rolls her eyes before stabbing him with playful dagger looks. 'We're civilised grown-ups, Patrick, and yes, Ollie knows that we've spoken.' With every word her voice becomes more strident. 'He just called to say hi and have a chat, what was I supposed to do, hang up on him?' By now she's almost yelling, and people are beginning to stare. She's deliberately breathing through her nose, which makes her sound almost hysterical.

'Yes, that's exactly what you should've done.' Patrick's almost yelling too, as oblivious to the starers as she is.

Claw lowers her voice. 'You liked him once too, I seem to remember...' And with a blink of her eyes and a finger by the side of her mouth: 'Or was it twice?'

Perhaps she's not being playful at all; I'm beginning to suspect a raw nerve. 'Claw, that's not nice,' I say.

'Yes, Ollie, I know. But we were married, for God's sake. For *years*!' While she stretches out her fingers on the table, her head makes short spasmodic jolts. 'And it may have ended badly, but I'm over it now, I'm much happier with Patrick than I ever was with Sigismund, so why on earth should I insist on being bitter?'

'Ended badly?' Now it's Patrick's turn to roll his eyes. 'After cheating on you with your future husband (twice, as you say, since we're sharing with Ollie), the man left you for one of his students, a boy half his age.'

'William is a very nice boy,' Claw retorts inconsequentially, sparking off one of their furious rat-a-tats:

'A very nice boy your arsehole husband practically abducted...'

'*Ex* arsehole husband. And it was hardly an abduction.'

'Alienated from his family and almost all his friends by keeping him holed up in some godforsaken place for almost a year...'

'Now you're just being silly! Since when has the gorgeous Barcelona, celebrated city of Miró and Gaudí, heroic epicentre of resistance to Franco, become godforsaken?'

'Then abandoned for an even younger girl, who by all accounts the civilised grown-up has also now dumped, no doubt to pursue someone else.'

'He's a pansexual, Patrick, not a predatory monster. Don't be so narrow-minded.'

'Oh, *a pansexual*, is that what he is?' While he whistles out air, Patrick rolls his eyes again. 'And what kind of name is Sigismund, anyway? Is he trying to pretend he's not from Grimsby? As if *Grim*sby gives a shit!'

When I laugh, so does Patrick. Claw tries not to, but when I tickle her, she does.

'Someone's in a good mood today,' she says as she slaps my hand out of the way.

They are a mystery, these two. They bicker constantly, and anyone who came across a bare transcript of one of their exchanges might reasonably assume it was heated, bad-tempered, aggressive. Nine times out of ten they would be wrong. The timing, the low, almost monotonous pitch of their voices and the vibrant good humour with which they deliver their lines come together beautifully to give their frequent arguments a lilting musicality that makes them a delight. I enjoy them so much that I sometimes suspect that my friends may in fact be putting on a performance for my benefit. But the synergy of their rhythms and gestures comes across consistently as so entirely natural that far more likely it is just one more expression, not of their affection for me, but rather of their love for each other. In the presence of these moments, I forget myself and feel almost human.

Has their argument today been an exception? The pitch of their raised voices has hardly been monotonous or low. Why would Patrick be so outraged by Sigismund all of a sudden? Why would Claw embarrass Patrick by confronting him with his own lapse? They have both come across as defensive. But perhaps this is a natural progression as they seek to expand their repertoire, turning even the worst of the past into theatre.

Now that I am able to be curious, I decide to test them both by playing along.

'How do you know this William is a very nice boy?' I ask Claw. 'You used to call him the poisoned Narcissus.'

'Oh, hasn't she told you? The poisoned Narcissus turned up on our doorstep one evening to beg her to ask Sigismund to take him back.'

'That's not true, the boy just wanted a shoulder to cry on, *and* to say sorry. He didn't beg me to do anything.'

'She stayed up with him all night and by morning she'd managed to persuade him that he'd had a lucky escape. Since then, he's a very nice boy who's always in our kitchen baking brownies and flapjacks with Claw. And eating them all, I might add.'

'William's extremely good at baking, and I'm happy I was able to help him move on.'

'She means she's been taking her revenge on him by making him fat.'

'Honestly, Patrick, you do talk some nonsense sometimes. Don't listen to him, Ollie, William's not fat. He's beefed himself up at the gym, not in our kitchen, and all the weight he's gained is pure muscle; he's got pecs and a six-pack to die for.' With a sharp intake of breath through her nose, Claw plumps up her lips as she slowly exhales. '*Anyway!* Returning to my ex, he may be a prize arsehole, but he does know a lot about the Arts. And he didn't like the name his parents gave him, so he chose one for himself, what's wrong with that?'

'The Arts, my arse. The man's a total fraud.'

Leaning back in her chair, now Claw rolls her eyes at the ceiling. 'Yes, we know you wrote a book and Sigismund hasn't, but that doesn't mean that Sigismund's a fraud. I'll say it again. When it comes to the Arts, he's ahead of you by a mile. Why? Because you're only interested in design, nothing else. A book on Le Corbusier's use of chrome is all very well, but its appeal is hardly universal. Whereas Sigismund's taste has always been far more eclectic. He makes sure he keeps abreast of the avant-garde, and consequently has his finger on the pulse much more than you do. Across *all* the arts, not just design. Admit it, your attitude to anything new is completely pooh-poohish, you think everything contemporary and remotely experimental is crap – you only read dead authors and you don't even like Damien Hirst.'

'Oh dear,' Patrick sneers, 'is *that* who you consider to be new and avant-garde?'

'Really,' I say, 'you don't like Damien Hirst? I thought that pickled shark was magnificent.'

From Sigismund's pansexuality and the abduction of a poisoned Narcissus to the Arts and pickled sharks. Ridiculous leaps that only in Claw's presence could have seemed entirely natural.

'His early work wasn't too bad,' I hear Patrick conceding. 'Nowadays I find him vulgar. That dreadful diamond skull was the last straw.'

'*For the love of God*,' says Claw. 'Wasn't the whole point that it *had* to be vulgar, to pose an interesting question on the intrinsic value of Art?'

'Oh, please!'

'It's called irony, Patrick.'

'Guys,' I say, 'we're going to be late.'

'Oh my God, so we are,' says Claw.

'Come on, then,' Patrick says with a sigh, 'let's go put our finger on the pulse.'

As we all get up, I give another muted chuckle. It has suddenly struck me that I wouldn't have wished any part of today to be different, that unbelievably I am also looking forward to They Them. But at the same time, I'm feeling very nervous. No, not nervous, petrified. That's not quite right either. I don't know exactly what I'm feeling, but I do know that I'm feeling it too intensely. And I also know that for a change what I'm feeling too intensely isn't grief.

TWO

The Cutting-Edge Arts Centre is housed in what used to be a pub. The old sign still hangs swingingly above the door: *The Slaughterhouse Inn.*

'Oliver plus two,' I say to the bondage-trousered youth at the door.

She looks me up and down, almost poking my eye out with her pointed Mohican. 'Oliver who?'

'We have tickets,' says Claw.

'Not anyone,' I say.

The Mohican clicks her tongue. 'Sure,' she says officiously, 'Alex said to give you the table.'

Claw's tugging at my sleeve. 'What table? Who's Alex? Tell them we've got tickets.'

The Mohican ignores her. 'Joe's set it up by the stage, know the way?'

'No,' I say, 'sorry.'

'Hey, Joe?'

Another youth, standing just the other side of a red velvet curtain, pops his head through, short-haired and preppy.

'Yes?'

'Not anyone plus two,' the Mohican explains.

'Ah!' the more demonstrative Joe almost yells, and looks from me to Patrick to Claw.

I raise my hand. 'Not anyone,' I say, 'and these are my plus two.'

Joe reveals more of himself: pink bow tie, winning smile, muscles bulging out of white short sleeves. 'Come through, come through, I'll show you to the table.'

Claw gives out a shriek, and through the curtain the three of us follow Joe in single file. Even in the semi-dark, I can see the place is packed. I can hear it, too. Feeling self-conscious (I hate being conspicuous in a crowd) and a little claustrophobic (the hubbub is raucously liquid, infusing the air with the dampness of too many breaths), I stare intently at the back of Joe's head as we make our way along a narrow central aisle past swarming rows of chairs arranged in a disordered semicircle that almost overspills onto the stage – a rectangular platform raised about a foot above the floor, bare but for a spot-lit wooden chair and freestanding microphone. The aisle comes to an end about a foot short of the stage, where a solitary table and three chairs have been set up.

'Here,' says Joe, pulling back the chairs so we can sit. 'Best seats in the house.' A folded card with GUESTS written on both sides in large letters sits diagonally at the centre of the table.

'Is this the only table?' I ask, shyly casting about.

'Yes,' says Joe. 'And this one's normally in the manager's office at the front. We only put it out for special guests.'

'Ah,' says Claw.

'There's a bar at the back, if you like you can bring your drinks back to the table,' says Joe.

'I'd *love* some Prosecco,' says Claw. 'Let's get a bottle.'

'You've got about ten minutes,' says Joe. 'There's been a minor issue with the sound that they're still trying to fix.'

'I'll go,' says Patrick.

'Right, I better get back or Dog will bite my head off,' says Joe. And then to Patrick, 'I'll show you the way.'

'Is Dog the Mohican?' asks Claw.

Joe smiles more broadly now and shakes his head. 'Dog's the manager,' he says. 'The Mohican's just Babe - she's actually my girlfriend.'

As soon as we're alone, her elbow on the table and her head flat on its side in her hand, Claw's glaring eyes have latched themselves like leeches onto mine. 'Oh, *Alex*,' she says.

'We had a cigarette together earlier, that's all.'

Claw makes a show of rapid blinks. '*Special guests*, the boy said.' And when I shrug, '"Not anyone plus two", what was that all about?'

'Just a joke we shared, no big deal.'

'A joke you shared with Alex.'

'Yes.'

Claw's head rises from her hand and is vertical again. As they shift position, her eyes cast a devilish glint. 'A joke you shared with Alex in the street.'

'Yes.'

'A joke you shared with Alex in the street while you smoked a cigarette.'

'Yes.'

Repeated rapid blinking magnifies the glint. 'And is Alex They Them?'

'I don't know. I think They Them is what the show is called.'

'By a poet like no other,' Patrick chirpily puts in, looming over us with the Prosecco and three plastic glasses. 'Looks like Sigismund might've got something right for a change. Oh, and Joe forgot to say we're invited backstage.'

'What, *now*?'

'Not now, Ollie, calm down. Obviously after the show.' Patrick has filled all our glasses and has taken his seat.

'This is so exciting,' says Claw. 'Where *is* backstage?'

'Joe said to wait here and he'll come back to take us through. But I think we should let Oliver go by himself.'

I'm blushing, and I know I'm blushing, and knowing I'm blushing makes me blush even more. I shift in my chair. Do I feel embarrassed or do I feel ashamed? I feel cornered, trapped into something I hadn't thought properly through. How did this happen? Just three days ago...

'I'm not sure I want to,' I say.

'You're not sure you want to go by yourself?' Claw leans over and puts one arm around me. 'Then of course we'll be happy to join you, even if it's just to say hi. Or perhaps the two of you could join us for lunch.'

Patrick sighs. 'Cheers,' he says, and takes a gulp of his Prosecco.

'No, I meant I'm not sure I want to go backstage. I'm not even sure I want to be here.'

But I do want to be here, so why am I lying?

Before I can think of an answer – Do I even have to think? Don't I know the answer already? Isn't the answer what's making me red? - the lights go out and there is music.

Emerging from the shadows in a smart black trouser suit and heavy platform shoes, Alex steps onto the stage in long strides and stands purposefully upright in front of the spot-lit wooden chair. Her long black hair has been let loose and its waves are agleam as she steps into the circle of brightness. She is not alone. In her arms to one side, she holds a ventriloquist's dummy, a painted *papier mâché* replica of herself but in a man's tuxedo, white shirt and white bow tie, with hair as short as Joe's, and somewhat incongruously sporting a pencil moustache. As if to enhance the contradiction, both Alex and her male simulacrum wear vividly red lipstick. Both now take a bow – an invisible hand controls the dummy's movements from inside. Everything moves: the head moves, the arms and legs move, and most importantly the lips move.

Watching Alex on stage, her presence so imposing that immediately it captivates the crowd, my own reaction is different: I see not Alex and a dummy, not a talented theatrical performer and her prop, but one more striking variation of the woman I had met in the street. Even as I think this, the words I have articulated to describe it make no sense, but merely signify that I am drawn less to theatre than to life. Life again, laying its claim afresh by caressing me with warmth and a shiver. And it's all I can do to deflect it by returning myself to the street, reducing my impression to a single insignificant thought: a tall narrow case; black; wooden; on wheels. Now I know what was inside.

'Good afternoon,' says the dummy in a masculine voice, jerkily scanning the crème de la crème of the Arts.

'Good afternoon,' says Alex in a different voice, more ambivalent than I remember.

'Good afternoon' the audience roars back, and I'm coming out in goosebumps already.

'I am Them and this is They,' says the dummy.

'I am They and this is Them,' says Alex.

'And together we are They and Them,' says the dummy.

Oh God, I can't help thinking, I hope this doesn't turn into slapstick.

It doesn't.

Head tilted slightly backwards, Alex draws in breath, deeply, and when the prominent lips are parted again, 'We would like to dedicate today's performance to someone who was almost not here.' With the movements of a marionette, her head now bends and her gaze is fixed on me. 'They are Not Anyone… and, everyone… please clap your hands.'

'She means you, Ollie,' Claw whispers, and then becomes the first to applaud. And when everyone has settled and the room is quiet, 'What did she mean, you were almost not here?'

'Shh,' Patrick says.

I was almost not here; it's true.

But how did Alex know?

And yet here I am, the six parallel lines dismantled if not yet disposed of – they have now become a fallback position, a reserve possibility. The concrete plan had crumbled into a smile, then a smudge, then a tumbledown assortment locked away in a box. Not abandoned, far from forgotten, perhaps not quite as failsafe as I had talked myself into believing, all the same the urgency of a substitute solution has receded. My presence in this hall is testament to something important that I don't know how to put into words, not yet. It has fallen to Alex, who already has proven her talent for persuasion (why else would I be here?), to communicate with meaningful pauses – Not Anyone... and, everyone... - secretly, only to me, an alternative to nothingness that yesterday I wouldn't have acknowledged, because yesterday, like Alex, or the warmth, or the shiver, it had simply not existed.

Forgive me,

Forgive me,

Forgive me.

Earlier I had sought Eden's forgiveness. Craving for aloneness had amounted to betrayal, a breach of every promise Eden had extracted from me.

'Promise me that you'll be happy again. Promise me, Ollie, this is what I need from you right now, a promise that I need you to persuade me you'll keep.'

And of course, I had promised.

I promise,

I promise,

I promise.

A promise I had never intended to keep; an impossible promise.

And now I seek Eden's forgiveness for a different betrayal,

A flutter of joy I am trying to suppress,

Only half-heartedly trying to suppress.

The keeping of a promise does not need forgiveness,

It is not a betrayal at all,

Eden herself would have said.

There are sixty days left.

Just three days ago there had almost been none.

And today?

They and Them are now seated, Alex in the spot-lit wooden chair and the dummy on her knee, its head against her shoulder, looking up at her whenever it is her turn to speak. As they recite their lines in turn, I am mesmerised not by their words, most of which elude me if taken one by one, but by the unexpected heartbreak of another interaction steeped in love. Although I am reminded of the earlier conversation between Patrick and Claw, which itself perhaps was charged with the effect of my encounter with Alex in the street, the sensation I am experiencing now is somehow very different. Patrick and Claw, although bouncing off each other to a unifying rhythm, had remained entirely separate. Here, in this captivated hall, Alex and the articulated dummy are not just bound together by a clever contraption and a voice that can be thrown, nor merely by the meaning of beautiful words or the undulating rhythm of sound. Something more essential is at work, a spellbinding coming together that everyone can feel. I feel it and the audience feel it too – for why else would the pantomime ruckus have so suddenly become a deathly silence, a uniform holding of breaths - and what we all feel goes beyond what we are able to perceive: by dint of some invisible force, They and Them are now They Them, an inseparable unit of one.

One plus one is one.

The invisible force has its roots in a tragic event.

A tragedy like mine, the tragedy of two broken halves.

I know this without knowing how. I know it like a reflex, in the physical way one experiences non-physical pain.

And yet the aura, in which I share, is of joyous overcoming. The triumph of mending. By the sheer force of remembering, not the pretence of forgetting.

Applause.

'Thank you,' says They.

'Thank you,' says Them.

'And now we'd like to share with you another dedication, to Someone... and to Everyone... who one day was here and the next day was not.' Alex leans her head to one side until it rests against the dummy's forehead. 'Without Them,' she goes on, 'I would not have been here either. Without Them I would not be who I am. The price of love is life and death.'

Now I understand. Them is a stand-in for "Them", not a resurrection but rather a constant reminder, both symbolic and real. The painted *papier mâché* replica is not a simulacrum of a person after all, but rather of a bond – one that it contributes equally to keeping alive.

"One plus one is one" takes on a different meaning.

Once the possibility of addition has occurred to me, its many permutations begin to assault me in a disordered and bewildering barrage.

Overwhelmed by its cacophony, my mind drifts to something mundane:

She? Or They?

It must make a difference to Alex; does it make any difference to me?

Not so mundane after all.

I remember arguing with Eden, in the months before her diagnosis, Eden as always on the side of the self, in whatever "other" form it happened – or it wished – to identify and manifest itself.

We had just got home after a party, where a fight had broken out over some idiot's provocation on the subject of multiple genders: he had left the party with a shiner and his tail between his legs: the punch had been administered by a muscular they/them.

Flippantly I had argued that the guy had been obnoxious and had probably deserved what he got, but he did have a point. All this talk of fluid identities and sexual variations – non-this, poly-that, queer- or neutral-the-other, the truth was it had all gone too far.

'And whose "truth" would that be?' Eden had demanded.

The truth of the myriad other problems in the world that were a little more serious than whether someone was post- or third-gender, which was pure self-indulgence, a symptom of rudderless times, a neither-here-nor-there affectation.

I remember the look Eden gave me. Ah, so it was language that bothered me, she said. And all the problems in the world would be solved if only people who felt different were deprived of their freedom to be who they were. Except that it wasn't just a matter of freedom. For them it was a matter that went to the core of their being, requiring not a courtesy of semantics but the opening-up of a generous space where difference could at least be imagined - with poetry, a space in one's heart.

I shouldn't be so lazy, she said. I should at least try to imagine. Difference might be hard to imagine, but the reality of difference was harder – and had to be lived, not imagined. Shouldn't we at least do our best not to make it even harder? Not "I know how you feel" but "I hear what you're saying". Hatred was when people could only imagine the worst, and hatred and indifference were not far apart, nor was laziness much better than indifference.

When she felt she had to be, Eden could be scathing.

I remember what I answered: 'I hear what you're saying.' And Eden had laughed.

Does love cross boundaries? While I attempt to imagine, I return to the room, and to the searing voice of They:

'Two strangers
Because of a moment
Are no longer strangers.
Excuse me, do you have a light?
An old-fashioned lighter
Sorry, would you like one?
A smoker, not a smoker
Really, I'd love one.'

I am not alone. The thought, so alien, has struck me like lightning, no sooner formed than it has caused me to flinch.

'Ollie, you're shaking, what's wrong?' While she whispers the words, Claw puts her hand on my forearm, and I become aware of the shivering glass in my hand, still half full.

'I'm fine,' I whisper back, laying down the glass on the table.

'Shush,' says someone in the row just behind us, and unusually Claw lets it go.

With a soundless sigh, once again I am back in the street, standing in the doorway, smoking that cigarette. Will it be the only one, I wonder. Then just as I remember the dead body and the dog out on a walk, the booming voice of Them cuts right through:

'Small world,' it says.

And I hear Alex answer in her own voice:

'So small that once again it has become enormous.'

Any ambivalence is gone. Boundaries are only imagined.

Sixty days,

Sixty days,

Sixty days today.

But suddenly numbers are light, divested of their weight by the insubstantial smoke of a single cigarette.

The voices from the stage are silent; throughout the performance, these shorter or longer pauses, judged precisely by They Them, their function almost that of a third interlocutor participating in the interplay being acted out on stage, have held the audience in thrall almost as much as the words. But this particular silence, the longest yet by far, appears to signify a discontinuation, as though a longer respite of calm is needed to more markedly usher in what will follow.

A tempest; a wuthering finale.

I brace myself, my mind already drifting backstage.

No, I need to stay present in the hall, I must, I have missed too much already.

I am literally on the edge of my seat, bent over the table, the only table, waiting for the words with baited breath, waiting for the silence to be broken.

And it is.

'Get your tits out!' someone yells from somewhere far. Behind me on the left.

There is uproar. Angry shouts reverberate across the hall. At the back, there is the noise of people rising to their feet. Perhaps the culprit is being forcibly ejected. Perhaps the force being used is excessive.

'Disgraceful,' says Claw in an angry voice. She has risen to her feet and has her back to the stage.

'Claw! Sit yourself down, for God's sake.' Patrick grabs hold of her arm and pulls her back into her chair.

The commotion continues, not all in one place; there are pockets of it everywhere, loud arguments erupting even nowhere near where the yelling had come from.

Where *had* the yelling come from?

Onstage, Alex and the dummy haven't moved. They seem immobilised, their poses statuesque.

I should stop calling Them "the dummy", I catch myself thinking, but really at that moment they both look like dummies, They and Them in suspended animation like the living mannequins I have seen in Covent Garden, frozen human statues whose literally solid backbone I have always admired.

But now there is movement. Them is shaking their head, looking up at They as though bemused. With a blink, Alex catches my eye. She smiles. She or They, it doesn't matter.

Then She, or They, bends towards the microphone, and is tapping at it, *tap, tap, tap,* the sound amplified and shrill. Alex, or They, clears their throat, about to say something.

'Violence,' they say. 'The final part of the performance.'

In the less than total silence of a pause, an identical but even louder yell by the same unmistakeable voice:

'Get your tits out!'

It comes again from somewhere far, this time in the back on the right. The same but only now recognisable as a recording.

'Violence,' Alex says again.

In the silence of another pause, the hush has now returned.

And then, unexpectedly,

'Thank you, goodnight.'

'Thank you, goodnight,' Them repeats.

The hush continues; They and Them are again statuesque.

The spot-lit wooden chair goes dark.

The hush persists, for a second. Then the hall becomes a blast of steady loud applause that suddenly takes on a rhythm, alive like a heartbeat, not broken but enlivened by the loud cries of "Bravo!", the loudest from Patrick and Claw.

Gradually the light returns to reveal an empty stage, and now some cries are clamouring for More! More! More!

But the curtains at the exits have been drawn, and the light is now bright and fluorescent, the stage dead under a plume of floating dust.

The applause dies down, and people are shuffling their way to the exits. The three of us stand up from our chairs and are putting on our coats.

'Oh, Ollie,' says Claw, quietly sobbing.

'Claudia, what's wrong?' Patrick asks.

Without answering Patrick, Claw throws herself instead into my arms. Still sobbing, the side of her face is pressed hard against my chest. 'It's you, it's you, you're the smoker, non-smoker who's made the world enormous again. Oh, Ollie, to think you're only here because of me, to think I had to *beg* you to come.'

'To think none of us would be here if it wasn't for Sigismund,' says Patrick.

'Or for Sir Charles and the Bodleian,' I say.

'You're both making fun of me but I don't care!' With a single mighty push against my shoulders, Claw is off my chest. She finds a tissue in her bag and dabs her eyes dry. Then she takes out her compact, but after taking one look at the smear of her make-up, she snaps the compact shut and returns it to her bag. 'I *want* her to see me like this,' she says.

'Her? I thought Alex was a they, not a she,' says Patrick.

'Oh, says Claw. And then, 'Oh,' she says again.

'Not that it should make any difference,' says Patrick.

'Well,' says Claw, 'doesn't that rather depend?'

'Yes,' I say, 'it depends on whether it makes any difference to Alex.'

'Alex is a she,' Joe says matter-of-factly, standing in the aisle behind us. 'Her partner was the original Them. Or would've been.'

'The dummy,' says Claw, looking flustered.

'Sam,' says Joe. 'Who as far as I know was a he, but he might have been a them, I'm not sure. Before the poetry, Alex used to sing and Sam was occasionally doing stand-up. Then one night they met here, at the bar, and Dog says that was it, everything for both of them, right from the start. They got married not long later. Alex wanted to, so Sam said yes.'

'But they're not together anymore,' says Claw.

'Sam died the winter before last.'

Alex is a She. They Them, Alex and Sam, a She and probably a He. I was right, a tragedy like mine, the tragedy of two broken halves, my half now feeling closer to hers, the closeness still divided by the enormity of Eden. I feel without being able to process.

'How awful,' says Claw. 'I'm not sure how, but I could sense that something terrible had happened. And after losing Sam, Alex *became* a ventriloquist?'

Joe nods. 'A good one,' he says. 'But just for this show, as far as I know. Without Them, there's no They. And vice versa.' Then turning to me, 'You haven't known her long?'

'He met her in the street this morning,' says Claw.

'Ah, the old-fashioned lighter,' says Joe. 'Hence the table, I suppose.' And then suddenly becoming brisk, while I contemplate what Alex might have told him and Claw is lashing me with probing looks, 'Right, if you're ready I'll take you through. And you can ask her any questions you like; she's very open, she talks about Sam all the time.'

'Maybe Ollie should go by himself?'

'Oh, stop it, Patrick. We're just saying a quick hello and then leaving.'

'Please come,' I say.

'If you're sure,' Patrick says.

'Yes, of course he's sure,' says Claw.

'It's this way,' says Joe. 'By the way, did you recognise my voice?' And when no one answers, 'Show us your tits. That was me.'

Claw gives out a shriek of delight. 'That was *so* unexpected. Just brilliant, brilliant! And by the end of the show, I was in tears.'

'She really was,' Patrick says.

'The place is littered with tissues,' says Joe. 'I wish people would take their rubbish with them.'

'Oh,' Claw says. 'I'm pretty sure I put mine back into my bag.'

And once again we follow Joe in single file, around the stage then through a door hidden just behind it.

Alex talks about Sam all the time.

Dog says it was everything for both of them right from the start.

Sam was the original Them.

Or would have been.

And Eden?

Eden was the original everything.

Everything and more.

Backstage is upstairs. Carpeted in floral oranges and yellows, the stairs are sheer and there are many of them; the ceilings downstairs are high. Photographs from past performances, all relatively recent, hang along the staircase wall in gilded frames; each bears the name of the act and a date. Bands, drag shows, solo stand-up comedians, a young female contortionist with her scantily clad male assistant. In some the auditorium has been cleared and everyone is standing up, dancing while clutching a pint. In none is there a table by the stage.

I wonder - might Sam be in one of the photographs?

I stop reading the captions.

Joe leads the way, slowly, holding the banister. At the top there is a narrow hallway with one door on the right and three doors on the left. All four of them are shut.

'There is another staircase at the front of the building, by the entrance, but that part of the upstairs is separate,' says Joe, bringing us to a standstill right in front of the last door on the left. 'This whole area here is just for the artists. They can even stay the night if they want, we get acts from all over the country, and from abroad. I've crashed here myself once or twice.'

'With Babe or without?' asks Claw.

'Babe and I aren't exclusive, she's my girlfriend but I've also got a boyfriend, and yeah, definitely with her a couple of times. We're not really supposed to, but Dog doesn't mind.' And pointing at the door to the right, 'That's the bathroom, if anyone needs it.'

'Ooh, yes, *please*, that Prosecco's gone right through me,' says Claw.

'But we're not staying long,' Patrick reminds her.

'Have you performed here yourself?' I ask Joe.

'Only for Babe and my boyfriend,' Joe answers with a cheeky smile. 'Once for both of them together. But never again. I'm yang and they're both yin, so it was never going to work, there just wasn't enough of me to go around.'

Patrick and I both nod.

'Right,' says Joe when Claw gets back, 'are we ready?' And before he gets an answer, he knocks on the door. *Tap*, then *tap-tap-tap*, then *tap* again.

Alex opens the door, almost immediately. She's out of the trouser suit, but still all in black: black jeans again, the black jumper I hadn't been wrong to imagine, and the heavy platform shoes she was wearing on stage.

'Not anyone plus two,' Joe announces with a hand on my shoulder. Then pulling Alex into a muscular embrace, he whispers loudly in her ear: 'You were brilliant today, everyone loved you.' And then he dashes off, disappearing down the stairs.

The room is cluttered with theatrical paraphernalia, an accumulation of leftover props and discarded items of clothing that hang untidily on a rail. There is a small blue divan in one corner, in another an Art Deco armchair that's seen better days. And between the two corners, a couple of chairs are lined up against the wall beside a large dressing table and a mirror surrounded by lightbulbs, none of which are on.

'Come in, please,' Alex says, 'and sorry about Joe, he gets overexcited.'

Claw lets out a gasp. 'Oh, but he was right, you were brilliant! It really was an unforgettable performance, thank you!'

'I'm Patrick,' says Patrick, 'and this is Claudia, my wife, who also gets overexcited.'

'Alex,' says Alex, smiling as she shakes Patrick's hand. 'Lovely to meet you both.'

'Claw, please, no one calls me Claudia,' says Claw. Then pulling Alex into another muscular embrace, 'Thank you, thank you, thank you,' she whispers loudly in her ear.

Alex peers at me over Claw's shoulder. 'Hi,' she says.

'Hi,' I say, raising the open palm of my hand.

'Oh, Ollie, she's beautiful,' says Claw, pulling back to look at Alex while still clutching the sides of her arms.

'Claw, you're embarrassing everyone,' says Patrick.

'Not at all,' Alex says with a short burst of laughter. 'As a matter of fact, Them whispered something very similar to me about Oliver while we were onstage.'

I feel myself wincing. 'They did?'

From on top of the case Alex had been wheeling in the street, Them is staring at me fixedly, with an iciness that makes me feel like an intruder.

'If you don't believe me, you can ask them yourself,' Alex says.

'Go on, ask me,' says Them in their masculine voice.

'Oh my God,' says Claw.

'Fuck's sake,' says Them without moving their lips, 'who *is* this hysterical woman?'

'Don't take any notice,' Alex says, 'they're just showing off.'

Claw lets out a nervous giggle.

'Well?' asks the impatient voice of Them. 'Are you asking me or not?'

'Go on, ask them,' Alex says, 'or they'll never shut up.'

'Okay, fine,' I say, clearing my throat as I turn to face Them directly. 'Is it true you whispered to Alex I was beautiful?'

'I might've said that you weren't too bad-looking. For a man. I don't think I'd've gone as far as saying you're beautiful.'

'That's just so clever,' says Claw.

'And a little bit creepy, I know,' Alex says. 'Has anyone seen *Magic*, with Anthony Hopkins?'

'Abracadabra,' says Patrick. 'Wasn't the dummy called Fats?'

'Is dumbhead calling me a dummy?'

Claw gives out another shriek of delight. 'Dumbhead, I love it!'

The slapstick I had been afraid of is now happening here, and I wish Patrick and Claw would go away. I want to be with Alex alone, and alone means also without Them – what *is* Them? A dummy or the ghost of Sam, whose presence must be as real to Alex as Eden's is to me?

'Right, time to go back in your box,' Alex says.

'Oh no,' says Claw, but already the case has been opened, and then closed with Them fastened inside it.

'Now let's all sit down and have a drink, I've had Joe bring up another Prosecco,' Alex says, as she picks up one of the chairs and starts moving it towards the divan.

'Let me out, let me out,' cries out a muffled voice.

Claw lets out another nervous giggle.

'I could've sworn I heard knocking from inside the box,' Patrick says.

'Trick of the trade,' says Alex, making a show of knocking gently against the chair with the tips of her fingers – the sound once again seems to come from the box. 'Sorry, sorry, now *I*'m showing off. That's it, no more evil-dummy jokes, I promise. Please, take a seat.'

'You're *so* talented,' says Claw.

'Claw and I will stay just for one glass,' Patrick says.

Do I really want them to go?

THREE

I met Eden in the foyer of the Coliseum. I had just picked up my ticket for that night's performance of *Così fan tutte* from the Box Office, and was about to meet a group of friends from work up in the Balcony. They had been insisting for months that I should join them, promising that I would fall in love with opera if I gave it a chance. I had my doubts, but finally I had agreed, to get them off my back once and for all.

'Don't look so miserable.'

I looked up from my ticket, almost certain the voice couldn't possibly be speaking to me. The British are uptight enough, I thought, but the British who like opera? They must be positively frigid. And what I saw when I looked up was Eden's smile, the two equal and beautiful curves that I would soon fall in love with.

She was looking at me, but even so I wasn't sure she was speaking to me.

'Let me guess,' she said, holding on to my gaze with the lightness of a tender embrace. 'This is your first time at the opera and you're dreading you'll hate it. Am I right?'

I felt the flutter instantly, and there was nothing vague about it.

'Damn,' I said, 'is it really that obvious?'

She nodded vigorously, and we both laughed.

'And on top of that I've got a crap seat,' I said.

'Let me see?'

Our shoulders touched.

'Oh dear,' she said. And leaning even closer, 'You're not wrong to look miserable,' she whispered in my ear. 'You'll hardly see a thing, and what you'll hear will make you want to tear all your hair out. But no, you shouldn't take my word for it, I *hate* opera.'

'Then why are you here?' In her Carhartt corduroy jeans and denim jacket she looked ready for a stroll in the park, rather than an evening of Mozart.

'I'm actually on a date.'

'Oh.'

'An *off* date - I thought I'd let him down very gently in the interval. But now I've changed my mind. And I'd like you to change yours and join me for a drink in Soho instead. I know a place where we definitely won't hear any opera. Oh, and I'm normally very reserved, but I just couldn't bear the thought of you being tortured in there for three hours. I'm Eden, by the way.'

I took the next day off. And the day after that, my friends at work were all giggling. My night at the opera had been a prank. They'd set me up: they all hated opera too. I giggled along, and then I showed them the unused ticket and kissed them one after the other.

From the foyer of the English National Opera to backstage at the Cutting-Edge Arts Centre.

From Alex to Eden and now back to Alex. Claw and Patrick have just left.

'Alone at last,' cries out a muffled voice from inside its box.

'This room,' I say, 'for some reason it doesn't feel real. And every time you do that, it feels even less real.'

'Do you mean this room, or do you mean this situation?'

Alex has taken Patrick's place on the divan, sitting with her hands clasped together in her lap. I have taken possession of the armchair, or rather the armchair has taken possession of me; flattened by the ravages of too many bottoms, its springs are no longer springy, and in spite of being relatively light (I have a swimmer's physique), I have sunk right into it.

'I mean this room with you and Them and me inside it. It feels like it belongs to a different world.'

'A different world that you've walked into and now you can't get out of. Can you even get out of that chair? I mean, look at you, you look like you're being swallowed. Sink any deeper and you'll probably come out the other end.'

When I lift both my arms from the armrests, I do sink a little bit deeper, and Alex and I share a laugh, which I cut short with a sigh. 'And that's kind of how it feels being in this room - like I've been taken out of one place and put somewhere else. In a place where nothing fits. A fictional place.'

'A fictional place where you feel out of place.'

'And the longer I'm here, the stranger it feels, but at the same time the less I want to leave. Or maybe it's like you said, maybe I do want to leave but I can't.'

Alex leans her upper body forward. 'Did I say I thought you wanted to leave?'

She looks at me and I see Eden's smile; suddenly I find the light touch of her gaze too familiar, and in spite of the flutter I turn mine away.

'It's probably because the room belongs to no one,' I say. 'I know it's just a dressing room, but it doesn't really feel like a dressing room either. It feels like a room that *should* belong to someone.'

'Holy shit, what a weirdo,' cries out a muffled voice, and automatically my gaze falls on the black wooden case.

'Don't take any notice,' Alex says.

'Don't take any notice,' I repeat, my gaze now caressing the rest of the room. Then I whip up the courage to fix it directly on Alex. 'Of what?' I ask. 'What shouldn't I be taking any notice of?'

'Honestly, it's just habit,' Alex answers inconclusively, but then she kicks off her heavy platform shoes, draws her legs up and sits on top of them, holding on to her toes, now bare but for a flimsy pair of socks. 'No, that's not fair, it isn't just habit – it's habit with a fair bit of insanity, just the right amount, more or less, to help keep me as sane as I am. And that's probably the best I could've hoped for.'

'Tell me about Sam,' I say. 'I mean the Sam you lost, not the Sam over there in a box.'

'Sam?'

'Joe mentioned him before we came upstairs.'

'Ahh.' Alex nods indistinctly, then she untangles herself and springs off the divan. 'I need a cigarette,' she says. 'Would you like one?'

'Are we allowed to?'

'Share a guilty pleasure? No, of course we're not allowed to. But Dog's a big softie, and we all take advantage.'

'All these dogs,' I say. 'If they're not out for a walk or reading poetry, they're being a big softie.'

This time it's Alex who breaks off the laughter, again with a sigh. She's standing by the dressing table clutching a packet of cigarettes, peering inside it. 'There's only one left,' she says. 'We'll share it.'

I stay silent. I should probably say it doesn't matter, it's her last cigarette, she should smoke it by herself. But I don't; instead, I dig into my pocket for my lighter. I flick it open and hold out the flame for her.

Alex bends down and lights the cigarette. She holds it in her mouth between two fingers while she inhales. Then, with an ashtray beside her, she perches herself on the armrest and takes one more drag. 'I'll sit here while we smoke it,' she says after exhaling. She passes the cigarette to me, and at that moment I'm thinking that the room has just become less unfamiliar. But then Alex speaks again: 'You've asked me about Sam, but you've also lost someone.'

I struggle to breathe; my heart is pumping. The blood is burning my ears; the hairs on my arms are bristling. In spite of the cold, I feel hot. I have just one puff and hand the cigarette back to Alex.

'I don't understand. When could she have told you, I've been with her all the time.'

'You mean Claw? She hasn't told me anything. No one has.' She takes one last drag and offers me what's left. When I refuse to take it (I look at it as if I've never seen a cigarette before), Alex puts it out in the ashtray. 'When I saw you in that doorway, I knew. I've seen that look often enough in the mirror.'

'You knew what?'

She stands up and moves the ashtray to the dressing table. Her head slightly bowed and her arms now tightly crossed, 'That you're grieving,' she says, turning to face me. 'That you've been grieving for a long time. And that you didn't want to be around people.'

Jesus. I stop myself from saying it out loud.

'You knew I didn't want to be around people, so you thought it was a good idea to come over and ask for a light.'

'I was trying to bring you back to the moment.'

'To distract me from my thoughts.'

'Yes. But then something happened I wasn't expecting. When I smiled, you smiled back.' She walks back to the divan and perches herself on its edge, and from there she smiles at me again. 'There, just like that,' she says. 'That's the smile of someone who isn't quite done yet. It reminds me of Sam's.'

It's true, I'm smiling.

'I hadn't realised,' I say. 'That I was smiling. I remember smiling in the street, but only because I remember you pointing it out, just like you did now. I also remember your smile when I lit your cigarette with my old-fashioned lighter. And I remember thinking that your stranger's smile reminded me of Eden's.'

Alex bends slightly backwards, clasping the edge of the divan with both hands. 'Just as yours reminded me of Sam's. I'm guessing Eden was your wife?'

'Yes,' I say, and I don't have time to say anything else.

'And you think *I'm* creepy!' cries out a muffled voice.

Neither of us laughs.

'I guess it is a bit creepy,' I say.

'Oh, don't take any notice of *them*,' says Alex, making a dismissive gesture in the general direction of the black wooden case.

'You keep saying that.'

'We just happened to both need reminding, that's all.'

'That's *all*? I mean, what were the chances? Eden, Sam, you spotting my miserable look in that doorway, me carrying a lighter, us both smiling, you inviting me to something I was coming to already...'

'It's in the nature of coincidences that the chances are small,' Alex says, sitting up straight with her hands again clasped in her lap.

'Small world, you said; you remember?'

'It wasn't me who said it, it was you.'

'But then you said it on stage.'

'That wasn't me either, it was Them.'

All my questions bounce back at me unanswered. What were the chances; and yet here we are. And I want to know why. Are we here because of Eden and Sam, are we here because I wear my grief for Eden too openly, are we here just because of the past? Or are we here because a flutter stirs in both of us?

'So small that once again it has become enormous,' I say. 'What did you mean?'

Leaning sharply forward, Alex puts an elbow on her thigh and settles her chin on her fist. 'Eden,' she says. 'It's a beautiful name.' And then, 'I'm guessing that you didn't lose her suddenly.'

'No,' I say. 'But you still haven't told me about Sam. The original Them, Someone and Everyone, who one day was here and the next day was not.'

'See? You already know everything. Except maybe one thing.'

I hold my breath.

'They Them, it's confusing,' Alex goes on. 'It's meant to be. Sam was the original Them, but Them isn't Sam and They Them has become something else.' Lifting her chin off her fist, she chuckles loudly. 'And you're literally scratching your head.'

'Because literally I'm confused.'

The world that has become enormous is once again shrinking. Perhaps Alex is as frightened as I am. Perhaps I have misread all the signals, mistaking the kindness of a stranger for more. Perhaps my own flutter has been a mirage, and tomorrow I will be counting back from sixty.

'Come on, let's go out.' Alex leaps off the divan. 'It's a beautiful day, let's go for a walk. Just the two of us. I say we leave the ghosts behind for a change.'

Tomorrow can wait.

'Yes,' I say. 'The ghosts and the dummy. But first I need your help getting out of this chair.'

It is already almost dark; the beautiful day is now a beautiful late afternoon that will soon break into a beautiful evening. This earlier part of December, when the shortening days mark with such imponderable mathematical exactitude the piecemeal advance into winter, has always been my favourite time of the year - something I had almost forgotten but has struck me just now once again with the searing physicality – *the pain*, I would say - with which my body is experiencing the cold. Suddenly I am in awe of my senses. The early twilight gloom, when daylight has faltered but darkness still hesitates, not for long around the winter solstice, seems in its innumerable shades of grey to form a perfect contrast to my mood, grey too until its colours were brought back to life by a flutter and the shiver of a warmth that I hadn't felt since Eden. And with the colours of my mood, the world has also come alive. The cold, so dismal, and the murk of lurking shadows have the contrary effect of steeping all the instances of humankind's resistance in an aura of luminescent exultation. The yellow shiver of streetlamps that fail to hold their own, the paltry twinkle of impatient Christmas lights flashing on and off in scattered windows, the red-and-orange pulse of faintly burning cigarettes, the pleasurable resignation with which I submit to at least the possibility of a different equation and a respite from dummies and ghosts, are all equal to each other and to a multitude of other illustrations that amount to nothing short of a blinding affirmation of life.

'There's nothing more depressing than tinsel,' Eden used to say, and we both used to laugh as we toured its most glittering manifestations in Oxford Street and Regent Street and Soho, where the silver of spangles mingled with the black of unsexy fetish leather in festive displays, before returning home to overdecorate our own enormous Christmas tree. And after New Year, the accoutrements of celebration were either stored away or discarded, and even when the thousands of dead trees had all been collected, shiny fragments of tinsel and evergreen needles persisted for weeks, adding to a melancholy sense of anti-climax the sense of a communal perseverance against all the odds that I found very moving. 'You mean of degradation and ugly excess,' Eden had half-joked, and I had not disagreed: what was life if not the volatile and thrilling fusion of opposing contradictions? Answering my rather rhetorical question as always on behalf of the many, Eden had had the last word: *Shit*, was what life was, while also being frighteningly short. Which in turn had proved nothing if it had not proved my point.

And so on, it would go.

Past the doorway where we smoked a cigarette, past the entrance, and the exit, to the station. At the barriers plastic tickets touch in and out, flaps swinging open, then shut. A mass of heavy coats going in, the shuffle of feet invisible in the congestion: *patter, patter, patter*, a greater mass going in than coming out. The black now a grey, dark but indistinct, like a cloud that will soon become a downpour.

Where are we heading to? Alex has taken the lead, and I follow without asking questions, happy not to know, happy to be led.

A man into his phone: *Are you sure?*

One plus one equals something.

Every day a step. Until what? Until when?

We are walking towards Brunswick Square on a cold Friday evening in early December, just a few spare minutes after four. Stunned by the brightness of night-time, so pale and blue-yellow it has faintly made the vista of architecture shiver with the fear its every contour might be about to fade away, I sigh deeply, and the mist from my breath unites with the mist from the breath of the woman beside me to conjure an illusion that I dare to imagine might not be an illusion after all.

As we pass the square on the left, 'For now we'll avoid all the greenery,' says Alex. 'In these narrow streets I like to walk near the traffic, especially at night. Not because I don't feel safe, I just prefer to be close to all the noises. To be part of the city. I hate it that new cars hardly make any sound, don't you?'

'I've never really thought about it,' I say. 'But I suppose they're easier to avoid if you can hear them.'

'That's also true,' Alex says, 'but it's not what I meant. I *like* the sound of cars. I like it when they whoosh through the rain or speed away from traffic lights, I like their thud when they go over speed humps.' And lowering her voice as she looks left and right before crossing the road, 'I even like the sound of crashing metal when they drive into each other; I mean, the last thing I want is for people to get hurt, but that clanging noise they make gives me a buzz, I can't help it. It's like laughing when you see someone trip and fall over, it's not because you think it's funny.'

'I'm not sure I do laugh when I see someone trip and fall over.'

She turns to look at me without slowing down. 'Really, you don't?' And before I can answer, 'Have you noticed how everything sounds different in winter, more distant? In the street, I mean. Not just traffic but also all the noises made by people. It's because the air is thicker, it slows everything down.'

'I've never really thought about that either,' I say.

'Hm,' Alex says. And then, almost in passing, 'I think we should both give up smoking. Today.'

We should both give up smoking. Alex has just said that *we* should do something *together.* I try not to read too much into it.

'But I don't smoke,' I say.

'Good. Then it shouldn't be too hard to give up.'

Another soundless sigh returns me not to a doorway or the street – I *am* in the street – but rather to the table at the foot of the stage at the Cutting-Edge Arts Centre, where I sit without listening through most of the Poetry Reading Event I am attending as the poet's special guest, unable to concentrate not because poetry is not really my thing, nor because all I can hear is a jumble of words with no meaning, but because my head is overrun by clashing thoughts that are not too dissimilar to life's thrilling fusion of opposing contradictions, but are so much more pressingly life-and-death. And yet, even as it fails to concentrate, my mind somehow knows how to cut through this internal upheaval at *all* the right moments – the moments, scattered in small clusters throughout the performance, that more or less obliquely make mention of my earlier encounter with the poet.

And now, back in the street with the poet beside me, I am able to recall one such cluster, as I could every other, word for word:

"Two strangers
Because of a moment
Are no longer strangers.
Excuse me, do you have a light?
An old-fashioned lighter
Sorry, would you like one?
A smoker, not a smoker
Really, I'd love one."

And I become nostalgic. The world is too full of finality already.

'Can we at least have one last cigarette?'

'That means buying a new packet,' says Alex, 'and if we only smoke two, we'll be wasting eighteen.'

'We could give them away, there's always someone dying for a cigarette.'

'I'd rather give them money for patches.'

'I don't mind buying us a packet,' I say.

Alex stops us both dead in our tracks. 'Is that really what you think the problem is, that I'm too mean?' Her voice is harsh, unforgiving.

'No, no, of course not.'

But Alex is laughing, and has already spun around and pinned her gloveless hands across my chest. 'Oh, look, you're blushing.' Freezing fingers pinch the tips of my ears. 'Now come on, let's find a shop.'

We're on Lambs Conduit Street, heading towards Theobalds Road. Alex leads and I follow, still uncertain if we have a destination, other than a shop for cigarettes.

Alex looks different. She is wearing everything I remember her wearing this morning, including her black scarf, her black coat, her black trainers (the heavy platforms must still be on the floor by the blue divan, where they fell after she kicked them off), and yet she does, she looks different. Walking slightly behind her, I can't keep my eyes to myself, and while taking her in I wonder if the only reason she looks different mightn't be that I am looking at her differently. And I can't deny it's true, I am looking at her very differently. I am looking at her in the dark of a cloudless winter evening, and I am looking at her in the light of everything that's happened since she asked me for a light on a sunny winter morning. I am looking at her with the eyes of someone who three days ago was almost at zero, and who now, because of her, is no longer counting backwards from sixty. And yes, I am looking at her with the eyes of a man.

The flutter has become more urgent, more fierce than the tingle or warmth of a shiver: I am attracted to a woman who isn't Eden with a force that feels like betrayal. It is not betrayal at all, Eden would have said, but Eden isn't here. What I need is to make peace with myself.

Night has quickly superseded dusk, at its shortest in early December, and all the artificial lights are now coming to their own, still primarily blue-yellow but brighter (more yellow, less blue), and dotted with the smaller jewels of colour that sparkle in the dark here and there. In the main road far ahead, traffic moves like brushstrokes of illumination that sweep across an ever-changing canvas with a rhythm as irregular as my own heartbeat. What Alex said about noise is true; it does appear to travel through invisible impediments that make its sounds more distant, and somehow also muffled. Our soft trainers barely squelch as our feet hit the ground in a rhythmical stride; as though sucking in the air that blocks their path, vehicles pass each other in a shush; conversations are low, like conspiracies pre-set to peter out.

'There!' Alex calls out, and the shrill sound of her voice makes me jump, causing me to literally trip. Alex steadies me by swivelling in front of me and taking the brunt of my forward momentum, our panoplies of heavy coats colliding with a thump. 'Are you always like this?' she asks me while we hold each other still in an embrace.

The cold mist of her breath again unites with mine as she looks at me. Its vague taste of tobacco brings me to, and through the many layers that protect us from the cold I can also feel the thud of her heartbeat, which might be the thud of my own, or it might be the cacophony of both. And while we stay in that position, through a purposeful paralysis whose effect is to intensify the thud, 'Am I always like what?' I ask her loudly, and for just the briefest moment my head is no longer full of thoughts.

'Like you're living in a daydream.'

A permanent mind-drift, Eden used to call it.

'It's a lot, what's happened in the last few hours.'

'And it hasn't stopped happening. I mean, it's anybody's guess what happens next,' Alex says, pointing with a flutter of her eyes at the entrance to the small corner shop across the road.

'Ah. I think I know what happens next.'

'Off you go then, genius, if you're sure you can stand up by yourself.'

'Admittedly that's never been my forte, but I'll try,' I say, smiling as the cold mist of her breath breaks away.

And soon we're on Theobalds Road with a packet of twenty cigarettes whose fate is not yet fully known - heading for Red Lion Square Gardens, Alex has decided. Much as she prefers tarmac and its noises to bushes and birds, a bench is a good place to smoke.

'The Walks are more spectacular, especially in winter, but I'm not sure we can smoke there.'

'The Walks?'

'The Gray's Inn Gardens.'

'None the wiser,' I shrug.

'The Inns of Court, where lawyers train to be barristers? Gray's Inn is one of them, and the Walks are how its Gardens are known.'

'Or not known.'

'It's my neighbourhood, so I know my way around pretty well.'

'And you don't avoid trees altogether.'

'No, not altogether. Their soundtrack also has its charms, I can't deny it sometimes suits my mood. But, in general, I'm not a nature person. All the ugliness that we're responsible for? I actually like it. The concrete and the cigarette butts and the tacky souvenirs, I love all of it. Oh, and all the fake stuff.'

'Like tinsel.'

'Except that I'm not sure about Christmas; the hype is so relentless it's oppressive. What I detest is the snobbery of good taste – which boils down to the rich telling the poor that they don't know how to live. Trying to take away all their pleasures.'

'But you're not poor,' I say, steering clear of a debate on the merits and demerits of Christmas, happy to keep tinsel to myself. 'I don't mean it as a criticism, I'm not poor either.'

Alex makes us stop so we can cross the road. Two double-decker buses dash past, a 19 and then another 19, back-to-back. I breathe in their brush of wind; it has a sound and a smell of its own, an aftertaste of metal.

'No, you're right. I'm not poor. And Sam's family are rich, so he was rich, and now I'm rich too, in a way.' As we turn left into Old North Street, the Gardens are already in sight. 'I'm not saying that everyone who happens to be rich is the same, just that rich people have power and most of them are bastards. Take your friends Patrick and Claw.'

No, let's not. 'I'm not sure we should go there,' I say.

'Why not?'

For different reasons that I don't feel like listing to Alex. Patrick and Claw are nothing like each other, and neither of them can be defined by a stranger's preconceptions. But I refuse to sanction *any* accusation by defending them.

'Because they're my friends.'

'And they were Eden's friends too.'

'Yes.'

'But that didn't stop Claw from seducing you.'

Something shatters, but the shock is quickly absorbed, and the momentary instinct to flee quietly dissipates. The thud, however, has intensified, and is mine entirely. We are already in the Gardens, our pace slackening as we approach the nearest bench.

'Here,' Alex says, almost cheerfully.

No one else is around, the small café is closed and we have the small oasis to ourselves. I prefer green to grey, and I prefer peaceful silence to noise. Why am I with Alex? A part of me still wants to walk away.

'A pocket of green we can hide in.' She makes a sharp circling gesture, as though to illustrate the smallness of the place. 'This is what I love the most about London, its treasures that are hidden in plain view.'

The shock has not been absorbed; rather it has morphed into irritation. Alex does *not* make a virtue of being casual while being indiscreet. And the swathe of her pronouncements is beginning to get on my nerves. Strangely the effect of these negative feelings is to slow down the thud and make me more relaxed. But all the same the number of unlikely coincidences and the accuracy of Alex's wild guesses are beginning to stretch my credulity. What might she be hiding? Is it possible her guesses aren't as wild as they seem?

'Who told you?'

We're not looking at each other. We sit side by side with our hands in our laps and we stare straight ahead.

'No one told me.'

'What, you just guessed?'

'It wasn't that hard,' Alex says. 'The way she relates to you, it's proprietary; it's obvious something's happened between you that's made her feel entitled, like I imagine she feels about most things in life, the way rich people do. Sorry, the way *some* rich people do. And it's just as obvious that what happened isn't something you'd've wanted. I'm guessing you probably think that you regretted it as soon as it was over, but really you never really wanted it to happen in the first place.' She bends a little to the side and turns to look at me. 'Am I wrong?' And before I can answer, 'I'm also guessing you told Eden straight away.'

'You're guessing too much,' I want to say. 'You're wrong about some things,' I say instead. And then, '12.30 is an odd time if you didn't want just rich people to come.'

Alex throws her head back and takes a deep breath. 'I love the way the trees smell when it's cold, don't you?' she says. And while still gazing at the sky, 'You said you're not poor either, are you rich?'

'I have enough money in the bank to be able to afford not to work for a while. But no, I'm not rich.'

'And what would you be doing if you did have to work?' Now that Alex has asked me the question, I find it strange she hasn't asked me before – it's usually the first thing people ask. 'No, wait, let me guess.' She makes a show of scrutinising me. 'Something creative,' she says. 'Advertising?'

'What, because I look so trendy?'

'Umm, I'd say more hipsterish than trendy.'

I rub my three-day stubble and I laugh. 'I'm usually clean-shaven.'

'Ah. So not something creative?'

'In my last full-time job, I was working in PR. And I didn't say I wasn't working. I'm still there part-time.'

'PR. That's *kind* of like advertising.

'And on the side, me and Eden had fun buying a couple of old properties and selling them on after practically rebuilding them from scratch. That's how I ended up with some savings.'

Me and Eden… Sharing joyful moments of our past with a stranger feels like both an obligation and a trespass.

'That sounds *very* creative.'

'Eden was a brilliant architect, so.'

Alex gives a thoughtful nod. Then with her hands still clasped together in her lap, at last she averts her gaze as she extends her body backwards for a stretch. '12.30 is a good time for students,' she says. 'And there was also an evening performance last night.'

'Oh,' I say. 'I didn't know that.'

The noises again, so distant in the night but so deafeningly loud in the quiet that we both now coalesce in, as though equally exhausted by the unfinished conversations about our two unfinished pasts that by dint of an old lighter have converged, with consequences still unknown, as hazy as the steam from our breaths.

Alex was right that London's many pockets of green are a treasure, and not only the ones that are hidden. Large and small, studiously designed or overgrown, they all serve their purpose - the larger ones as social oases, the small ones as intimate hide-outs where aloneness feels different, at one with the colours and smells of the earth, more at peace with coming closer to the end. In Waterlow Park, just a few yards up the hill from where I live, the unkempt graves of the modern Highgate cemetery can be seen from the paths, the wildness of greenery mingling with carvings and fragments of stone as though seeking to unite life and death. There are benches everywhere from which to contemplate the smallness of this distance, every one of them inscribed with words that remember a loved one. The price of life is love and death...

'We're about to lock up now,' says a man.

'Could we *please* smoke our cigarette first?' Alex pleads with him.

'Sure,' says the man. 'We're supposed to close when it gets dark, but I reckon it's unfair, some people like the dark, they like the quiet of it. I like it too if I'm honest. I'll be sitting over there, out of your way behind old Bertrand. Take your time.'

'Is that Bertrand Russell?' I ask when he's gone, nodding at the black metal bust in the distance as I take the cigarettes out of my pocket.

'I believe so,' Alex says. She bends down again to lean on her knees, but then propels herself backwards to face me. 'People like Claw, they take what they want and they also somehow manage not to get all the blame.'

I take two cigarettes out of the packet and offer her one. 'She didn't force me,' I say.

'What, you mean you wanted to?'

I dig into another pocket for the Dunhill. 'No, not exactly. But I could've walked away and I didn't.' I flick it open. A strong reek of petrol, a flame feeble and blue. I raise it and Alex lights her cigarette. Then I light my own and I suck on it hard. 'I told Eden that same day. "Good," she said. "Everyone has sex with Claw once, but the first time is always the last." And then we made love.' I let the smoke out, then the cigarette is back in my mouth and I take another drag.

Alex makes a gesture with hers. 'So, no one got the blame. And you all stayed friends.'

I prefer not to mention the lump, or rather its coinciding with what happened between me and Claw.

'Claw's a doctor,' I say. 'She has her own private general practice, but when Eden fell ill, she was there for her.' Six parallel lines are again in the forefront, traces of leftover mercy, of kindness I had almost abused. 'You know earlier on stage, right at the beginning of the show when you said I was "almost not here", what did you mean?'

'When I met you before in the street, you were on your way somewhere, no one stays in doorways forever, you didn't just look like you were grieving, you also looked like you were having second thoughts, like you'd much rather be somewhere else.'

'These days I think I always look like that.'

'You don't look like that now.'

A few minutes ago, I almost walked away, so I must have had second thoughts then. But I didn't walk away, I'm still here.

Why?

Why am I still with this semi-crazy stranger who knows all my secrets and doesn't like Christmas?

My distance from Eden is growing, and so is my distance from Alex; my distance from Eden will never be anything other than nothing, and that certainty causes my distance from Alex to shorten. I shut my eyes, then I open them again and take a breath. I can smell the darkness; I can even smell the noises. With every breath, I feel the cold in my lungs. When I look at Alex, what do I see?

'I asked you about Sam,' I say, 'and all we've talked about is me.'

Alex stubs her cigarette out on the stones, picks up the butt and puts it in the bin next to the bench on her side. Then she plucks what's left of mine out of my hand, and the sequence is repeated: stones, butt, bin.

'We should go,' she says, and she's already on her feet. 'Thank you,' she calls out to the man, and he waves without getting up. Then to me, 'Would you like to come over for something to eat? I live just round the corner, and I can pick all my stuff up from the centre tomorrow. Or even the day after. Or maybe not at all.' She laughs as we exit the gardens, heading back the way we came. I wait for her to tell me she's not normally so forward, but she doesn't, because probably she is.

'You're not performing tomorrow?'

'Is that a yes?' Alex takes me by the arm and we walk on, in step and bound together, turning right, back into Theobalds Road. The yellow fog of streetlamps and headlights is broken by the bright red of brake lights blinking as the traffic hesitates or stops. A red light, then amber, then green and they go, accelerating for a distance then again slowing down, a forever stop-and-go with an improvised rhythm that brightens up the sky, moonless tonight, its blackness prey only to the enterprise and noises of stubborn human beings.

'Yes,' I say.

'Good!' Alex squeezes my arm without letting go. 'And no, I'm not performing tomorrow, what you saw today was the last of They Them, so later we're going out to a club.'

'A club? What for?'

'For a dance to the music of time! Not the painting, nor the novel, my favourite DJ's special two-hour set tonight at *Frustration*. It's not far, and I promised I'd be there.' She pokes me with her elbow. 'Like you promised you'd come to see They Them.'

'It's snowing,' I say. A drift of scattered flakes far apart, it may become a snowstorm from one moment to the next.

It doesn't; the drift remains a drift. Unsteady and sparse, its slow motion jars spectacularly with the whirl of city lights.

'Isn't life beautiful,' says Alex, holding on to me more tightly as we cross Gray's Inn Road, breathing in the freshness of the cold, some perfect shapes of frozen wetness resting on our hair, and our sleeves, and our shoulders, for a fraction of a second before they dissolve.

Can life be beautiful again, in spite of all the sadness that will never go away? I see a freedom in Alex's eyes that I envy, but I can also see the sadness behind it that sometimes spills over and clouds it.

'We're missing just a car crash to make our first day perfect!' And tugging at my coat sleeve when I look at her sideways, 'Don't worry, I'm joking.'

Our first day. How would I rate it? Perfection is made up of imperfections, someone said. But how many imperfections wasn't specified. Nor the type of imperfections that might qualify, or wouldn't.

'The last of They Them,' I remember, 'what does that mean?'

'Here,' says Alex, and we turn right into Hatton Garden. Some of the shops are still open, their windows brightly lit, glistering with fairy lights and jewellery and gold and silver tinsel. Security men stand on guard, traders dart about, shoppers gawk outside or go in. 'Nearly there,' as we turn left into St Cross Street.

'The last of They Them, a poet like no other,' I say.

'I told you, They Them belonged to Sam, and I'm no poet without him.'

'Him?'

'That old chestnut. I know, I know, it's confusing,' Alex says. We stop in front of an enormous double door. 'This is us.'

FOUR

The building must have been light-industrial before being converted. Even in the semi-darkness, its brutalist straight lines and large metal windows are squat and no-nonsense, a testament to its original utilitarian intentions. It has a geometrical solidity about it that residential streets in London generally lack, except in its most affluent parts. Along two sides of the naked brick walls of the lobby, large black-and-white photographs narrate the history of the building; the machinery suggests an old printing works. Painted cast iron columns, with intricately moulded capitals, frame the entrance to an enormous lift. The metal grills of its sliding scissor gate open like a concertina, to an interior buzzing with a constant phosphorescence, an ooze of yellow luminosity that sounds almost radioactive.

When Alex pulls open the gate, I follow her in. 'Second floor,' she says.

'I'm not judging, but you're rich too, *in a way*? This feels like more than just rich *in a way*.'

'Wait till you've seen the apartment,' says Alex, and I laugh.

'You're always being so mysterious,' I say. 'You never give straight answers to anything.'

'That's because there are no straight answers.'

As the elevator climbs with an almighty jolt, the light temporarily flickers and the buzzing intensifies. But everything steadies when it clangs to a stop. Whitened by the light, Alex looks like a ghost, and I imagine I do too.

'I love this elevator, but it's scary,' I say, cautiously peeling myself off the wall.

'It's like a fairground ride, Sam used to say.' Alex opens her front door and waits for me to go in first, then she flicks a switch, turning on the room's phantasmagoria.

'Wow, this is enormous,' I say.

And it is. It's the largest room that I have ever seen, an entirely white kitchen that gives in to an almost naked dining room that opens up to a sparsely furnished living room, their minimalism as much the effect of high-ceilinged white emptiness as of design: a square wooden table that looks like it belongs in a carpenter's workshop, four chunky wooden chairs with tall backs and armrests that remind me of Andy Warhol's grim screen-print images of the electric chair, a bright red sofa shaped like a comma, an oblong chrome-and-glass coffee table and a Bauhaus 1930s sideboard, are all arranged at odd angles to each other that do not give the impression of not being haphazard. Bare lightbulbs hang at different heights from four random spots on the ceiling in the area around the sofa, their inadequate glow complemented by the fierce white light emitted from three holes in the bleached wooden floor.

Not just a room but a grand loft apartment in Clerkenwell. Does the dogged understatement prevent its pervasive good taste from amounting to snobbery?

'And this is far from all of it,' says Alex with a mischievous chuckle, and pointing in some vague direction, 'Two en-suite double bedrooms, each with its own walk-in wardrobe, guest bathroom, plus a storeroom in the basement.'

"Not just not poor" doesn't quite cut it.

I walk over to one of the several windows, all curtainless and iron-barred, set in a solid cast iron frame.

'Not much of a view,' Alex says as she joins me, 'but then I like looking at bricks.'

'It must be worth millions,' I say. 'Is it yours?'

'Yes, but I didn't buy it. The whole building belonged to Sam's family, and when it was converted, they gave him this apartment.'

As we both turn around, again our shoulders brush against each other's, then settle just a quiver apart.

'There's so much to take in,' I say, but really there isn't.

In terms of the economy of its geometry, its clever lighting, deliberate sparseness of furniture and dazzling preponderance of whiteness, it is a stunning apartment that could feature on the cover of a lifestyle magazine. But impressive as it might be in the two dimensions of a photographic composition, as an inhabitable space, through which to move and breathe, its calculated flawlessness renders it soulless: it's as if by depriving it almost completely of the warmth of human touch, the intention is to simulate instead the coldness of an execution chamber. An exaggerated first impression, I am aware that it doesn't fit at all with my impression of Alex. I am also aware that it is partly a reflection of my own state of mind, and to some degree the consequence of a comparison I am unable to resist: I can see Eden's hand sweeping through the room and transforming it to a style of decoration as wholehearted in its championing of clutter as our own flat had been - our walls covered in a mayhem of 60s abstraction, our furniture littered with glorious bric-a-brac, every piece of textile harking back to the decade of colour, and all of it together amounting to a style that like Eden's architecture was conducive more to living than appearance. Here, in this overly-illuminated dungeon, there is not one cosy corner to escape to.

But perhaps I'm just being blinded by nostalgia.

'So, what's the verdict?' Alex asks, leaning into me as though to prompt me to say something.

'There's no art on the walls, not a single painting, how come?'

'Art isn't decoration, that's what Sam used to say. Everything you see belonged to him; I haven't changed a thing.'

'But you lived here together.'

'When we got married, I moved in. And now I can barely afford the bills. But I don't want to sell.'

We've taken our coats off, and Alex disappears for two minutes and returns in a blouse.

'Take your jumper off if you like, the place is very warm.' And when I've stripped down to my T-shirt, 'Now then, what shall we eat? I make a mean spaghetti carbonara.'

'With or without cream?'

'No cream and no bacon, I make it like they make it in Rome. Guanciale, pecorino and eggs.'

I've never heard of guanciale or pecorino.

'Carbonara sounds good.'

'Come and have a drink at the table while I make it.' Alex leads the way and I follow, counting my steps: twenty-four to the table.

Why hasn't Alex changed a thing? She can't possibly *not* find the emptiness oppressive. Perhaps it helps her feel Sam's absence more intensely. I still live in the flat I shared with Eden, and I haven't changed anything either. In amongst her clutter, I am constantly aware of Eden's presence.

The chairs clunk as we pull them away from the table. 'Is it time for my execution already?' I ask.

'Oh, the electric chairs,' Alex says, after just a moment's hesitation. 'They are a bit severe, but they're Sam's own design, so I love them. You like wine?' She dangles a bottle of Pinot Noir. 'I only have red.'

'Sure, I'd love a glass of wine. And I wouldn't mind a glass of water. But may I use the toilet first?'

'Through there.' Alex points again in the same vague direction. 'First door on the left.'

More steps. This time I count forty-three. The guest bathroom is another lack of ostentation; I continue to resist answering or asking questions on behalf of the poor. After washing my hands and throwing a splash of water on my face, I retrace the forty-three steps back to the table.

'They're actually quite comfortable,' I say, settling in the electric chair that faces the kitchen. Alex has her back to me humming a song, so quietly I can still hear her cracking the eggs; one, two, three – the extraordinary room's acoustics are also extraordinary.

'I'm starving, aren't you?'

'I suppose so,' I say, sipping from the wine I found waiting for me with the water at the table.

It must be late, but *how* late? I have no idea what time it is; just before the performance I switched my phone off, and it's still off now. In all the hours we've spent together I haven't asked Alex for the time, worried she might think I was either getting bored or being impatient.

Being impatient for what?

Perhaps to avoid answering the question, I attempt calculations instead. How long was the performance? How long were we upstairs, in the room that felt unreal? How long did we walk before we found the shop where I bought cigarettes, eighteen of which are still in my pocket? How long were we in the gardens that shouldn't have been open after dark? How long was the walk to St Cross Street? The time that has passed since a radioactive lift delivered us to this remarkable apartment already feels like an eternity, one I know can be counted in minutes. The same fluttering that causes this distortion is also what prevents me from

74

even roughly measuring *any* of these fantastical fragments of time. And they *are* all fantastical, each as though a fraction of a separate fictional whole in which I feel out of place - one unfathomable labyrinth that leads into another.

Breakfast was a single slice of toast and some cheese, and that was the last thing I ate. In spite of having smoked, I should be feeling hungrier than I do, and no sooner has the thought occurred to me than I suddenly feel famished. The smell of frying meat that may not be bacon but sizzles not unlike it wafts over to the table enticingly, egging on my appetite. Reminded of its emptiness, my stomach starts to growl.

'Not long to go now,' Alex calls out reassuringly, looking at me over her shoulder. 'Early dinner or very late lunch, take your pick.' None the wiser, I look at her vacantly, and she laughs. 'You've no idea what time it is, do you? It's not that late, it's not even seven yet.'

'If you're not guessing my past or how I'm feeling, you're constantly reading my mind,' I want to say, but instead I laugh too.

If it's true that time passes quickly when you're having fun, then these jigsaw-puzzle hours of interlocking fragments, which Alex has now quantified precisely, can't have amounted to fun; for me at least, they have not passed quickly. And I wonder if this might be because I have been in two places at once, with one foot rooted firmly in the past while timidly the other, with an eye to a different future, dares to dip only the tip of a toe in the present. The labyrinths have not consisted of the sounds and lights and colours of the day as it progressed into night, or of all my uncompleted interactions with Alex – uncompleted because, without ever settling, they have constantly swayed between Eden and Sam. They have consisted of the morass of my own opposition, my holding on to distant voices I wrongly attribute to Eden, while in breach of my promise resisting a flutter that makes me feel almost alive.

I promise,

I promise,

I promise.

The keeping of a promise does not need forgiveness,

It is not a betrayal at all.

The labyrinths of subterfuge dissolve, and with them *all* second thoughts. I let go of the past, and now, in the present, I know that I want to be here.

If only it were that simple.

'Tuck in and I'll tell you about Sam while we eat,' I hear Alex saying, and I stare into the plate in front of me unsure for how long it has been there; when I look up from it, Alex must have been already eating for some time.

'It looks delicious,' I say, because it does, but eating it seems like an impossible task. It feels as though my stomach has shrunk into a knot that keeps getting tighter. I take a gulp of my wine hoping it might cause it to loosen, but if anything, it has the opposite effect.

And now Alex has stopped eating too. She watches me with heedful eyes, attentively, with a smile that signifies affinity and the sadness of a deep understanding - the unbounded solidarity of a comrade who knows better than to lazily mistake similarity for sameness. Not a spoken "I feel what you feel" but an unspoken "I give you space to feel it differently".

In this shared space, this emotionally *over*charged oasis, I feel hungry again.

I use just my fork, twirl it around the spaghetti, skewer a chunkier piece of pork than I could imagine any recipe demanding, and take my first mouthful.

'Mm,' I say, shaking my head this way and that while I chew, and when my mouth is no longer too full, 'This really is delicious, thank you.' Then lifting up my glass of wine, 'Cheers!'

For a moment Alex seems bemused; her brow again slightly pinched, the heedful eyes narrow as she gives an indefinite nod. But then there is the wheeze of a sharp nasal intake of breath, and she breaks into a smile as she exhales. 'Yes, cheers,' she says, clinking her glass against mine.

'Good wine too,' I say after we've both had a swig.

'It's nothing special, it's been on offer in Tesco all week,' Alex says, and when we've each had one more mouthful of spaghetti, 'So, Sam and They Them, the true story. Well, the true story from *my* point of view, I should say.' Her fork jingles as she uses it to gather all her leftover spaghetti into a pile, her other arm still holding up her glass of wine. 'Sam wasn't just the Sam of They Them,' she goes on. 'He was many different things to many different people, people who would all tell different stories, and all these incompatible stories would be more or less equally true. And I say "more or less" because I know Sam himself would have gauged them all differently.' She has a sip of her wine, then another, peering at me over her glass, prodding me to follow suit. I do, washing down another bite of carbonara. 'He liked to question everything, and was open to everything too, so he rarely made final decisions.' Alex leans back against the sheerness of the wood as though the moment has arrived to get strapped in. And smiling faintly after dabbing her mouth with her napkin, '"We're all of us queer," he would say, "I just choose to be queerer than most." It was by far the biggest part of who he was, that unrelenting need to be curious, to never settle, to never be contained, to never take the slightest thing for granted. Except maybe me.' Her gaze, fixed on mine, seems more awash with gratitude than grief or resentment. 'And I thought that was enough. Whenever I was with him, he always had that smile - the smile of someone who isn't quite done yet. But I wasn't always with him.'

I feel touched by the affection and depth of her openness, and ashamed that I had thought it one-sided.

But now a silence is needed, and while we let it run its course, we both finish eating. Alex replenishes our glasses, and opens a second bottle. When she resumes, her tone is more matter-of-fact, and she concludes her story without pause, as though finally a truth she has held on to with enormous effort is being purged by being told.

'I only ever knew Sam as a man, but being a man didn't define him, I think nothing defined him, not even life. "Don't let them try and label me," he said. "I'm everything and nothing, and I love you." I should've asked him who he thought might try and label him, but I didn't, and by the time I understood what he meant it was already too late. And that's our true story in a nutshell, and all of it together is They Them.'

'Not very literally,' I say. 'But then it's meant to be poetry, so.'

'So most of it goes over your head, especially if you're not paying attention.'

'I *was* paying attention. I remember hearing words and knowing their meaning without knowing how.'

'And what did you think was their meaning?'

'A tragic event; something broken. But then you improvised, and also spoke words about me. Not Anyone... and, everyone, two strangers because of a moment are no longer strangers, the smoker, not a smoker...'

'Ah, you really do remember.' There is again the wheeze of a sharp nasal intake of breath, but the smile this time is broader, less uncertain. 'What I hoped They Them would be was an outlet for both of us, me and Sam. That it would keep us grounded and give us some focus. Without Sam it felt more like a love song, a *happy* love song, not a dirge, then today... today it became something else.'

'And now?'

'And now it's done, it's come to an end. Like all things do eventually, don't they?'

We both sit stiffly erect in our chairs, our arms over the armrests, our hands like claws as they cling on to the roughly bevelled edges. I feel at a loss - my head swimming, my body inert, my emotions frozen, all separated from each other, adrift in a sea of incoherence. Right now, any prospect of electrocution would not feel like a terrible option. Not because of a renewal of my desire to be dead, but because I have reached another impasse, or rather reached the same impasse again: no sooner have I found a way through it than it once more finds itself in my way, one more insurmountable hurdle in a race of insurmountable hurdles playing out in a never-ending loop.

Alex claps her hands, and another impregnable impasse is broken.

'Let me get these to the sink, and if you don't mind walking over with the wine, I'll join you at the equally uncomfortable sofa.'

'Honestly, the chairs look more uncomfortable than they are,' I say.

'I wish I could say the same about the sofa.'

We each make our way to opposite parts of the room, Alex with the dirty plates to the sink and I with the bottle of wine to the sofa; I then have to return to the table for the glasses, which means Alex is now waiting for me at the sofa, whose low back tapers as it slopes in a curve towards the tail end of the comma.

'Sit while I pour the wine,' she tells me when I arrive.

'Somewhere in the middle,' I decide.

'And I think I'll recline at its apex,' Alex giggles.

But the hilarity is short-lived, and while Alex fills our glasses, I stay standing. And once again my instinct is to flee. Why am I here? It's unnatural, the speed with which a flutter and a distant warmth have culminated in whatever either of us might choose to call this. Are our expectations the same? Is that a question whose answer I am ready to confront? A shiver and a brushing touch have already caused me turmoil. How will I be able to withstand what might come next?

'I don't know what I'm doing here,' I say. 'Whatever's going on, it doesn't feel right.'

Alex is still standing too. 'Whatever's going on...' she says mullingly, but then lifting up her gaze from the floor she gives a shrug. 'This is strange for me too,' she goes on. And smiling as she gives a second shrug, 'It's been strange from the moment we first spoke in the street, but it hasn't felt wrong.'

'You're right, it hasn't,' I say, 'and that's probably what doesn't feel right.'

'I'm glad you're here,' says Alex, and I nod at the equal and beautiful curves of her smile, not quite able yet to say I'm glad too. But words appear unnecessary, and in silence we both sit, almost simultaneously, Alex at the comma's apex and I half-facing her from somewhere in the middle.

'Sam took his own life,' I hear myself saying, speaking out the words almost before I have thought them, and as soon as I have spoken them, I want to take them back. "Taken his own life." Is that also what I almost did to myself? Is it even possible to "take" what already belongs to you? Or is the word deliberate, used to imply that all our lives also belong to other people? "Take." A word I cannot easily dissociate from blame, and I would not have blamed myself, so how could I be blaming Sam?

Other words would have been better, and perhaps no words at all would have been best.

'I'm sorry,' I begin, but Alex reaches out and places three extended fingers softly over my mouth.

'I always struggle with the words,' she says. 'I know it's not words that have taken Sam away, but I still think they're important. Or maybe what I can't come to terms with is what happened, not how people choose to describe it. Maybe, but I don't think it's as simple as that. "Took his own life", "died by his own hand", "committed suicide", they all suggest a violent act, the *doing* of something violent, because how can an unnatural death not be the consequence of violence? And then there are the graphic images of self-disembowelling and self-immolation, which are intentionally violent, in protest or self-punishment. But that's not what Sam was doing, he wasn't protesting and had nothing to punish himself for.' She pauses, as though to give one final thought to her conclusion: 'I think he just wanted some peace; he lived life so intensely it exhausted him.' And now Alex takes her hands from her lap and intertwines them, then raises them and bends her head forward until they're almost covering her mouth. 'Or do you think I'm making excuses? Is it natural not to feel angry, or resentful? Does it mean I've not been grieving?' She looks at me over the overlap of fingers. 'Even feeling sad seems disrespectful.'

I remember Claw's phone call, and being persuaded to attend an unforgettable performance while playing with six colourful parallel lines made up of pretty shapes; would it have been an act of violence if I had gone through with my plan and washed them all down with a bottle of the most expensive vodka I have ever possessed in my life? Would it have made anyone angry or resentful if I had? Would anyone at all have felt sad? I know I am being self-indulgent, neither asking the right questions nor answering the questions Alex asked.

How would I have felt if Eden's life had not been snatched by illness but surrendered by Eden herself? How would Eden have felt if I had faced the dilemma of the colourful pills in her lifetime, and had resolved it by swallowing them all? These, too, are meaningless questions, unrelated to the questions Alex asked, which again I am avoiding to answer.

Is that why she asked me for a light in the street? Had she seen in my eyes something she had seen in Sam's eyes too? Had she then decided to save me because she had failed to save Sam?

'Anger, sadness, resentment, I still feel all those things all the time,' I say. 'But I don't know how I'd feel if dying had been Eden's own choice - I can't even imagine her making that choice, that wasn't who she was. And I don't think there's a recipe for grieving, people grieve in different ways.'

I have spoken too coldly, but right now I don't feel able to regret it, and I feel worse because I know that my coldness isn't Alex's fault. Over her fingers, she has been looking at me all this time, and all this time I have been looking somewhere else.

When she speaks, my coldness is unanswered. 'That wasn't who she was, you say that so conclusively.'

'I think I knew her pretty well.' I answer too quickly, and the coldness hasn't gone.

Alex too answers immediately, now rebuffing my coldness with warmth. 'I thought I knew Sam pretty well.' I can feel her gaze drifting to something behind me, to the whiteness that envelops the room. 'And I knew he sometimes struggled, but it never crossed my mind that he might do what he did. I always had the fear it might happen by mistake, but he made sure everyone knew that what happened was intentional, not an accident or a mistake.' With a smack she brings her hands down on her thighs, and gets up as though on cue.

I'm almost certain she's about to ask me to leave, and I want her to, because I want to leave. I also don't, and I'm also almost certain of that.

'Wine,' Alex says. 'Unless you've had enough.'

'Enough?'

Alex laughs. 'Enough wine,' she says. 'Hopefully you haven't had enough of me yet.'

'No,' I say. 'I mean yes, I'd like some wine.'

This morning I had been alone with Eden, with her but also without her, and then I had met Alex who had been alone with Sam, with him but also without him, and soon all the comparisons and contrasts had become overwhelming, causing time to become jumbled up, the past cutting through and almost derailing the present as though in that way past and present might both have been different, as though in that way I might still be with Eden and Alex might still be with Sam. But then Alex had answered my coldness with laughter, and her laughter had returned us to the room.

FIVE

While Alex is filling the glasses, I begin to think ahead, breaking up what's left of the evening into segments. I wonder what will happen when we've drunk the second bottle of wine. A third is not an option; already I feel tipsy and the last thing I want is to get drunk. Clubbing... I've not even been to a bar since Eden died. Just thinking about clubbing should be making me feel silly, and it does, but I also feel ashamed that I'm measuring my silliness by how long it's been since losing the woman I loved.

My mind is in another tangle, and once again I attempt to untangle it by filling it instead with calculations. It must be around eight o'clock. If I leave at nine, I can be back before eleven. I live halfway up Dartmouth Park Hill, a good ten minutes' walk from Tufnell Park, the nearest Underground station, which is on a different line to Farringdon, the station nearest to Alex, which means I'd have to change at Kings Cross, so a thirty-minute journey door-to-door, give or take. Which isn't too bad by London standards, and if we're really going clubbing, first I definitely need to shower and change my clothes.

I am already looking forward to the journey home and back. I love walking alone on a dark cold night, it's something I've always enjoyed, unlike Eden, who hated both the dark and the cold. Alex seems to like it all, the cold, the night, the walking, but then, other than Christmas and the rich (or some of the rich), there's little Alex doesn't seem to like. She also likes dancing, and later we will dance together to the music of time - her favourite DJ's set at a club called *Frustration*.

And later still, when the clubbing is over?

'Here,' Alex says, handing me a glass half full of wine before returning with hers to her perch at the apex. 'And there's enough for one more glass in the bottle.'

'You don't have any photographs,' I say, speaking out loud a thought that has only just occurred to me – might this be the absence that's making the room feel so soulless? 'Of Sam, I mean.'

'Sam hated photographs.'

'But Sam's not here,' I say, and I know the conversation is as much about Eden and myself as it is about Alex and Sam.

Alex knows it too. 'No, Sam's not here, you're right, and Eden isn't either, but you were also right that people grieve in different ways.'

'I have photos of her everywhere. Even though she wouldn't've liked it.'

'If it helps you, then she wouldn't've minded. And the same is true of Sam.'

'But they're not here.'

'But they're not here.' Alex smiles bittersweetly as she raises her glass. 'To Eden and Sam, who will always be here.'

'To Eden and Sam.'

'Other people call you Ollie. But I'd like to carry on calling you Oliver, if you don't mind.'

'Oliver is fine.'

'My name is actually Alexandria, not Alexandra.'

'Like the city in Egypt,' I say.

'Like all the many cities everywhere named after Alexander the Great.'

'I can only boast Oliver Cromwell.'

'Not really much of a boast.'

'They did cut his head off quite some time after he died... And then had it on a spike for thirty years.'

'They did?'

The last of the wine has been poured, and I'm grateful to have moved off the subject of Eden and Sam and what they might or might not have approved of. But Alex is one step ahead of me always.

'We should set off around eleven, and it's not even half past eight yet. Would you like to have a lie-down for an hour? It's been a long day.' Then filling the awkward silence with a smile, 'Spare bedroom, remember?'

'Yes. I mean, no, I need to go home for a shower,' I blurt out, and I expect Alex to laugh at me again.

But she doesn't. 'Why not have a shower here? Saves you an unnecessary journey.'

'Clean clothes,' I say.

'You're Sam's size exactly, I think. And there's a wardrobe full of clothes he's never worn. Including underwear, in case you're squeamish.'

There are no excuses left to be made.

Past and present are becoming jumbled up again. We met just half a day ago and Alex is asking me to have a shower and go to bed in her spare room before getting up to go clubbing with her in her dead husband's clothes.

'Are you sure we should be doing this? It really doesn't feel right.'

'This?'

'We've just met, and you're asking me to put on Sam's clothes and go dancing with you. I mean, aren't we both supposed to still be grieving?'

Alex gives a shrug I can't interpret.

'I'm sorry,' I say, 'I think that came out sounding wrong.'

'Wrong how? I thought it was a good summing up.'

'It sounded unkind.'

Now Alex shakes her head. 'Oh, it was brutal,' she says, 'but no, it wasn't unkind. Everything you said is true, and it's also fair to ask if I'm sure we should be doing this. I'm still not exactly sure what "this" actually is, but yes, in spite of that, I'm sure. And we'll always be grieving, so I don't think that should stop us. As for wearing Sam's clothes to go clubbing with me, they're just "things", things Sam never used, and honestly? I can't think of a better use for them.'

'But not because you'd like to be reminded of Sam.'

It's becoming a dangerous habit - speaking out my thoughts even before they have become fully formed. Is that my real objection? That I remind Alex of Sam, that this goes back almost to the moment when we met, that the smile that had reminded her of Sam might be the reason we are together in this room?

'Oliver, I don't need to see you wearing his clothes to be reminded of Sam. In a way, that's the biggest surprise, that you *don't* remind me of Sam, and you still wouldn't remind me of Sam even if I dressed you up in his favourite clothes.'

'And the smile of someone who wasn't quite done yet?'

We speak rapidly now, our voices low and flat but not cold.

'Is that why you were looking for a photograph?'

'Your smile looks just like Eden's. But that's not why I'm here.'

'When I first saw you, I was worried about you. I saw signs that I'd ignored in Sam. I've told you all this already.'

The smile of someone who wasn't quite done yet but very soon might be - so that's what she meant when she described me as someone "who was almost not here", that I was "almost not here" like Sam wasn't here. Had my state of mind as I stood in a doorway really been so obvious? Had it been obvious to everyone or only to Alex? Am I shocked more by my vulnerability, or by my failure to hide it?

If I had been able to hide it, I mightn't be here.

'You suspected me of thinking about killing myself.'

Alex shifts in her seat, and her eyes become swollen with moisture. 'Yes, but that's not the whole story.'

'There's a story?'

'But I don't know what it is anymore.' She speaks with effort now, her voice still low but somehow more brittle. 'Maybe you're right, maybe things are happening too quickly.' And after pausing as she looks at me intently, 'But I don't seem to be able to help it, I'm sorry.' She makes a sweeping gesture with her hand and suddenly she seems bedraggled, her hair over her face in disorderly clumps.

'Let me,' I say, and with the fingers of both hands I caress the stray tufts out of the way, the tingle of touch shooting through me with the tremble of an even warmer warmth. 'There, that's better. And there's no need to be sorry.'

Alex sniffles as she brushes the back of one hand over her face, emerging from behind it looking fresh and no longer bedraggled: her eyes clear and bright again, the beam of her smile recomposed.

I say the first thing that comes to my mind: '"Things", you said. You don't think they're important?'

'They are if you think they are,' says Alex. 'I thought they were important too, the first few months, when I still thought I needed reminders.'

'You still have all his clothes.'

'I still have everything, even this uncomfortable sofa. But that's because I'm lazy.'

Do I believe her? Time after time she seems to go out of her way to make a show of being blasé, as if trying to make some point that escapes me completely, so perhaps she's trying to make it to herself.

Compartmentalising everything too neatly comes across as denial, and denial is another of the stages in the process of grief.

If that's what it is, I try to counter it by *not* being blasé: 'I still have everything too, but not because I'm lazy. It doesn't feel right, giving things away that aren't mine.'

'But they are yours now.'

'And almost everything comes with a memory.'

'With time, memories become more abstract. We can't hold on to everything forever.'

I listen; to some extent I even understand. Things are not important; things get in the way of moving on. I would have heard it all from Eden too if she were here. If Eden could have been here, she would have thrown her things away herself. But I can't do it on Eden's behalf, I don't want to; I won't even move them out of the way. I don't want abstract memories, I want to *feel* Eden's absence as though it were a physical thing, something I can actually touch; abstract memories are just a ruse, a substitute that borders on betrayal.

But that too is a form of denial, and I haven't forgotten my promise.

I promise,

I promise,

I promise.

People grieve in different ways, and the flutter has not gone away.

I lock my gaze softly onto Alex's, and again I say the first thing that comes to my mind: 'I'm glad you're holding on to this apartment.'

'For now, at least,' she answers. And then, leaning closer to me, so close that my neck can feel a tickle when she speaks, 'I know it'll sound like a ridiculous question, but do you have any hobbies?'

It is a ridiculous question. But instead of reading anything into it (I have been reading too much into everything), I choose to think about it and then answer it. It reminds me of *First Dates*, and the clumsy questions people who had been paired up by the producers would ask one another over dinner. Eden and I used to watch it together religiously. There was something heart-warming about the tension and the awkwardness, especially when there was obviously a mutual attraction. Both of us would root for happy endings.

There is little that is tense or awkward about Alex, all the tension and awkwardness, except at that one moment, has been mine. But there is obviously a mutual attraction.

Isn't there?

And can there ever be a happy ending?

I promise,

I promise,

I promise.

'What kind of hobbies?' I ask.

'Collecting. Things like autographs, or vintage toys, or 1950s furniture. I collected Barbie dolls when I was small.'

I laugh. 'Really? Barbie dolls?'

'The pleasure was in having one more, and it didn't last for long. My mind was always on the ones I didn't have. On the day I turned sixteen, I put them all in two laundry bags and carted them off to the charity shop round the corner. I remember walking out of there feeling really happy. And that was twenty years ago today.'

'You mean it's your birthday?' And when Alex nods that it is, I lean over the short distance that divides us and give her a kiss on the cheek. 'Happy Birthday,' I say.

'Best one in a while,' Alex says. 'By far.'

I feel overcome by a sense of euphoria, familiar because I have felt it before, but unfamiliar because, until now, I had only ever felt it with Eden.

'So, hobbies,' I say, snapping myself out of once more overthinking how I feel. 'Well, Eden loved 60s tat, and we went around markets together almost every weekend, but I've never really been a collector myself – I remember as a kid I used to break all my toys, deliberately smash them or rip them apart. I suppose rebuilding houses was a hobby, something I enjoyed doing with Eden. We never made much money, so it wasn't about that.'

'Exactly,' Alex says.

'On the other hand, your Barbie dolls must've been worth a fortune.'

'Mum was furious when I told her what I'd done, which made me feel even happier.'

Overthinking why Alex does anything, which I seem unable to resist, I return to the ridiculousness of her question, wondering what hidden motive lay behind it.

'Hmm,' I say. 'I'm missing something, aren't I?'

'Oh, you know,' Alex says. 'Just *things*.' And then becoming more serious, 'Since Sam, I haven't been able to talk about any of these *things* with anyone else. And suddenly being able to with you, an almost total stranger, feels so... I don't know, *good*? Or is that too prosaic?'

'Mm, maybe. For a poet like no other.'

'Ah, but I told you, the poet is no more. And I don't think I was much of a singer, but I'm a songwriter too, and not a bad one either, so I think that's what I'll stick to from now on.'

'You write songs for other people?'

'Just the lyrics.'

'Anyone famous?'

'I couldn't possibly say.' She pinches forefinger and thumb and drags them very slowly over her lips.

My whole body is getting stiff. It really is an uncomfortable sofa. I want to get up and stretch out, but I worry it might give Alex the impression that I'm bored. I never had such worries with Eden, and making another comparison has filled me again with unease. Something still feels wrong. *This* feels wrong, this whole situation, including every step that has led up to it - and it also feels wrong that I keep thinking *this* feels wrong.

Because *this* also feels right, and it is this recurring contradiction that has filled me with unease. Can all these different feelings *ever* be reconciled?

Alex gets up and one after the other she raises her knees to her waist, up, down, up, down, marching on the spot.

'Helps to loosen my back,' she says, panting as her thighs rise and fall.

'Good idea,' I say. And getting up too, I lift one knee up first so that my thigh is at ninety degrees to my body, then lower it and lift the other, and once I've got the hang of it, I fall into the same rhythm as Alex, up, down, up, down, and like soldiers in step with each other we thump on the modern wooden floor with our trainers.

'That's enough,' says Alex. 'We don't want you pulling a muscle from straining too much – you can do that later in the club.'

We both breathe heavily, and Alex catches me – just as I also catch myself - looking at her in a way I haven't looked at her before, not just with the misted-up eyes of a man, but wantonly, in a way I prefer not to have to think how to describe more precisely. I am grateful to Alex for knowing not to tease me for blushing.

'Right,' I say, and not joining Alex on the sofa when she sits, 'I think I should go home now.'

'Why?'

Do I know why?

'Hopefully the walk will clear my head.'

'You can have a cold shower here,' I imagine Alex saying.

'You're going to *walk* home?' she asks me instead.

'I'll catch the tube to Tufnell Park, and from there it's a ten-minute walk to my flat.'

'I think you should sit down for another five minutes.' And when I hesitate, 'I haven't been completely honest with you, and I think it's only fair you know everything. Then you can decide if you want to come back.'

Then I can decide if I want to come back...

I fall back onto the sofa in the swoon of a slowly deflating balloon.

'Everything like what?'

Once again, Alex gathers up her legs and sits on top of them. 'This morning, when I walked up to you and asked you for a light, well it wasn't a coincidence.'

This morning wasn't a coincidence... But how could it have been anything else? My mind is blank, as hollow as the rest of me; I am functioning only mechanically. I know Alex has been watching me, scrutinising my reaction and encountering only its lack - my expression is vacant and my gaze must be as blank as my mind. Hers seems to wander. She casts about, glancing over from the coffee table to the table in the kitchen, craning her neck, and I know what she's looking for.

'They're in my coat,' I say.

Alex nods. 'While you're getting them, I'll get an ashtray,' she says, and disentangling herself she springs off in the direction of the kitchen. 'And maybe another bottle of wine. Oh, and some nuts.'

One minute I'm leaving, and the next we're having a picnic, so that Alex can be honest and tell me what she hasn't told me yet.

For a while we puff away in silence. The ashtray is on the table next to the bottle of wine, and Alex bends forward to flick the bending ash off the end of her cigarette. She takes another drag and puts it out. I suck on mine too deeply, and hardly any smoke comes out with my cough – it all filters out through my nose.

'That's it, my last cigarette,' I say, still coughing as I stub what's left of it out with one violent squeeze. I sit back with my glass, slightly tilted towards Alex, who now locks onto my gaze solicitously.

'Are you okay?'

'I'm fine,' I say, not quite pacifying the tickle in my throat with a swig of my wine.

'I owe you an explanation,' Alex says, paraphrasing what she's told me already. And then, 'Where to begin...' Her hands slightly shaking, she makes an awkward gesture through the air.

'If there's a story, you should begin at the beginning,' I say.

'There are many stories, and none of them have clear beginnings.' She holds one hand with the other in her lap and stares down into her open palm as though struggling to divine the right beginning.

'Alex, come on.' I should feel angry with her but I don't. All this cloak-and-dagger stuff, it's as if it no longer means anything. Instead of becoming impatient, it's all I can think of that my attraction to her is becoming more physical, a longing whose warmth has become an unbearable heat.

'Yes,' I hear Alex saying, but again she falters, and her eyes begin to well up.

'Hey,' I say, 'it's okay.'

She gives an equivocal smile as she nods, and after clearing her throat, 'Sigismund,' she says, and automatically she reaches for another cigarette. 'You want one?' she asks me, but I shake my head to say I don't, then I watch as she flicks the lighter open and lights up, the reek of petrol even stronger as the blue flame dies out.

The flutter tightens, my heart beats too fast. The past again, but Sigismund? I haven't seen or heard from him in years, how could he have anything to do with this morning? How does Alex even know him?

'Sigismund,' I say, as I pick up the ashtray and set it down between us on the sofa. *Hopefully it will burn and she'll have to replace it*; the absurdity of the thought is almost amusing, causing me to almost smile. I try to think of something else to say, but I can't. The whole scene has become so absurd that I feel myself apart from it.

'You're right, I'll start from the beginning, or one of the beginnings,' Alex says. She drinks some wine and takes a slow drag of her cigarette, and the smoke comes out in short shallow breaths. 'This morning wasn't a coincidence, when I walked up to you and asked you for a light, I knew who you were and I knew where you were going.'

'It wasn't a coincidence.' I shut my eyes tightly for a second, as though to snap me out of being an echo to all the absurdities. 'I mean, you say that you knew who I was, but who am I? I don't understand.'

'You're not anyone, right?' She doesn't wait for me to answer. 'Sam took pills,' she says, and she takes one more drag and another gulp of wine. 'At the time he was just on one prescription for anti-depressants, but he must've been hoarding everything else, benzos, sleeping pills, anti-psychotics, I'm not sure what else, and then he took them all at once, with alcohol and drugs. Which means he wasn't acting on the spur of the moment, he didn't throw himself under a train or jump off a cliff. He had a plan, he was thinking it over, and there was time for him to change his mind.'

'But he didn't.'

'But he didn't.' The smoke at last escapes in a spiral.

This morning wasn't a coincidence. Sigismund. Sam took pills. The absurdity has now become more tragic, but it's still an absurdity.

'I don't understand how anything's connected,' I say. I don't feel like more wine, and I put my glass down on the table.

'You're right,' says Alex. 'So, I'll start with Sigismund. I met him shortly after he left Claw for William, and over the years we've become quite good friends.' After inhaling one last time, she puts her cigarette out. 'Or is that still too disjointed?'

In the silence that follows, I almost get up, but I know that if I do, I will leave, and I'm still not sure I want to leave.

I decide I want to stay. Whatever Alex has such difficulty saying, I want to hear it. I need the ugly truth.

'You're becoming restless,' says Alex. 'And it's not surprising, I'm sure this is all very confusing.' She rests her hand lightly on my forearm. 'Sigismund was married to Claw, I was married to Sam, and Sam was Claw's patient. Let's leave Sigismund to one side for now and make that the beginning instead.'

Sam was Claw's patient. Then he took pills. And Alex wants to make that the beginning of the story that connects her to me. Has everything today been part of a performance? If that's true, then Alex is an even better actor than a poet. I want us to fast-forward to the end…

'Go on,' I say. 'Sam was Claw's patient and what else?'

'The whole family were.'

'But you weren't.'

'No, today was the first time we met.' Her head inclines towards me, her eyebrows slightly raised. 'I was never part of the family, and I don't like the idea of private doctors. Nor did Sam, but he liked to keep them happy. Well, I say happy… "They're all so fragile, they live under the same cloud of neurosis," he would say, but really, he was the one who was fragile. All his childhood he'd been bullied by his sister, and both his parents were manipulative drunks – still are, I imagine.'

'I take it you didn't get on with them.'

Alex gives a chuckle. 'Oliver Bridge, master of the understatement,' she says, her head still inclined but her eyebrows now level as her lips unfurl again into equal and beautiful curves.

She knows my name, all of it, and she has known it all along: "not anyone" is Oliver Bridge. What else does she know? Should I ask her now, or should I wait? Wait for what? For the story to catch up, for my own part in the story to come out. Whichever story it was that was being told.

'I like it, by the way. Oliver Bridge. It has a ring to it.'

'Let's go back to Sigismund,' I say. 'You say that you've been friends since he left Claw.'

'We met through a mutual acquaintance.'

'And he also knew Sam.'

'For a short time, but Sam kept his distance. Sigismund was my friend, and Sam was Claw's patient, he didn't want to hear Sigismund's stories. He looked up to Claw, she made him feel safe.'

'Fair enough.'

'Sigismund liked Sam a lot. It upset him that they couldn't be closer. But we've agreed all that's for later. So, back to Sam's family, and no, I didn't get on with them. They were never unpleasant, but still they made it obvious the first time we met that they thought I fell short and they didn't approve. And they were never going to, so I hardly ever saw them after that, we kept out of each other's way, and to be fair they never tried to interfere, probably because they didn't want to lose him. Sam couldn't care less, he was already used to keeping everything separate, not just Claw but also his family and most of his friends. Then after we got married, he would meet his parents once a week on his own and everyone was happy, or pretended to be.' Alex raises her glass and looks up at it against the light. 'Sam left letters, but of course they still blame me.'

I regret my impatience. I have been the Echo to my own Narcissus, playing all the parts while suspecting Alex of theatre.

I take the glass from her and put it on the table. 'No more wine,' I say.

Alex looks at me blankly, her arm still raised, her hand now empty, suspended in mid-air. 'And I'm not sure I shouldn't be blaming myself.' Her gaze becomes alert, and her hands become pincers as this time she clenches my forearm with both of them. 'I thought I knew him better than everyone, I thought I understood him. But in the end, and all that time before the end, he must've felt so alone. I know it doesn't matter what anyone else thinks, what matters is the truth, and it's a part of the truth that I failed him.'

I swivel round and use my free arm to grip one of her forearms as tightly as she's still gripping mine. 'Alex,' I say, and she blinks. Then as I watch the focus in her gaze begin to soften, 'Did you ever have a choice? Would Sam have let you do anything differently?'

Our bodies are not far apart, and she bends her head and rests its side against my shoulder, tickling my neck with her hair. I feel my spread-out fingers tremble with the rest of my body as I rest them in a spider's arc over her crown.

'No,' she mutters. And then, 'Thank you.'

We stay like that for seconds that exemplify the paradox of time: an infinitesimal fragment can amount to an eternity that lasts but for the briefest moment, and is already nostalgia before it has ended. As we separate, I no longer feel whole, as if a part of me that was missing already has again splintered away. And it has: Eden, whose loss has been renewed by being re-enacted in that split-second physical coming apart of two bodies. I remember Nick Cave talking movingly on TV about his grief for the loss of his son. When someone dies, everyone who has already died dies again; every new separation brings to life every past separation. But if death is separation that can never be mended, then there may be a possibility a future still exists: even as I ponder the meaning of time and the endless repetition of death, my body and the body beside me still breathe.

Eden doesn't breathe; nor does Sam.

Suddenly I feel very tired, exhausted by the thought of endless death: any future, *every* future, will always contain it.

Six parallel lines dismantled but not yet disposed of, a reserve possibility guaranteed to bring relief.

Not Anyone… and, everyone… how easily no one.

'Oliver? You're crying, what's wrong?'

Her body is again against mine, the side of her head against my shoulder, tickling my neck with her hair. But the old separation has still not been mended and this time our breaths are just air.

'You said drugs,' I say. 'You know what kind?'

'Drugs?'

'You said pills with alcohol and drugs.'

The echo of her pulse as it quickens runs from her chest into mine.

'Is that what your cocktail is missing? You have the pills and alcohol and you want my help to clinch the lethal dose?'

The quandary of sums: one plus one, what does it equal?

Every day a step. Until what? Until when?

Every step draws nearer to another separation, every step an endless repetition of death.

And yet,

My body and the body beside me still breathe.

As ever with a head full of thoughts, and now also with a head against my shoulder, pondering again whether, by some means or other, I should cease to exist: sixty-three minus three is still sixty.

And here I am again.

Fogbound in the mist of my thoughts, the warmth of a body beside me, now warming, now not warming my heart.

I imagine the scene from above: ants, mechanically acting out our existence, gathering, consuming, occasionally mating. Clinging on to life in clouds of smoke, we belong to the recalcitrant few, poisoning ourselves with tar and nicotine.

The man into his phone: *Is it really any wonder?*

Broken by subtraction, contemplating an addition, in dread of another subtraction, forever in a quandary of sums. I have now become not anyone but everyone and none, a dot in an infinity that always leads to zero.

In the periphery of my vision, a shifting, then a voice, this time my own.

'My dose is pretty lethal already,' I say. I swivel again, and when Alex shuffles back into her upright position at the apex of the comma, I hold her by the shoulders. Her long-sleeved blouse is thin, and I very softly pinch the protrusion of her bones. 'Was it really that obvious?'

'It wouldn't've been obvious to anyone else.'

'You're still being mysterious,' I say, smiling while I gently shake her.

'There,' she says. 'The smile of someone who isn't quite done yet.'

I follow her gaze, and we both look at the packet of cigarettes. Then we look at each other. 'Maybe later,' I say. 'Just one more.'

Alex shrugs, and the protrusion of bones rises with my fingers. 'Okay,' she says, whistling one more breath through her nose. 'Sam's pills, or most of them at least, they came from Claw. And I know for a fact, because Sigismund's told me, that she overprescribes.'

Is a link being made between Eden and Sam? Is Alex suggesting that Claw might have harmed them both intentionally? Sigismund's word is hardly sufficient to make such an absurdity a fact.

'I don't know what that means, that she "overprescribes". You think she gave Sam pills knowing what he would use them for? Because I don't. Claw was Eden's best friend, and it was Eden who begged her for help with her sleep and to manage the pain. It gave her peace of mind; it was nearly the end, and there were times when she clearly needed more than what she was being given. And when Claw agreed, Eden was grateful. We both were.'

'And where did *your* stash come from?'

Another mental leap.

I let go of her shoulders and stand up. 'Let's go sit at the table,' I say. I want this conversation to be separate, I want us to be alone somewhere else.

'Oh,' Alex says. 'Really? Okay.' She gets up too, and when she goes to pick up the wine and the cigarettes, I motion to her not to. 'No last drink or cigarette before the electrocution? I'd call that both cruel and unusual,' she says as we make our way together to the table.

'My stash,' I say too loudly, and the words are repeated by the vastness of the room; it's as if the emptiness has its own voice.

We sit opposite each other, Alex with her hands entwined together on the table, I with mine in my lap.

'Your *leftover* stash,' she says. 'Am I wrong?'

I shake my head. 'I was about to kiss you,' I say.

'Yes, I could tell. Why didn't you?'

Now it's my turn to shrug; I hold my shoulders up for a long time, pursing my lips. 'My leftover stash,' I say, breathing out a secret deep breath.

'Listen,' says Alex. And when I bend forward to reach for her hand, 'This is a really strange way of getting to know you, but I swear it's not what I'd planned. I'm not sure what I'd planned, but it definitely wasn't this. I know you'll think it's weird, but I wanted to find out what had happened to Eden, I knew from Sigismund about her illness and her friendship with Claw. And then when Claw told Sigismund that she was worried about you, even though I didn't know you I wanted to make sure you were safe.' And after a sigh, so deep that I can feel the air caress me as she lets it out slowly, 'We've both got so much baggage, and yet here we are, moving from one end of the room to another just to stop ourselves from kissing.'

'To stop ourselves from kissing while you're telling me a story.'

While we're telling each other a story.

'But you're safe now, aren't you?' Alex looks straight at me. And when I don't answer immediately, her body lightly shivers while she sobs.

'Hey,' I say, and letting go of her hand I get up and walk to her side. 'Hey,' I say again, crouching down as I clasp my arms around her, enfolding her entire upper body and holding it away from the hardness of the tall wooden chair, tightening my grip as the shiver intensifies.

'It was here,' she says, sniffling as she sobs, 'this is where I found him,' her voice breaking up, 'slouched over the table in this chair.'

And, of course, I will promise.

I promise,

I promise,

I promise.

'I am, I'm safe, I promise,' I say, and we kiss while Alex is still telling me a story.

SIX

Our kiss lasts a very long time; it is several kisses at once: the kiss we should have had in the street when we first met, the kiss we should have had on the blue divan upstairs at the Cutting-Edge Arts Centre, the kiss we should have had on the bench in Red Lion Square, the kiss we should have had on the bright red sofa shaped like a comma, all the kisses we hadn't had with Eden and Sam - our kiss is all these kisses too.

But the story hasn't ended, and when our endless kiss comes to a pause, which is also a beginning, we are back on the sofa, closer to each other than before, and when the story resumes, I want to know every detail.

'How did you know it was me? In the street, I mean, when you asked me for a light. Was Sigismund there, hiding with you round some corner so he could point me out when I came out of the tube?'

'Oh, it was much worse than that. He gave me your address and I staked out your flat until I saw you coming out, then I followed you all the way to Russell Square.'

'You didn't.'

'No, Oliver, I didn't. But actually, the truth is even more convoluted. Your three tickets were marked, they all had a big X on the bottom right-hand corner, and the idea was that Deborah would spot it at the door and Joe would take you to the table and then offer to bring you upstairs. But then there you were, hiding in a doorway just outside the station, I'd seen a photograph of you and Eden with Sigismund and Claw and I recognised you straight away. And I did want a light, so I thought I'd take my chances and I improvised.'

I get up and walk over to my coat. I get my They Them ticket out of one of the pockets and it's true, the bottom right-hand corner is marked with an X. I put it back where I found it and return to my place on the sofa.

'Jesus,' I say.

'You looked so miserable standing there alone, too miserable to be left on your own. And I know I must sound like a hypocrite, almost romanticising Sam's letting go, while at the same time blaming Claw and being terrified the same thing might happen to you.'

'You couldn't save Sam, so you want to save me.'

'Maybe it was like that at the beginning. I want more than that now. I want you not to need to be saved.'

'Not to need to be saved.' I repeat the words slowly, brooding over their meaning. Then, 'Huh,' I go on in a mild exclamation. 'You know what the irony is? That if it hadn't been for Claw, I probably wouldn't be here. On the night she called to rave about They Them, because Sigismund had seen you in Brixton and had told her you weren't to be missed, I already had the pills out on the table with the vodka, and I can't say for sure, because I didn't want to break my promise to Eden, but I think I was about to take them.'

'You also wouldn't've been here if it hadn't been for Sigismund. He knew from Claw you weren't well.'

'Ah, more euphemisms.'

'And he knew she'd been prescribing drugs for Sam, so we suspected she might be doing the same for you.'

'Everything you know about Claw comes from Sigismund, doesn't that worry you? They had a filthy divorce and probably a terrible marriage, he's not exactly unbiased.'

'No, but on balance I trust him.'

'Claw's never prescribed anything for me.'

'Probably because you never asked. You thought you already had enough.'

I don't want this to become our first row. I don't care about Sigismund, I only care about Alex, and although her obsession with Claw is unhealthy, I understand that the reason for it isn't just that she lost Sam but that she lost him in a way that makes her feel she let him down.

I slap her thighs gently with the flats of my hands and I smile. 'So? What happens now?'

'Now you need to also keep your promise to me.'

I promise,

I promise,

I promise.

No, I don't regret making it, not yet. 'I know,' I say.

'Good! Can we please have our last cigarette now?' She points with her eyes at the packet on the table.

'Not yet,' I say. 'Is Deborah Babe?'

'Sorry?'

'The girl who was supposed to spot the X at the door.'

'I hadn't realised you'd become so familiar.'

'And did Sir Charles know the tickets were marked?'

Alex pulls a face. 'Who?'

'The hideous little man who runs the National, old friend of Sigismund's from Oxford, apparently they used to wank each other off every Wednesday afternoon in the Bodleian.'

'I haven't a clue what you're talking about.'

'The man Claw got our tickets from.'

'Claw got your tickets from Sigismund, who got them from me, and I swear to you I've never wanked him off, in the Bodleian or anywhere else.'

'She definitely told me that she got them from Sir Charles, she said they met at his club and he was rude to her.'

'And I know for a fact that she got them from Sigismund, on Wednesday evening at a wine bar in Carnaby Street.'

Is Claw part of the conspiracy too? There have already been so many tangled webs that I'm almost becoming addicted, craving the next hit.

'If she was lying, she must've known about the tickets when I picked mine up last night from her practice,' I say.

'Claw? No, of course she didn't know. The only two people who knew apart from me were Sigismund and Babe.'

'But then why would she...' Before I finish the question, the only possible answer occurs to me. 'Because she didn't want Patrick to know she was getting the tickets from Sigismund.'

'Well, that wouldn't be surprising. Sigismund said she made a pass at him.'

Sigismund said this, Sigismund said that: it sounds like he'd say anything. Do I believe Claw made a pass at him? I find it much more likely that she lied about Sir Charles just because she's a liar.

Alex was right. The truth is convoluted, and it is veering via a kiss back and forth from the tragic to the absurd. There is an undercurrent of hilarity that feels almost obscene. Everything is "almost"; almost this, almost that. Everything except the kiss. The kiss wasn't almost a kiss, it was more than a kiss, and I wonder if it mightn't be that aggregate excess that feels to me almost obscene.

There is only one way to find out.

'I think we should have that cigarette now,' I say. 'But can we kiss again first?'

Our second kiss also lasts a long time, and would have lasted an equally long time as our first if the doorbell wasn't ringing, and then ringing again.

'It must be them,' says Alex.

'Is someone bringing home the dummy?'

'The dummy?' She holds my face still with both hands, our lips barely parted, our breathing still fast. Then, 'Oh,' she says with a chuckle. 'No, no, not Them. *Them* - Sigismund and William.'

'Sigismund and *William*?'

William the Conqueror, as Eden used to call him when Claw wasn't there. When Sigismund upped and disappeared with him, we had gravitated towards Claw not only out of sympathy and a lack of an address in Barcelona - we were both drawn to Patrick much more than I had ever been to Sigismund, and Claw and Eden were like chalk-and-cheese sisters who couldn't stay apart, so Claw had easily prevailed, like bad habits often do.

Alex is halfway to the door. 'Didn't I say? They're together again.'

'And they're here? Now?'

I haven't seen Sigismund since he left Claw, and I've never met William, who Claw had given me the impression was still baking cakes in her kitchen (and eating them too, according to Patrick).

'They're coming clubbing with us. I thought I'd surprise you.' And before I can answer that she has but I would rather she hadn't, 'Hello?' she says into the intercom, and then, 'Come on up, I'm here with Oliver.'

'I'm not sure about this,' I say. 'You should've warned me, at least.'

'I know, I know, I've been bad,' says Alex, trotting back to the sofa and squatting down in front of me. 'But please don't go.' My face is again in her hands, and as she raises herself to stand back up, our lips come together for our briefest kiss yet. Then she takes me by the hand and hoists me off the sofa almost weightlessly, and together we walk to the door.

When she opens it, Sigismund and William are already waiting on the other side.

'Oliver - Ollie! It's so nice to see you again,' says Sigismund.

I had always found him too enthusiastic.

'Hi, Sigismund,' I reply while already I'm being squashed in an embrace.

'Let me see.' Without letting go, Sigismund pulls back to survey me. 'Looking well, looking well,' he says, but his voice has suddenly become unstable, and he dives into my shoulders in sobs, blubbering, 'I'm sorry, I'm so sorry.'

Really? He's just now remembered to be sorry, so sorry that he's burst into tears? But perhaps I'm being unfair. He may be as indifferent to me as I have always been to him, but he had never been indifferent to Eden, nor Eden to him - she was sad they had lost touch.

Alex peels him off. 'Come on, let's all sit at the table,' she says. 'William, this is Oliver.'

'Hi, William,' I say, taking William's hand and shaking it firmly.

'Hey, Oliver, good to meet you finally,' says William in a very deep voice. 'I've heard a lot about you.'

'While baking?' I'm tempted to ask. 'Good to meet you too,' I say instead.

But really, William has not made a bad first impression: good handshake, good voice, and a generally likeable vibe. Dressed youthfully under his heavy army coat, he's wearing very baggy blue jeans and a tucked-out loose black shirt with its sleeves rolled up already. Sigismund is wearing a skinny tartan suit that is probably a Vivienne Westwood – he was always a fan.

At the table, 'Gin and Tonic if you have it,' Sigismund says without waiting to be asked.

'William?' Alex asks.

'Just water for me, thanks.'

'I'll give you a hand,' I say, but when I go to get up, Alex pushes me back down.

'Stay,' she says. 'G&T for you too?'

'Oh, why not,' I say.

'Have you been smoking again?' Sigismund asks Alex, who's already on her way to make the drinks.

'We both have,' I say.

'I thought you quit years ago,' says Sigismund.

'I did, and then I met Alex.'

'We didn't need the tickets in the end, I saw him standing in a doorway and I asked him for a light. And fortunately, even though he doesn't smoke he still carries a lighter.'

'But how did you know it was him?' Sigismund asks.

Not because of an X on a ticket. Isn't Sigismund embarrassed for his part in a plot so ridiculously elaborate that it had even involved a ventriloquist's dummy? But the reason I'm here is no longer the same as the reason our tickets were marked with an X, and whatever the conspiracy's intention, I can't honestly say that I'm unhappy with its outcome so far – just less happy than I would have been if Sigismund and William weren't here.

'I recognised him. You'd shown me that picture of the four of you together, remember?'

Sigismund is shaking his head in disbelief. 'She's incredible,' he says. 'Honestly, in that picture you're *so* small.' He makes a gesture with his forefinger and thumb to show how small he means – minuscule, almost microscopic. 'You'd remember it - we were in that fancy seafood restaurant in Lisbon and the waiter took the picture with Claw's phone. We both liked it so much we had it printed.'

'And when he left Claw, he stole it,' Alex says, arriving at the table with a tray full of drinks. 'I met her finally. She and Patrick came with Oliver backstage. And before you ask, no, I can't say I liked her.'

'There's a lot not to like,' says Sigismund, drinking almost half his gin in one gulp. 'But she's not all bad.'

'You didn't seem too keen on Patrick either,' I say to Alex, wanting to test Sigismund's reaction.

'I didn't actively dislike him, I just assumed he wouldn't be dissimilar to Claw.'

'Patrick's actually okay,' says Sigismund.

I dart a dirty look at him. 'He's more than just okay and you know that very well,' I say. 'And he's very dissimilar to Claw, who definitely isn't all bad. When Eden was sick, both of them were there for us 24/7, and they've been my only friends since Eden died.'

William fidgets with his fingers on the table.

'Alex and William both know about what happened between me and Patrick,' mutters Sigismund tetchily, after drinking some more of his drink.

Sitting back in her chair and holding her drink with both hands without lifting it up from the table, 'Let's not talk about Patrick and Claw,' says Alex.

'It's a very nice photograph,' says William, obediently changing the subject. 'I'd've stolen it too.'

Yes, I remember it. But I would rather the past and the present were kept separate.

'Thanks for getting us the tickets for earlier,' I say to Sigismund, deciding not to mention the X. 'Claw made up some story that she got them from Sir Charles, but Alex said she got them from you.'

'You mean Sir Charles who wanked me off every Wednesday afternoon in the Bodleian?'

'I thought you wanked each other off,' I say.

Sigismund dissolves into hoots of laughter, for a few long seconds he just rocks in his chair and laughs uncontrollably. 'Oh God, so we did, so we did... yep, guilty as charged... Oh God, good old Charles, how utterly vile he's become...'

'Anyway, I don't know why Claw lied,' I say, 'but that's not the point.'

'Oh, Claw's always been a fibber,' answers Sigismund, 'and that's never been the point.'

'The point is, I'm grateful,' I say. 'If it hadn't been for you, I wouldn't be here, and I'd've missed a great show.'

Sigismund becomes subdued again. He glances at me briefly and gives a little nod. Then with another big gulp he finishes his gin.

'A stunning show,' William says in his deep voice. 'We saw the preview in Brixton a couple of weeks ago. I thought the idea of Them and a dummy with a voice of its own was so brilliant!'

'Stop calling me a dummy or I'll smack you,' says the voice of Them from somewhere near the red comma sofa – even though the dummy itself is still upstairs at the Cutting-Edge Arts Centre.

'See what I mean?' William enthuses with big gestures while everyone laughs. 'The idea of Them was brilliant and the poetry was really, really moving.' And reaching over to squeeze Sigismund's hand, 'I was in tears on and off throughout the show, wasn't I, Ziggy?'

'He was,' says Sigismund, and his face turns bright red.

'Ziggy? That's so cute,' Alex says, patting William on the shoulder.

'I think so too,' says William, taking back his hand to run it through the curls of his black hair. His features are plain, but fit together in an unexpected way that somehow makes him look very handsome - unlike Sigismund, whose slickness cancels out his good looks.

'I know it's not my business, but I got the impression from Claw just this morning that you two had gone your separate ways,' I say.

'We split up for a while, but now we're back together again,' says William.

'But Claw doesn't know yet,' says Sigismund, holding up his empty glass, and Alex is already on her way to the kitchen.

'Patrick seems to think you've run off with someone else,' I say.

'He ran off with me to Barcelona,' William says.

'Then we got back and William got the wrong end of the stick.'

'I thought he was cheating with a woman, so I left.'

'And you went round to Claw's,' I say.

William makes noises by circling his finger round the rim of his glass, watching himself doing it with his face slightly scrunched. 'I thought I owed her an apology, maybe I was curious as well, and she was nice to me at first, so I went round a few times and we baked. Then one day...' He looks up at me with his big eyes. 'But she's your friend, I don't want to bad-mouth her. And Ziggy wasn't cheating, so it's all in the past now.'

In an awkward silence, in which I don't ask any questions, Sigismund's drink has arrived and Alex has returned to her seat.

Now it's Sigismund who's fidgeting, twitching as he fumbles with his gin, picking out the lemon and then putting it back, while all the time his gaze flits about. Then with a jerk he fixes it on William, still twitching as he attempts an awkward smile.

'We're having a baby,' he says. 'The girl I was meeting, she's agreed to be the surrogate. And yes, I should've discussed it with William first...'

'But now he has,' William cuts in, 'and we're both as happy about it as each other.'

Now I understand the drumbeat introduction, and I'm trying very hard not to laugh. It's like having a bit part in a soap opera I wouldn't watch. Am I being mean for not being able to take any of it seriously?

'That's lovely,' Alex says. 'Congratulations!'

'Yes, congratulations,' I say with all the enthusiasm I'm able to muster.

Alex gets up and kisses them both, Sigismund first, then William. And on the way back to her chair, she stops and kisses me too, but on the lips.

'Oh,' says Sigismund.

'You said this would happen,' says William, sounding genuinely excited.

'But I never imagined it would happen *today*,' says Sigismund.

'Nothing's really happened,' Alex says.

'Nothing... and everything,' I say, and I'm no longer in the same soap opera, far less in one I wouldn't watch. No longer just a shiver, or a tremble, or a warmth, the flutter has become a state of being, a part of an inseparable wholeness, as palpable as any of my limbs.

'Yes,' Alex says, smiling two equal and beautiful curves while meaningful glances are briefly exchanged.

'You both look so happy,' says William. 'I think it's really cool.'

'Thank you, William,' says Alex, and her eyes are glazing over with wetness again.

'Cheers!' says Sigismund, raising his glass. 'To all of us.'

'To all of us,' says William, raising his water.

'To Eden and Sam,' Alex says.

'Always,' says Sigismund, raising his glass even higher.

'To Eden and Sam,' William's voice resounds through the room.

'And to the baby,' Sigismund remembers.

'Yes, cheers,' I say, and as my glass clinks absent-mindedly against all the others, once again the fluttering becomes a frail and distant vagueness countered by the knot of self-destruction that I imagine is the only way to honour the past, even as I hear Eden's voice yelling at me that it isn't, that the past is safe - that it can no more be erased than the present, that it does *not* need human sacrifice. But these are Eden's words, and if I am to reconcile the present with the past, I must now find my own.

'Whose baby will it be, have you decided?' Alex asks. 'Biologically, I mean.'

'We'll have our sperm tested and leave it to the doctors to decide which is best,' says Sigismund.

'I think it should be yours,' says William. 'To me it's not important who the father is.'

I hear them, their words like vacuous background noise that makes me want to scream. Veering from the tragic to the even more absurd - from blubbering to baking to babies, via another toast, courtesy of Alex like the last one, "to Eden and Sam" - an undercurrent of hilarity persists, and it now feels not *almost* obscene but completely.

'Oliver, you're shaking, are you okay?' When Alex reaches out with her hands across the table, I pull mine away, and I decide to speak my feelings aloud.

'Am I okay? No, not really. This morning when you saw me you thought I was about to top myself, but now

William's decided I look really happy, because people who're not happy don't kiss.' My chair scrapes against the floor when I push it back to stand up. 'All *this*,' I say, making wild, frenetic gestures, 'I'm sorry but it's just too confusing. One minute Sigismund's sobbing, the next we're chitchatting and laughing, then we're raising our glasses to Eden and Sam to celebrate babies and kisses. I mean, Jesus! It's kind of obscene, don't you think?'

With a gentle movement, Sigismund extends his hand to stop Alex from speaking.

'Ollie, you're right,' he says, 'I should've known better. But if I've seemed to you too casual tonight, it's because I find it easier to be casual than to express how I feel without bursting into tears. Alex goes along with it, she says she doesn't mind the pretence, in fact she claims it helps, but I had no right to assume you would feel the same way. At least I've tried to be there for Alex, and I know it's my fault that I've not been there for you, but I didn't want to meet you and lie.'

My anger dissipates and now I'm filled with dread. The room has the hush of the Cutting-Edge Arts Centre at the end of They Them. I can only hear Alex and William holding their breaths, and I'm deafened by the sound of what hasn't yet come next.

Still on my feet, looming over the table, 'I don't understand,' I say. 'Lie about what?'

'After Eden got sick, she called me a few times and we met, somewhere for a coffee or a walk, but she asked me not to tell you. All she ever talked about was you, about how much she loved you and how amazing you were being and how she hoped you'd be able to cope when she was gone. But she said that if you knew we were meeting, probably you'd think the opposite was true, you'd imagine you were doing something wrong, and she really didn't want that.'

'So, that's what she was doing all the times she went missing.'

'It was never for more than an hour, but she always insisted on switching off her phone.'

'She used to tell me she'd forgotten to charge it.'

'I know you must've worried, but it wasn't very often and I think it did her good. I'm sorry. Staying away was the wrong thing to do, Eden asked me to look out for you and I didn't.'

Time collapses.

I am raging with that same sense of total helplessness that I had felt throughout Eden's illness: no matter what I did, nothing could have made her better. I had cared for the person I loved most in the world knowing there could only be one outcome, and I had cared for her with all my heart. Until today, until just now, it had not even occurred to me that Eden might have needed something more, that the hard shell of our love had not encased her in the same way it is still encasing me, that someone else might have been able now and then to do some small but significant thing – have a coffee or take a walk with her, just for an hour - that "did her good" not although but precisely *because* she wasn't doing it with me.

I am no longer raging; rather, I feel humbled by my own self-centredness. Eden's illness had not belonged to me, any more than Eden had: I had been more needy than my dying wife, who had thought more of me than of herself even in those moments she had spent away from me, moments that the tunnel-visioned nature of my love had forced her to keep secret from me. In just the last few minutes I have come to see Sigismund differently; my view of him has become less black-and-white, dotted with the colour of Eden. But I also now feel differently about myself. If I'm able to become less stubbornly possessive of my grief, then its darkness might become less opaque. Remembering Eden's entreaties, all of them relating to me and the future she insisted on envisaging for me, I already feel an unaccustomed lightness in the burden of my promise to continue to live.

For how long now have I loomed over the table? It is impossible to calculate the amount of time it has taken the jumble of thoughts and emotions to form and then swarm inside my head like an army of ants, but it has taken just the sharp gust of air of a long exhalation to disperse them.

Past and present have for once found common ground. I have heard Eden's voice again, reverberating across time that I thought had been lost to demand from me the keeping of my promise.

I stand up straight before I speak, my lungs now full of strength. 'Thank you,' I say to Sigismund. 'Eden was always very fond of you, and I'm glad she was able to turn to you.' Then to Alex, 'If you'd like me to, I'll go.'

'Please stay,' Alex says.

'Yes, please stay,' says William. 'We promise not to talk anymore about babies.'

'Or baking,' says Alex.

I sit back in my electric chair, which I have scraped back into place. 'No, if I'm staying then you can talk about whatever you like. And, Sigismund, it's my fault we lost touch, not yours. I'm sorry I was so mean with my grief.'

But Sigismund waves my apology away with another gentle wave of his hand. 'I was glad to hear from Claw that she and Patrick were still managing to see you. At least you weren't completely alone.'

'I've told Oliver about our suspicions,' Alex says to Sigismund.

'I would call them accusations,' I say, wondering why Alex would have chosen this moment to dredge all that nonsense back up. Does she think that by becoming more amenable to Sigismund I may have also become more amenable to accusations against Claw?

'Concerns,' Sigismund proposes. 'Eden told me she was grateful to Claw for helping her manage her pain, and we know she was prescribing drugs for Sam. These are the facts, and then there are our own interpretations of the facts.'

'Suspicions,' Alex insists. 'But we said we wouldn't talk about Claw. If you're all free on Sunday afternoon, we can meet here at five to talk about whatever we feel like.'

'That's a great idea,' says William.

'But now we should be making a move,' Alex goes on, 'or we'll miss Joanna's set.'

'I can't believe we're really going clubbing,' I say, finishing my Gin and Tonic in one gulp.

SEVEN

Frustration is buzzing with the shudder of young bodies, fizzing as they bop to the ear-splitting sounds of wordless techno music. The tunes come in screeches and booms, and the experience is as physical as I remember. Eden would have loved it.

'We're too old, they're never going to let us in,' I had thought to myself as we made our way on foot to the club. The night, black and fierce, was refreshingly freezing, once again restoring me to life by cutting through the cobwebs in my head in pang after pang of deliciously excruciating pain: iced-over cheeks that felt ready to crack, the hurt of hardened blinks and the grinding of clattering teeth, rigid hands that shallow breaths failed to thaw. This sustained accumulation of assaults, much more vicious at this hour than the prickling sensations of dusk, had caused me to feel energised, hyper-conscious of my body's state of being to an altogether different degree.

It was too cold to snow, but a solid layer of ice had managed to conjure itself out of nowhere. Catching the sheen from the street lamps, its hardness was somehow majestic, unfolding before us in a panoramic vista of glistening concrete and tarmac, the roads scoured like pencil drawings by the heat from passing cars.

Only William wasn't too old; Sigismund and I definitely were, and unlike Alex had nothing to make up for it with. We had crossed Farringdon Road, and past Smithfield Market had taken a left and then a narrow turning sharply to the right. The winding queue we had walked past had offered no reassurance – a long line of chattering youths who shivered as one in their T-shirts, clearly more impervious to the cold than to the cost of depositing their coats in the cloakroom.

Too old and not dressed for it – I had neither showered nor changed into Sam's clothes, and couldn't wait to shed my winter bad taste and strip down to the blandness of T-shirt and jeans for the dance floor.

Alex had led the way straight to the front, to another guest list and another Mohican, who had greeted us like stars, each one of us receiving a welcoming kiss and the stamp of an F on our wrist. And now the four of us are standing on the edge of the dance floor with our drinks – we have switched from Gin and Tonics to Vodkas with Red Bull, all except William, who spasmodically sways to the music clutching a bottle of water.

We might as well be invisible, which is good, the sign of an electric atmosphere. People are either deep into the music or loved-up, smiling at each other with abandon. One or two are gurning, not hostile but too high – off their faces too early. I remember the look, more gruesome in the shifting frantic lights. But as a mass, the dance floor is a glorious celebration, a collective embracing of the intrinsic absurdity of wild bodily movements that only vaguely correspond to the ebb and flow of sounds blurted out by the speakers.

'Too loud?' Alex yells in my ear.

'I like it,' I yell back.

'Me too, it's cathartic.' Her voice is like a knife, slicing through the boom.

'Like the noises outside.'

Alex makes a gesture that I don't understand. 'There's no seasons in here,' she says. Then switching to my other ear, 'I'm glad you came.'

When I turn around to speak to her, our heads collide and we both laugh – laughter we can see but neither of us can hear. 'Me too,' I would have said. But our faces draw nearer instead, and the equal and beautiful curves of her mouth, blurred already by the flickering lights that dance with all the bodies and the dark, become invisible as they unite with mine in a kiss. Drunk with alcohol and longing, I feel momentarily lost, although the moment, my consciousness of it distorted by the flutter's machinations, lasts much longer than I will be able to recall.

And in the moment that follows, we are once more apart, but transported to the middle of the dance floor, separated from the others and frenetically dancing, our limbs manoeuvring around one another's precisely, our bodies ever closer without touching, as if the very purpose of each movement is to taunt us. But no such thing exists as mathematical impossibility on the dance floor, and refusing to be taunted I wind my arms around Alex and lock them. We sway less as we become more synchronised, and now we dance as one, not alone but together in a crowd to which we also belong.

'Joanna's just come on, she always plays this first,' Alex yells without detaching.

'This is ancient,' I yell back, and then I remember.

Loops & Tings, I know it, one of the few records Eden took from her father. I remember clearly the first time she played it for me on the cheap record player she had bought in Camden Lock. We listened to it holding hands, and our eyes had danced together while she tightened or loosened her grip in tune with every second of the music.

I feel the track's manic rhythm once again course my veins, the harrowing repetition of sound broken again and again by the sorrow of the rolling single verse – *Do the thing that bring the smile to your faces*, and the emotion chokes me.

.

The track doesn't mix into the next; it stops, and blends instead with the moment of silence that follows. 'She always does that. And now she's going to play it again, but at 33 rpm instead of 45. She does it with a lot of tracks, it's what she's known for.'

The slower speed intensifies the sorrow, and the dance track has now become mournful. I know I am heaving with tears, and the feeling on my cheeks of tears over sweat is peculiar.

'Oliver? Oliver, what's wrong?'

I can hear her but I don't want to answer; I need to confront this alone. Sparked by lightning memories of single moments, I know it will happen again, and I will find a painful pleasure in it when it does, in the same way I find a painful pleasure in it now – in the unfolding of a different world in which a part of me is still attached to Eden. Pleasure is perhaps the wrong word, and as I search for what might be the right one – yearning? wholeness? - I realise that I'm not on the dance floor anymore. Alex has me by the hand and we are walking through some kind of tunnel, past the bulk of shadows that crouch against its walls. I can still feel the tickle of tears, not the first since They Them but so painfully absent for too long before that. And all of them have been the consequence of an astonishing collision, between my grief and today's hints of joy.

Another turn, and now there is light, muted but constant, and low music that shuts out all other sounds. There are no other sounds, no one else is here.

'Chill-out room,' Alex says, as we sit beside each other on one of many platforms laid with cushions. 'It fills up later, no one feels like chilling out while Joanna is on.'

Rows of heavy velvet drapes are hanging from the ceiling like enormous banners, cleverly dividing the room into intimate sections that still belong to a space shared by all. A steady stream of air causes all the drapes to ripple lightly, adding to the room's impression of calm.

'We're missing her set,' I say.

'She's on for two hours, and we were there for the best bit.'

'The bit that made me lose the plot.'

Alex knocks my shoulder with hers. 'It does us good to lose the plot.'

'You lose it too?' I turn around and take her hand into my lap, and when she bends her head and leans against me, I can feel her body gasping for air as it rises and falls. 'I keep forgetting,' I say. And then, 'I'm sorry.'

With a jerk she digs her chin into my shoulder. 'What for?' Her sideways gaze is fixed on me.

I shrug. 'For being so stuck in the past, like I'm the only one who has one, like I'm the only one who's lost someone they loved.'

The chill-out music changes its tempo, almost as if we're being watched and the music is a soundtrack, alive to the smallest variation in our movements and words – bending to our bodies the way our bodies bend to all its rhythms when we dance.

'I was terrified you might tell Sigismund and William it was my birthday,' Alex says.

'If I'd remembered, I probably would've. But why didn't you want them to know?'

She takes in more air while the room stays deadly still. 'Two years today since I lost Sam. Well, it's after midnight now, so two years yesterday.'

'On your birthday.' I can feel my face tighten as I attempt to wipe it dry on my sleeves. 'That was cruel,' I say.

'It was probably coincidence; he never remembered my birthday. Nor did I until two years ago. And I'm glad this year I spent it with you.'

The music stops abruptly and the light becomes more muted, while the banners flap about in air that now somehow feels much colder.

As though to counter that illusion of coldness, we turn towards each other and we kiss. Then while our lips and our foreheads still touch, 'Come on, let's go dance and celebrate some more,' I say. 'Sigismund and William must be wondering where we are.'

The night ended on Saturday morning, and at three in the afternoon I was making the journey from Clerkenwell to Highgate on foot. My legs were hurting already, but I didn't mind them hurting more.

On Friday early evening, and then much more intensely on the way to *Frustration,* I had experienced all the pains inflicted on me by the cold as a pleasure, my body reawakened by a sense of its apartness; then on the dance floor, while listening to *Loops & Tings* I had wept in a yearning for wholeness. And when later this yearning was sated in Alex's bed, I had not been unprepared. The earlier prompts had prepared me in a way I had not been aware of, by somehow aligning the dissonant parts that made up who I was, or rather who I had become after breaking. That last climactic act, in which by a union to another I myself had become reunited, had signified a final letting go, but the process had been underway since that moment in the street when Alex had asked for a light. The past had not been laid to rest, rather it had been assimilated into a new beginning that embraced it. There had been no conflict, no comparisons, no sense of betrayal.

I had wanted to walk back to Highgate not because the approach of another freezing night promised more physical pain. Pain was no longer my purpose. My body had already fought its way back to life, but by keeping it alert I was able more acutely to savour the entire accumulation of sensations that far from superseding served to magnify each other as though merely through the fact of coexistence. Nothing could have happened unless everything had happened, and from that unity had sprung the intensity of each component part. And yes, people tended to philosophise more after sex. Not everything could be reduced to mathematics.

The route was not especially scenic. As I approached Kings Cross, there was little that made an impression. But I was experiencing everything differently, enjoying the small pleasures that would have escaped me if I hadn't spent an afternoon walking with Alex – revelling in all the sounds I would have normally shut out: the rustle of electric black cabs that blew past like drifting leaves, the moan of buses as they swung their doors open to let passengers off, the whizz of racing bicycles, that varying hum of voices wherever there were clusters of people. In the cold of winter afternoons, everything was distant and muffled but amplified too - the noises, the pauses, the spells of longer quiet. And in parallel the light that fell from street lamps or escaped from shop windows, that shone behind the blinds of offices or poured out of pubs, that slipped out of the road at the approach of passing cars or lurked inside the rooms of houses hiding Christmas trees and secrets, as I walked past them fell upon me like caresses from a long-forgotten loved one intent on drawing me out of my estrangement.

Would Eden have approved of Alex? It was an impossible question. If Eden were here, there would have been no Alex to approve or disapprove of. But I was not asking Eden, I was asking myself, and just as I had known Eden well enough to know she would have loved the unforgettable performance by They Them, I had known her well enough to know she would have also loved Alex – we had rarely disagreed about people. She would have loved Alex, but what would she have made of Sam? And what about my own opinion? In Eden's place I would have judged Sam self-indulgent and selfish. But I had not gone through what Eden had, and could not judge Sam as harshly. I had, after all, confronted six perfectly parallel lines of my own, and was well aware that selflessness was no match for despair.

London was life, like every other city. But in spite of its long distances and ugly terraces, and even its disparities and inequalities, there was something about it that set it apart – a special warmth in its diversity and even in the coldness of its humour, and above all a uniqueness in the music and buzz of its youth. Far from all was perfect, but the feeling was of always moving forward, of taking one more step further away from little England. It could also be harsh and enslaving, sometimes even murderous; I was not unaware that I was judging it romantically, in the way I liked to judge all my fellow human beings, who sang together and were kind and made love, but could also be the monsters on tabloid front pages.

Eden and Sam. Everything was clouded with the thickness of the contrast – of a life that was taken away and a life that was surrendered. Before yesterday, I would have judged that the two lives could not have been equal, and that loss would have distributed itself unequally too. By changing fundamentally not just my opinion but *me*, Alex had succeeded in bringing me back from the brink: as soon as I got home, I would safely dispose of my colourful collection of pills. Eden would have been as grateful as I was. If Eden were here, she would not have judged Sam harshly - in spite of the contrast, she probably wouldn't have judged him at all.

Kings Cross was no longer lurid; its thick air of transgression was gone. In my rebellious adolescence it had retained some of the end-of-days edge that had made its nightlife haunts so legendary in the 80s and 90s. But "progress" had wreaked havoc, its wholesale demolitions pushing everything towards the east or further south, out of dilapidated warehouses and into purpose-built establishments like the one hosting *Frustration*, where the young still managed to have fun, making atmosphere out of themselves and the music.

The long stretch of York Way led all the way to Camden Road, past the repositioned gasholders and modernised brick buildings of Granary Square, so successfully transitioned from a sprawl of dereliction to a gathering of fashionable chic, then past the tall apartment blocks that had sprung up to accommodate commuter needs, veering up the hill through road works and the hold-up of temporary traffic lights to a patch of unkempt housing and down-market shops, then across the road to Brecknock Road and the upsurge in affluence on the approach to Tufnell Park.

I liked the unhidden contrasts, not because they were desirable or just, and absolutely not because I found them picturesque: precisely because they were ugly, their starkness made the best case for change. London, in that sense, was honest; it wore its many cruelties on its sleeve – it did not confine its worst to the margins. I was being romantic again, and it struck me just how long it had been since the last time I had felt romantic about anything. And then it struck me that the reason I was suddenly feeling romantic about everything was that I was feeling romantic about Alex.

Dartmouth Park Hill was steep but it would lead me home. I was cold and exhausted, and pain, as though affronted that it hadn't been my aim, was afflicting every part of me - in my legs it had become almost unbearable, and each separate part of my face was in agony, writhing like an animal being torn by shards of ice. It was dark now, and the night's play of lights seemed to mock me, the swirls of yellow shimmer from the street lights laughing as I attempted to walk through them, only to be blinded by the headlights whizzing past. My breathing became heavy, congealing in my throat like lumps of fat, and as I leaned against the heavy iron railings of the water reservoir, I could feel my body slowly leaving me, or perhaps I was leaving my body. And I even felt romantic about that.

'Ollie? Ollie, wake up.'

I came to, still slouched against the railings, warmed to life by Eden's breath.

'Eden,' I said, but then I floundered, almost falling back into unconsciousness.

'Stay with me, Ollie, that's it, keep your eyes open, well done.' I managed to stand up, away from the railings. 'Now let's get you home.'

She had an arm around my waist and we trudged our way together up the hill, along the straight approach that would deliver me home.

'Thank you,' I said, and Eden smiled as she tightened her grip, two equal and beautiful curves that gave me the strength to go on.

And we made it. With Eden beside me I climbed the few steps to the entrance, then I was inside, unlocking my front door.

'Alex, are you there?'

EIGHT

I wake up in my bed feeling hazy. My sleep has been uneasy and my dreams uneasier still. The bedside lamp is on, and provides the only light in the room, low and slightly orange. Outside it must be night. The curtains are drawn, but daylight seeps in even in winter, and flickers dully around the edges. The edges now are charcoal-grey and still.

I am wearing my pyjamas, even though I can't even remember undressing. I can't remember getting into bed. Can I remember getting home? When I try to sit up, I break into a cough, but the congestion in my chest fails to clear. I am hot but I feel cold; I am probably running a fever. I need water, I suddenly feel very thirsty. I try to get up but have no strength, and as I fall back into bed my cough starts again. The painful spasms are hoarse, dry, and as each one of them propels me forward I can feel my stomach burning with acid.

Whose name should I call out?

I remember hearing Eden's voice. I remember the feel of her touch as she helped me off the railings, and I remember her smile as she tightened her grip when I thanked her for bringing me home. Then I vaguely remember calling for Alex as I grappled to unlock my front door.

Older thoughts crowd me as I struggle to find meaning in becoming someone else – someone able to hold on to Eden's presence but without being entirely possessed. It had never been her wish to possess me, and I had asked for her forgiveness for my stubbornness: I had refused to let go, unable to imagine an existence without her.

But then I had imagined an existence with Alex, sequestered from the part of me that would remain forever Eden's.

Then I had doubted myself. It had all been too easy, indecently quick. The pain had been a pleasure, but then it had become my punishment, badly masquerading as philosophy and romance.

And at the moment when I needed help, it was Eden who had come to me. She must have known that at that moment I was thinking not of Alex but of her.

Eden had saved me. It was *her* voice I had conjured as I stood on the edge, ready to step into nothingness. It was *her* voice I had heeded. And yet it was Alex I had called for when the voices were no longer in my head.

The parts have become even more disunited, not just separated from each other but falling apart as I break into pieces.

Inside the single drawer of the bedside table there is a large framed photograph of Eden. It had stood beside the lamp, whose dim orange light made it look just a little out of focus, phantasmal without being funereal. On the night when I lined up my concoction into orderly columns, the central ceiling light had been on, flooding the room with the brightness of an operating theatre. Eden had requested the excess of light as though it might have boosted the effect of medication. Or perhaps she had become afraid of semi-darkness. For me the opposite was true. It was the glut of brightness that hurt. It had become unbearable because it had failed us, only serving to register more starkly the disease's daily toll. And yet Eden had insisted on it, and in it we had had our last embrace. Since then, the room had remained dimly orange, making Eden's photograph appear almost holy. Apart from that one time, the central light had not come on again.

But the photograph had gone into the drawer when the pills had come out, and had stayed there until now. I lean on to my side, taking it out and putting it back on the table. Another fit of coughing takes possession of me, searing me with sharp stabs of pain. With effort I prop myself up on my elbow and turn the frame slightly to one side, so that Eden's smile is aimed directly at me, its equal and beautiful curves drained of blood, drenched instead in the shiver of an orange luminescence.

Whose name should I call out?

I have never really been a collector, except of leftover pills, whose combination with vodka I had hoped would be lethal. They must still be in the drawer; I will look for them later. My promise to dispose of them had been to myself, and I intend to keep it, and by keeping it I will also be keeping my promise to Eden. I have made the same promise to Alex, and I have Alex to thank for having also made a promise to myself.

Sam is still on my mind, and I can't help making the comparisons, although perhaps the comparisons are false. I didn't even know him, so how can I be sure Sam had a choice? Does it even matter if he had? What does it even mean, to have, or not have, a choice?

What matters is that Alex is helping me heal. She couldn't help Sam, but she is helping me. I am easier to help. I want to be helped. I want Alex to help me. She already has.

Hasn't she?

Whose name should I call out?

No, not Eden's. Eden now belongs to my dreams.

I am not dreaming now. Lying in our bed, in our slightly orange room, I am looking at her photograph and muttering the words:

Forgive me,

Forgive me,

Forgive me.

A knock on the door interrupts me. 'Ollie, are you awake?'

It can't be Alex; she doesn't like calling me Ollie.

The door opens quietly, the light from the corridor making angled lines on the ceiling and the wall and the floor. Another knock, then the door opens wider and Claw is in the room, making her way towards the bed with a glass of water.

'Claw, it's you.'

'Try not to sound so disappointed,' Claw answers cheerfully. And then, 'Of course it's me, who else could it have been?' She hands me the glass and sits beside me on the bed, then she places the back of her hand on my forehead. 'You gave me quite a fright – you were in a *terrible* state. But you're better now, and tomorrow you'll be right as rain.'

'Tomorrow,' I repeat uncertainly, then I drink most of the water in one gulp.

'And if you're working on Monday, you should take the day off, just in case.'

'I don't understand, what day is it today?'

Eden, then Alex, now Claw. Against the railings I had almost collapsed; Eden had delivered me home; I had called out for Alex; Claw has just entered my room; I am in bed in my pyjamas. These are the parts I know, but how do they connect? I seem to be stumbling from puzzle to puzzle...

'Saturday,' says Claw, but then she looks at her watch. 'Well, it's already after midnight, so technically it's Sunday.'

Sunday. My mind skips back to yesterday, and to the day before, filling up with Alex, then with cold and with pain, then with Eden... I can't find the thread that leads to Claw.

'Then I can't've been asleep for very long.'

'You were asleep on the sofa when I got here, and first I turned the heating on and then I undressed you and rubbed you *everywhere* with Vaseline – I had to, or you'd've never warmed up – then I rolled you into your pyjamas and I managed to get you to sleepwalk to bed. I got here just after five thirty, so you've slept for six hours at least.'

A shorter burst of coughing, tearing at me from inside like an animal's claw.

'I still don't understand, did someone call you?'

'You did, and I thought you were drunk, you could hardly string two words together, but you also had this awful-sounding cough, so Patrick drove me over to make sure you were okay.'

'And I opened the door for you?'

'I did ring the bell, but when you didn't answer, I let myself in, I still have the set of spare keys Eden gave me when...' Claw purses her lips and sighs deeply and loudly. Then she takes my hand and after giving it a squeeze she presses it against her lips. 'I'll sleep on your sofa tonight, just in case. And I have something to help you get to sleep.'

'I don't need help to sleep,' I snap, taking back my hand. Have all the "suspicions" and "concerns" that are really accusations suddenly become more plausible, or am I just being ungrateful? I'm too exhausted to decide. 'And you've done more than enough for me already, you don't have to stay. Really, I'm fine.' I make an effort to smile and Claw smiles back.

'I'll call myself a cab in a minute,' she says. 'But not before you've told me *exactly* what happened between you and Alex on Friday afternoon after we left. *And* what happened to you yesterday.'

'Yesterday?'

'When you almost froze to death. Isn't that what happened? You were mumbling on and on about it in your sleep.'

And before that, Alex and I had made love – at least I hadn't mumbled about that. So much has happened since They Them, so many alternating moments of warmth and rage and then passion, of hope and then despair. At the door I had called out for Alex, but then apparently I had telephoned Claw. The irony isn't lost on me and I almost want to laugh.

'Wasn't she lovely?' Claw speaks through her hand, and her voice now is serious as she takes in Eden's photograph.

The sudden change in tone takes me by surprise, causing me to take myself by surprise: 'Alex is a friend of Sigismund's. And she was married to a patient of yours.' Again the words fly out, almost of their own free will. I would have spoken all of them eventually, but I would have separated Sigismund from Sam. Now Claw will be suspicious.

Suspicious of what? She either has something to hide or she hasn't. Eggshells make no difference either way.

I look at Eden's photograph and then I look at Claw. This room more than anywhere else is pervaded with the friendship that had bound them so closely together, unbreakable even by betrayal. I had always sensed that Eden could see something in Claw that I couldn't – that perhaps no one else could. Had I been wrong to trust her instinct?

As though to flee being scrutinised too closely, Claw gets up from my bed and walks over to the window, parting the curtains for a brief look at the night outside before letting them fall back into place.

'I thought it might be snowing,' she says distantly. The orange of the bedside lamp dissipates before it can reach her, and in the grey that encases the window she isn't much more than a blur.

'Aren't you going to ask me what happened to the man Alex was married to?'

'You mean my patient,' says Claw, her voice suddenly confident again. 'Why? Is it important?'

'Well, he's dead and you were his doctor... "Without Them I would not be who I am. The price of love is life and death." Ring a bell? No? Joe even mentioned his name.'

'They Them.' Claw's voice is now a whisper, and I can't see her well, but I know she must be trying to make sense of all the dots. How long will it take her to join them together? Not long. 'Sam,' she says.

'Sam, that's right.'

'And Alex knew who I was when we went upstairs to meet her?'

My head is heavy, my chest still hurts, Claw is here to help and what am I doing? I haven't thought things properly through, and I've blurted out too much already. 'No, not exactly,' I say eventually.

'Not exactly?'

'I mean no, she found out later, when Sigismund came round.'

'Came round where?'

'The apartment in St Cross Street. We went for a walk first, and then Alex invited me round for a drink.'

'And Sigismund was there?'

'He came later.'

Claw peers through the curtains again. 'I was never invited,' she says. Then turning around, her features still obscured by heavy shadows, 'I only ever saw Sam at the practice. I did find it curious that I never met his wife, that she didn't reach out even after what happened. I suppose some people like to draw a line, but it's very unusual not to want to know every detail, especially in cases like Sam's – people's instinct is to look for evidence they're not at fault.'

'Alex knows she's not at fault.'

'Sam loved her very much,' Claw says mournfully. 'Will you tell her I said that?' Already she has left the darkest grey. 'And if there's anything she'd like to discuss with me...' One more step towards the orange, then she stops again. 'But I'm curious. How did it come up, the connection?'

'Coincidence,' I say. 'Sigismund and Alex have been friends for a while, and he also knew Sam.'

'Really? Sam never said... But then why would he? He was my patient, not my friend, and he was also very sensitive, and although he and Alex shared a very open lifestyle, probably he thought I'd be embarrassed, knowing he'd found out about my ex running off with a boy.'

'Probably.'

I am shocked by Claw's lack of emotion. She speaks of Sam as though she had been fond of him, but at the same time she seems preoccupied with trivial details, her tone inflated as though to either hide or disguise her true feelings.

'What I do find odd is that Sigismund should bring it up that I was Alex's dead husband's doctor. It's not exactly a topic for light-hearted conversation, a young man's tragic suicide.'

She knows I'm not telling her everything, and that not everything I'm telling her is true.

'The conversation was already not light-hearted - we were talking about Eden, then we got talking about Sam. And Sigismund knew I'd been to see They Them with you and Patrick.'

'Ah yes, that's true.' Three more strides, and at last I can almost see her clearly.

'Because apparently he gave you the tickets.'

Fully orange now, Claw gives a loud laugh. 'He's *always* liked to spoil my funny stories! And you still haven't told me *anything* about what happened between you and Alex, so lots to talk about later.'

Hilarity again. "Claw's refuge", Eden used to call it, as always manufacturing excuses for her friend – "she's Claw, and everyone has sex with her once" was another example. Whatever Eden might have called it, it offends me.

'Right, then. I'll be back around noon with some lunch.' Her smile is orange too.

'There's really no need,' I say. 'I've a fridge full of stuff to make lunch with, and at five I'm meeting Alex in St Cross Street.'

'Oh. I see.' The orange smile becomes more strained. 'And will Sigismund also be there?'

'With William.'

I instantly regret my provocation, but remarkably Claw lets it pass unremarked. Instead, she bends over and kisses my forehead. 'No fever,' she says. 'Now you should rest, and don't go anywhere unless you're feeling well.'

'I won't, I promise.'

'Good. Then I'll order a cab and shut the door behind me when it's here. Oh, and there's a sandwich ready for you in the fridge if you're peckish.'

'Thanks for everything,' I say. 'And say hello to Patrick.'

When I hear the front door shutting, I let out all the coughing I've been struggling to hold back, terrified that it might stop Claw from going. Then I prop myself up on my elbow again and turn to look at Eden's smile.

'Hi,' I say. 'I miss you so much.' Then I open the drawer and feel around with my hand. I pull it out further and almost lose my balance as I lean over to look at what's inside. Nothing; it's empty. The square plastic container with the broken smile of pills has disappeared.

I fall back into my pillows wide awake. My breathing has improved and my chest feels less congested, almost normal. In my throat I can still feel the tickle of the cigarettes I smoked with Alex, and the aftertaste of burning tobacco brings to life the succession of moments in which we smoked each one - my most recent recollections, of the cigarettes we smoked on Saturday before and after sex, are so vivid that it's as if Alex herself is right beside me. But Alex has no place in the bed I had only shared with Eden, the bed in which Eden had died, and I blink her away.

'Every time I go to bed, I feel like I'm rehearsing my own death,' I used to say to Eden before she got sick. 'Stop being so morbid,' she would chide me, and I would always answer back that talking about death wasn't morbid at all – even death itself wasn't morbid. I remember Eden laughing. 'Yes, yes, death smiles at all of us and all we can do is smile back - I've seen *Gladiator* too. Now come on, Russell Crowe, get yourself over here and let's do *Annie Hall* instead - turn all the lights off and play hide the salami!' Then the lump under her arm put a stop to all the jokes about death, and when the time came there was no smiling back.

Just now, when I looked inside the drawer for the lethal cocktail, what exactly had been my intention? Feeling romantic about Alex had made me feel romantic about everything, and yesterday afternoon, as I trudged my way uphill in the freezing cold, almost giving in to death's warm embrace just a few yards short of home, I had also felt romantic about death. And there was still something romantic about death being so readily at my fingertips, affording me the opportunity to constantly oppose it.

No longer in a drawer next to my bed, all my pills are gone.

Someone must have taken them.

Claw – who else?

But she couldn't have known they existed, and unless she knew they existed, how would she have known where they were?

A fresh bout of coughing, dry and scratchy.

When I get up for the bathroom, I feel disoriented and weak, and my movements are uncertain and slow. Will I be well enough to make it to St Cross Street in just a few hours, or even tomorrow to work? I need to have my phone by my side, in case of an emergency and also to keep track of the time. But where is my phone? In my coat pocket, and my coat must be hanging by the door. I need to have my phone because I want to call Alex.

Alex has been calling me. She called six times, and has left one voicemail message. She has also sent several texts. I stop at the fridge and take out the plate with the sandwich Claw prepared. Cheese, ham and tomato, a little soggy by now. I replace the top slice of bread with a fresh one and make my way back to the bedroom, the plate in one hand and my phone in the other.

I put the plate down on the bedside table, puff out my pillows and lie down, turning over to the side that is less orange, as though to hide my phone from Eden. The screen lights up, and I scroll down to the earliest message.

I've just popped out to Tesco and it's freezing outside. I hope you had the sense to take a cab. Let me know when you get home. Missing you already.

The next one is from half an hour later.

It's been ages since you left, you must be home by now. Call me.

And fifteen minutes after that:

You've probably dozed off, please call me as soon as you read this.

Then there was a gap of one hour.

I'm getting really worried now.

At eight in the evening:

Oliver, I hope you're OK. Please call me, even if you're having second thoughts.

And finally:

Everything's happened too quickly and it's my fault. But I need to know you're safe, at least send me a text.

The first text message is from 15.56, about an hour after I had set off for home, when I must have been approaching Tufnell Park, although I couldn't say for sure how long any part of my journey had lasted. I had been so absorbed in my thoughts, and in soaking up the city's vital signs, that any sense of time had been lost. Nor have I a single recollection of extraneous sensations that ought to have forewarned me of my imminent collapse, or of wilfully not heeding my body's admonitions. The last text is from 10 o'clock last night – it is already the early hours of Sunday morning.

The voice message is from 21.34, less than half an hour before her final text. I should listen to it now but I can't. It must be frantic too, perhaps even more frantic than her texts, and like her texts it has also gone unanswered. I'm too frightened to play it, to hear the change in Alex's voice, to hear the panic and the disappointment I have read in her texts. I should speak to her instead. But it's after two in the morning, isn't it too late to call her now? Should I text her instead? Or should I wait until the morning?

Paralysed by indecision I have turned onto my back, pulling myself up against the pillows. When the phone begins to silently vibrate between my fingers it makes me jump; my phone jumps too, out of my hands, landing buzzingly on my chest.

It's probably Claw, feeling the injustice of everyone's suspicions telepathically.

It's not; it's Alex, feeling the injustice of my long procrastination.

'Hello?' My voice is rough, hoarse from too much coughing.

'Oh, thank God, you're safe!'

The sound of her voice, which I was so afraid to hear in her message, is now flooded with affection and relief, and with all of the accumulated warmth of the time we have already spent together.

'I'm sorry I worried you,' I say, wishing I could find better words. 'My phone was on silent all this time, I've only just this minute seen your messages.'

'But you sound unwell, what's wrong?'

'You were right. I should've taken a cab. I nearly collapsed on the way here, and I did collapse as soon as I got in.' I mention passing fever and Claw, but I omit the Vaseline and Eden's voice. 'Really, I'm fine now,' I say, 'I just have a bit of a cough.' As though goaded by being mentioned, my cough starts again, even drier and scratchier than before.

'You poor thing,' Alex says. 'And there was selfish me feeling neglected.'

'I was stupid, walking all that way in the freezing cold.'

'I was going to say you need to see a doctor, but you already have.'

'Claw stole my pills.' The curse of even more escaping words. As though unformed until they were spoken, they hover in a heavy silence, then dissolve. Alex is giving me time to explain, and the only explanation that will do is the truth... what *is* the truth?

Alex has been waiting too long. 'What pills?' she asks me at last, and I can hear the alarm in her voice. She *knows* what pills, and I know that the question she wants me to answer is different: how did I know the pills were missing? In other words, why had I been looking for them in the first place? I have already asked myself the same question, but now I will answer it differently. "Romantic" and "death at my fingertips" would not sound reassuring to Alex.

'The pills you guessed I had,' I say. 'They were next to the bed in a drawer.'

'And now they're not.'

'But I wasn't going to take them. I was looking at the photograph of Eden I keep on the bedside table, and I just wanted to make sure they were still there.'

'You think the two are connected? Looking at the photograph and wanting to know if the pills were still there?'

Leaning on my elbow, I drag my body further up the bed, coughing as I struggle to sit up. 'I'm not sure. If they are, I swear I don't know how.'

'Insurance,' Alex breathes into the telephone. 'In case things don't work out.'

It's not even properly Sunday yet, and I am speaking on the phone with a woman I have only known since Friday. Is it possible these thirty-six hours are already so significant that they qualify as "things"?

'I don't know, maybe.' I clear my throat and cough again. 'It's true that everything's been happening too quickly, but it's no one's fault, I'm just struggling to keep up.'

'That's what Sam used to say; that he couldn't keep up.'

'I think that's why I wanted to walk home – I was hoping it would help clear my head. But I couldn't even manage that without nearly killing myself.'

'I'm coming over,' Alex says, and it isn't a question. 'Text me the address.'

NINE

The heating has been on for too long, and my flat is stiflingly hot. Even if I am still running a fever, keeping my body relatively cool should help bring my temperature down. But if I turn the heating off, it will be uncomfortably cold very quickly, so I turn it down instead. I also open the window in the bedroom by an inch, but an icy waft of wind hits me like a slap in the face, and I slam it shut again in a hurry. I drag myself into the bathroom, throw some water on my face and take a fleeting look at myself in the mirror. I look pasty and drawn, like a sick man twice my age but with a heavy mop of thick dark brown hair: I resemble the Ghost of Christmas Past with a wig on. I should never have agreed to Alex coming round, but it's already far too late to put her off; any minute now she will be ringing my doorbell. I make my way to the living room and open the window overlooking the street. The flat is open plan, and I walk over to the sink in the opposite corner and pour myself another glass of water. I drink all of it, then I walk back to the window and shut it; I am beginning to feel feverish again.

My flat isn't mine at all, or rather it is but feels like it isn't. It is mine and Eden's, not just mine, even though Eden is dead and neither of our names is on the title: we were renting until we could afford to buy our dream – a ruin we would rebuild into something magnificent. In the meantime, this had been our only home, and it makes me feel a little less alone that every room, every piece of furniture, every painting, every piece of 1960s junk is exactly as it was when Eden was still filling every corner with her presence. Only one thing has changed; as though to mitigate the pain of her absence, photographs of Eden are everywhere: four on the sideboard in the hallway, two on the larger coffee table in front of the sofa, three on the bookcase in the alcove by the window, and one on my bedside table.

And now a woman I have known for only two days – a woman I have more than gone to bed with already - is about to arrive very shortly and shatter the spell; suddenly *everything* has changed, and what jars are the photographs of Eden.

What does that say about Alex? No qualms - is it bravery or brazenness? I ask myself the question theoretically; it does not correspond to any similar equivocation in my feelings. I am glad that Alex is coming. I am glad that events are unfolding at breakneck speed. I am glad that my emotions are being put to the ultimate test. But this absence of equivocation does not preclude the parallel presence of opposite forces; there are still barricades. I am glad that Alex is coming – and yet earlier I had blinked her out of bed; I am glad that events are unfolding at breakneck speed – and yet earlier I had questioned if they qualified as "things"; I am glad that my emotions are being put to the ultimate test – and yet yesterday I had all but surrendered myself to the cold. There are still barricades, but permanent limbo is hardly an option, and reality *needs* to be put to the test. If Alex can co-exist with Eden in a physical space so loaded with the past, then the present may be able to diverge from it at last.

Forgive me,
Forgive me,
Forgive me.

The plea is repeated by rote, perhaps as a test. There is no need for forgiveness, Eden would have said, but what Eden would have said has mattered very little until now. Let go, she would have said. Move on, she would have said. You've grieved enough, she would have said, it's time to live the rest of your life. But I had not been interested in the rest of my life until a woman in the street asked for a light.

And that woman is now at my door. *My* door, because Eden isn't here anymore, because Eden just *isn't*. But even as new memories are formed, Eden will not be forgotten. There *is* no opposition; the fever has helped make up my mind, its blur a useful spur to mental leaps. I am not unaware I have had all these feelings already, but it's only now I don't just feel them in my head.

'My God, you look dreadful,' Alex says, while at the same time I am thinking how perfect she is, how flawless and fresh even at three in the morning.

Her hair absolutely suits her. Its waves break unevenly against her face and neck to make her features softer, playing with the curves of her smile and giving radiance to the unfathomable darkness of her eyes, so fierce without being violent. And her neck as she uncovers it by taking off her coat, rises out of her sweatshirt like a statue's, the carved severity of its elongated posture contrasting superbly with the almost liquid joy of her whimsical smile.

'I know it's selfish of me just turning up, you'd probably be asleep if I hadn't said that I was coming over.' From the threshold she gestures at the sideboard. 'If you think I'm intruding, I should go. I shouldn't have... I mean...'

'Don't, please.' I smile and step back so that the door is wide open. 'You're not intruding. I want you to be here. But come in, before we both freeze to death.'

Alex doesn't just come in. She drops her small red rucksack on the floor and somehow falls into my arms, but lightly, as though in a featherweight swoon: her embrace is unclutching, an enfolding caress that makes me feel fragile and precious. 'At least you're not burning,' she says. 'But you shouldn't be up, let's get you to bed.' And then, unexpectedly, 'Sigismund was right, Eden really was very beautiful. And her eyes – they remind me of yours.'

'I thought you were about to say that they reminded you of Sam's.'

'No one's eyes remind me of Sam's. And I hope that if you saw them, they wouldn't remind you of mine.'

I don't ask why. We cling on to each other and I guide us to the bedroom in small steps. 'The place is like a shrine,' I say as we're about to go in. 'I know it's unhealthy.'

Alex draws me closer. 'Why?' she asks. 'Whatever this is,' she points tenderly at the photograph of Eden on the bedside table, 'I don't think it's unhealthy at all.'

The day after her father's funeral, her mother gave Eden a small framed photograph of him, and Eden thanked her and put it in her bag. 'Shrines are unhealthy,' she said to me, putting it away in a drawer as soon as we got home. If the display of just a single photograph could constitute a shrine, I had always assumed that so would that of ten. And if Eden thought a shrine was unhealthy, until now it had never crossed my mind that it might not be, or even that it was a matter of opinion whether it was or it wasn't.

'I take it you've been taking your temperature?' Alex asks me as we untangle and I sit on the edge of the bed.

'Claw said it was normal.'

'We should take it again just in case.' And after puffing out my pillows, 'You better lie down first.'

'I'm not sure I still have a thermometer.'

'Then it's just as well I brought one with me.' When Alex comes back with her rucksack, she takes the thermometer out and takes it to the bathroom to wash. 'Mouth or armpit?' she asks when she comes back.

Mouth, and after a few seconds it beeps.

'Let's see,' Alex says. And then, 'Oh no, 37.5, no wonder you're delirious!' She gives a quiet chuckle and brushes back my hair with her hand.

'I look like a ghost with a wig on, I know.'

Her chuckle now is louder. 'I love your hair,' she says. 'But you're obviously poorly, and we'll need to keep an eye on your temperature, to make sure it isn't rising.' She sits beside me on the bed and bends to the side to look at Eden's photograph. 'May I?' she asks, and when I nod, she picks it up. 'She really was very beautiful,' she says again, and the curves of her smile widen until they are equal, as if to mirror Eden's smile in the photograph.

How do I feel about Alex? How do I feel about her holding Eden's photograph and smiling Eden's smile? I articulate the second question because the answer, which I already know and has already surprised me, serves to make the answer to the first more emphatic. I must feel a lot about Alex, because her presence here – in this flat, in this room, on this bed, sharing Eden's orange glow - does not feel in the least like an intrusion. And my short-lived surprise, far from triggering doubt or rekindling remorse, has already given way to the same feeling of freedom I had envied in Alex's eyes – the freedom to feel all these feelings while at the same time feeling Eden's presence too.

'You think I don't need them,' I say. 'The photographs, I mean.'

Alex furrows her brows. 'How would *I* know what you need? How would anyone?'

'But you must have an opinion.'

'Because you think you know what *I* need?' The question is sharp, and Alex doesn't wait for an answer. 'I would like you not to disappear,' she goes on softly. 'That's my only opinion.'

'You're more practical than I am,' I say. 'I have photographs and you have strategies.'

'Mmm... I do have strategies, you're right. And now I also have you.'

Say it,

Say it,

Say it.

I can't. I bend my head instead towards the bedside table. 'That's where the pills were. In that drawer.'

Alex opens it, and then closes it. 'And you're sure Claw took them?'

I shrug. 'Who else? I mean, they were there on Friday, and they're not there now.'

'You definitely didn't flush them down the toilet...'

'I might have, I suppose, but then where's the plastic box they were in? I definitely couldn't've flushed *that* down the toilet.'

'If it was Claw...'

'I told her about Sam, but that was later. The pills must've been taken before that, while I was out of it.'

'And that?' Alex points at the blue-and-pink capsule on the bedside table.

'Oh,' I say. 'That's supposed to help me sleep.'

'Claw?'

'Yes.'

I know what will happen, and inevitably it does. The moment, *our* moment, again becomes waylaid, and now belongs to Sam, and to Claw.

I should never have mentioned the pills, and I should have got rid of the capsule.

Now Alex picks it up. She has a closer look and then she puts it down. 'She prescribed these for Sam for a while. And she shouldn't have. You don't prescribe *these* to an addict.'

'Sam was an addict?'

She narrows her gaze, its darkness more impenetrable as she averts it from mine. 'Sam was open about everything, and would've told Claw that he regularly used recreational drugs – except that there was nothing recreational about them, not the way Sam was using them. He already had problems with his moods, and the drugs made everything worse. Claw should've known that prescribing even more drugs was definitely not the solution. At the very least she was negligent.'

'But she couldn't've known...'

'She should've known there was a risk.'

Her reasoning is flawed, based on unreliable conclusions that are themselves based on unprovable assumptions.

'And she took my pills today because she realised who you are, and was worried she might get into trouble?' The idea is so far-fetched that it's almost fantastical.

But the irony is lost on Alex. 'Something like that.'

'I don't think so,' I say. 'I mean, how would she have known I had the pills in the first place? She can't have.'

'Maybe not for sure. But she told Sigismund that you were always feeling down and she was worried about you. It was his idea that she should bring you to the show, and then you all turned up and found a table waiting for you....' Her gaze is sharply focused on the grey around the window. 'She wasn't Eden's doctor; she shouldn't've prescribed her anything. If she realised who I was, then maybe she suspected a set-up....'

'That's too many "ifs",' I say. Too many *ridiculous* "ifs", I should have said.

Now Alex looks straight at me. 'There's no "if" about your pills going missing.'

'It's possible she found them by chance and took them away to protect me.'

'Took them away and left you alone without mentioning anything? That's hardly protecting you.'

And suddenly I've had enough.

'Is that why you're here? To cross-examine me about Claw while pretending to care that I'm sick?' Sitting bolt upright, I am stunned by the sound of my words, even as my vehemence drives me further down a spiral that I make no attempt to escape. 'Is that what the last couple of days have been really about? Collecting evidence that you and Sigismund can use in your vendetta, trying to pin the blame on someone else because otherwise you'd have to accept the simple truth that Sam was selfish - that he did what he did because he wanted to, and would've found a way to do it no matter what? I mean, it's not that hard if you're really determined, and good for Sam that he obviously was - the only reason I'm still here is because I'm a coward!'

Alex hasn't moved. I have felt her gaze stay fixed on me throughout my rant, and have avoided it by staring straight ahead at the room's gloomy shadows, beyond the edge where the orangeness fades and then becomes grey as it fails to reach the walls, all of them bare in the bedroom since Eden became ill. From one day to the next, the posters of horror films – *Halloween*, *Friday the 13th*, *A Nightmare on Elm Street* - that she used to collect, luridly depicting crazy murderers and bloodthirsty monsters had become too disturbing, and with the excuse that they were giving me nightmares, which Eden had pretended to believe, I had taken them all down. 'Sleeping better without sweet Freddy Kruger staring back at you?' she had teased me, and I had answered dryly that I was. I had lost my sense of humour the day I had lost hope, unlike Eden, who had clung on to hers till the end.

Alex still hasn't moved; nor has her gaze. I am lost in the fuzz of grey and orange that seems to contain us, shrinking the room to the edge where the two colours merge in a haze. What do I expect is going to happen? Did my outburst have any expectation in mind? Do I even know where it came from? It must have come from somewhere, and the various possibilities of where it might have come from are unfolding in my mind all at once.

'I feel shivery,' I say, and I know Alex is helping me lie down so that the duvet can cover the whole of my body. 'Thank you,' I want to say...

'Oliver...'

The shadow of a sound, distant, like an echo through fog.

'Oliver...'

A murmur; a caress of affection, unwanted. A trespass.

'Oliver, wake up.'

A breath on my neck; a hand on my shoulder. Eden has broken away, out of my reach. Unable to see, or move, or speak, paralysed in darkness and silence, I am alone and awake in a dream.

'Wake up.'

The smell of our bed; of our bodies, both naked. My palate dry, my lips dehydrated. Quivering eyelids, disturbed. A sensation of light too intense; painful. Half awake, annoyed; thoughts barely forming, inchoate. A longing for sleep, uninterrupted. For dreams; for a lifetime of dreams. Eden, my Eden; a wholeness of being. A glorious pit in my stomach. Real, all too real.

'Are you awake?' The voice now above.

Abruptly on my back with one turn. Arms outstretched; fists clenched, then unclenched. Eyes still shut.

'Oliver, wake up.'

The gasp of a sigh, then movement. The sound of muffled footsteps, one, two, three, four; no more than six. Darkness slowly dissolves into light; light and shadow mould into shape. My eyes now wide open, focussed on hers.

'Alex,' I say.

'Still here.' Her smile is reassuring.

A conflict I thought had been settled has resurfaced in a dream: how do I hold on to Eden without losing Alex; how do I hold on to Alex without losing Eden?

In an effort to recover my consciousness fully, with slow movements I turn towards the brightness behind me. The curtains have been drawn, and the orange blends with daylight, dissolving in the brightness of a winter morning sun.

Almost blinded, I return to the preponderance of orange.

'I haven't drawn the curtains in ages,' I say, with a limp wave of my arm towards the window.

Alex has pulled over the small armchair from beside the dressing table, and leans forward in it by the bed. 'Would you like me to close them again?'

I lie. 'No,' I say, 'the light is lovely.'

'Yes. It's another gorgeous day. You were asleep for quite a while. And I also nodded off for a couple of hours.'

I cough just once, and then I cut through the small talk. 'I'm glad you're still here. I'm really sorry about before. All those things I said, I'm not even sure why I said them.'

Alex doesn't recoil. The warmth has returned to her eyes. But when she speaks her voice is flat.

'You were right,' she says. 'Not that I was here to cross-examine you, or that I was just pretending I care. I'm here because you need me and I want to be here. You were right that I'm obsessive about Claw, and I do think she's dangerous, but it's also true that Sam was determined, and if his mind was made up, nothing anyone did would've made any difference.' She stops and runs her fingers through her hair, pulling it back and then letting it go. 'I know why you think Sam was selfish, but I promise you that's actually the last thing he was.' Her voice now is tender. 'He was just completely exhausted.'

With another limp wave, I fumble for her hand, and she gives it to me.

'What I said was out of order. And I'm grateful you're here.'

'Please don't be grateful.' Alex feels my forehead with the back of her hand. 'When I'm with you, I can't imagine being anywhere else.' Her head moves a little to the side, but her gaze stays fixed on mine. 'Or is that too much?'

'For a man on his deathbed?'

Two equal and beautiful curves break into laughter. 'Oh, I think you'll live.'

'Now that Claw's got my pills.'

'You were right about that too, it's not hard at all if you're really determined. But I don't think the only reason you're still here is because you're a coward. No coward would've put themselves through a lunchtime poetry reading at the Cutting-Edge Arts Centre.'

'An "unforgettable performance" by "a poet like no other", how could I resist?'

'No real poet is like any other.'

'No other poet I know of performs with a dummy.'

'I'm not a poet without it. I'm not a poet full stop. It was Sam's performance; I was just filling in.'

'But you improvised.'

'Only because you were there.'

The words now dance with our eyes, flirtily playful but peaceful.

Alex reaches out to stroke my hair, and I clasp her hand and bring it to my chest, threading all my fingers through hers.

'Last night, just before I passed out, I wanted to say thank you.'

'You did,' she says. 'And *then* you passed out, which was exactly what your body needed.'

My energy is back, my chest is less heavy and my cough has almost stopped; my breath still catches in my throat every now and again, but that's probably the cigarettes. The cigarettes...

'Have we given up smoking?' I ask Alex, holding up her hand so I can look at it - there is so much of her still that I couldn't describe.

And I fail to resist one more comparison: my total grasp of Eden, and of the parts that made her whole, had always been beyond photographic; it was physical, a deep familiarity approximating an equation. The stages of her slow deterioration, and then the imagery of the final few days, so bodily and yet so insubstantial, had imprinted themselves on my consciousness indelibly, and for a while after her death had prevailed over even the most vivid recollections of joy. But not a single one had become irretrievable, and very slowly my memories began to mingle with each other almost randomly, the good, the bad, the indifferent, spurred by life's reminders. And the most joyful became my worst tormentors, leading me to crave for aloneness, leading me to crave for the end, leading to a neat arrangement of colourful parallel lines.

'Mmm... I think we should, don't you?' Alex answers non-committally. And then, while our hands float together in mid-air, 'Neither of us is wearing a wedding ring.'

'We stopped wearing ours the day after our wedding,' I say.

'I've made ours into this.' With her other hand, Alex pulls the chain around her neck over her sweatshirt, and takes the small ball of gold that dangles from its end between her fingers.

'Ball and chain,' I say. But then, very quickly, 'I don't know why I said that. It's beautiful.'

'"I'm your ball and chain." Sam said that to me once. It wasn't true but he believed it – he never said anything he didn't believe.' For a moment she becomes melancholic. 'If your photographs of Eden are a shrine, then so is this.' The small ball of gold catches the light as she lifts it, and her gaze grows brighter in its glow.

'Eden thought it too towards the end – that she'd become a burden. I told her all the time it wasn't true.'

'Sam thought he was to blame for making me sad, and it's true I was sad, but it was no more his fault than your sadness was Eden's. Blame is ugly.'

I want to say something, to make a distinction. I want to exonerate Eden by apportioning *some* blame to Sam. The blanket equation seems to me unequal, the claim of equivalence unjust.

But Alex is right. Blame is ugly. Sam is not to blame for what happened to Eden, nor Alex for the burden of my grief.

'I have a confession,' I say.

Alex shifts in her chair, and her smile turns with her gaze to face me intently. She clears her throat, as though offering to speak on my behalf.

I clear my throat too, as though insisting I should speak for myself. 'I was judging Sam, and I wanted you to judge him too. I thought it was unfair he had a choice and Eden didn't. I thought that of course he was selfish and of course he was to blame, and it bothered me you didn't think he was.' I speak quickly, but my cough has made me short of breath, and every so often I need to take a pause and draw in air. 'I found it offensive that you thought your loss and mine were the same - I thought *my* loss was somehow more worthy. I was wrong. And obviously the reason I compared in the first place is because I'm self-centred, still behaving like the only thing that matters is what happened to *me*, like everything else revolves around it – and if it doesn't, it should. Which of course I know is nonsense. I'm an idiot, and I'm sorry.'

Retrieving her hand, Alex lifts herself out of the armchair and leans the side of her face against the side of mine, while holding me in place by clutching my neck. She smells of bright and chilly weather, of rain and wetted leaves.

'I also have a confession,' she whispers in my ear. Then she sits beside me on the bed and bends towards me, swathed in orange sunshine. 'I've judged Sam too, many times; at the beginning I was really, really angry. And not just with Sam, with the world. Which I think is the same as what you're describing.' Her voice is light and musical, her words spoken breezily, lacking the self-critical portentousness of mine. 'And I've also judged you, by the way - people judge each other all the time, so you're not the only idiot, the rest of us are all idiots too. But it's not a competition, you're right about that too.'

Briefly relieved that Alex has lightened the mood, now I want to ask questions. I like everything to be explained, I like it to be clear. I feel too much with my head – that's what Eden used to say. 'It's like you *live* in there. My God, relax! You can't just stay locked up in your head all the time. Come out and have some fun.' Eden was right, and Alex will no more know the answers than I do, because there aren't always answers, and questions shouldn't always be asked.

'Eden used to say I live too much inside my head.'

'And I live too much inside *other* people's heads,' says Alex. 'Can't we just both be who we are?'

'"Get out of there and have some fun," she used to say.'

'And we did, on Friday night.'

I look at her sideways and laugh. Perhaps she does have all the answers after all. 'What's the time now?'

Alex looks at her watch. 'Time to have something to eat, it's almost one o'clock.'

'Fine, we'll order something. And then I'll get ready and we'll go back to yours. You haven't cancelled Sigismund, have you?'

'Oliver, you need to rest. I think we should stay here.'

'You think I'm ill?'

'No. I think you caught a chill and you're exhausted.'

'I *was* exhausted. I'm feeling fine now. And my cough's almost gone.' The tickle in my throat is still there, and I know that if I try to clear it, I'll probably start coughing again, so I don't.

'Let's eat first, and then we can decide,' Alex says.

'And I don't mind talking about Claw if you think it might be useful.'

I feel an openness with Alex that I haven't felt since Eden, but still in shock from its unlikelihood I am unable yet to feel it all the time without guilt.

We ordered pizza, and Alex made a salad from ingredients she found in the fridge – there was lettuce, tomatoes and rocket, all still usable. I pulled down the Formica-top counter that served as a kitchen table, and we sat on stools to eat. Eden and I used to always have our breakfast here, and occasionally lunch at weekends, but dinner at home was always something light – a sandwich or a soup or a salad, followed by some fruit - and we would have it from trays in our laps while watching the news on the sofa.

I hadn't completely recovered. I was still feeling weak. My cough still lurked, barely held in check by a tickle; my breathing was steady but uneasy. I had spent too long in bed, and longed for some fresh air, or imagined I did – I could hardly have forgotten that an excess of exertion and fresh air had caused me to be ill in the first place. Filling up my lungs with yet more freezing moisture was probably the last thing I needed. I was restless and wanted to get out of the flat, but my restlessness implied neither wellness nor the least desire to be social. The bedroom, which I had shared with Eden, had become claustrophobic, and the bed, where I had watched her fade, had come alive with voices and feverish ghosts. I wanted to be with Alex, but not here. I wanted us to share a bed, but not *that* bed.

After eating, we moved to the sofa and Alex dozed off in my arms. She must have had a terrible night on the armchair, which ruled out the armchair as an option for another night's sleep – a bed really was imperative, and St Cross Street was the obvious - the *only* - solution. But not at the cost of entertaining Sigismund and William for several hours – in my present condition, that was too high a price to pay. I needed to rest; Alex had said so herself. If I asked her to, she would be happy to cancel. But if she did, what reason would there be for us not to stay put? The reason was the bed, but how would I explain that to Alex? We had already slept together in the bed she had slept in with Sam, but somehow the bed I had slept in with Eden was off limits? It was sacrosanct? Why, on what rational grounds? Ghosts were hardly a good excuse.

Overwhelmed by overthinking about beds, my mind turned to thinking about Claw. Eden and I had experienced first-hand how ruthless she could be when it came to trying to get what she wanted. But all the same she had been a good friend, and whether it was legal or illegal for Claw to prescribe them, Eden had been grateful for the additional drugs. They had eased her suffering, and by easing hers had also eased mine, which was perhaps part of the reason Eden took them, and perhaps part of the reason she didn't take them all: while she lived, she would have wanted to feel as alive as she could. Throughout her illness, Eden had attempted to conceal from me the extent of her pain, and I had gone along with the pretence. And once the outcome had crystallised, her concern had been primarily for me.

'I'm not afraid of dying, not anymore. But I can't help worrying about you. Promise me that you'll be happy again.'

And, of course, I had promised.

I promise,

I promise,

I promise.

An impossible promise that was now coming true.

'But not in our bed.' I speak the words out loud.

'Mm?' And now Alex is awake, looking at me from her perch on my shoulder. And when I don't answer, 'You said something.'

'Did I?'

'About a bed.'

I shrug my shoulders lightly. 'I must've been dreaming.'

'Of Eden?'

'Mm?'

'"But not in our bed," I think you said.'

'It's probably the pizza. Eating too much cheese gives me nightmares.'

'It didn't sound like a nightmare. It sounded like a gentle conversation.' She slips out of our embrace. 'Like the one we're having now, but with Eden,' she says.

'With Eden,' I repeat uncertainly. 'I'm not sure what you mean.'

'She's here, I know. I mean, she's probably everywhere, but here she's almost real.'

Almost real makes me wince. But it's true all the same. *Here* is where Eden comes alive, *here* is where I feel closest to her. And *here* is also where I feel most conflicted. Which is a paradox; if Eden really were here, she would want Alex sharing our bed. If Eden were here, she would kiss me good bye.

'You talk to her, don't you?'

'Every day.' In my daydream I answer truthfully, and I don't regret it. 'You don't talk to Sam?'

'Yes, of course I do. That's really what They Them was about. But I know he's not there.'

I am still in my pyjamas, which are striped, like a prisoner's uniform. And over them I'm wearing the old-fashioned dressing gown Eden gave me one Christmas. When I first tried it on, over the same pair of pyjamas, 'Let me see.' Eden made a show of pressing down on my lapels while she looked me up and down. 'Now we know what grandpa Oliver will look like,' she said, and when she roared with laughter, so did I.

But now suddenly I'm feeling like an inmate in a mental institution.

'You think I'm crazy,' I say.

'Crazy?'

'You said you talk to Sam but you know he's not there.'

'Oh, and you thought... No, that's not what I meant.' Balancing herself on the edge of the sofa, she looms over me. 'I used to ask Sam for advice all the time. He had this rare gift - he knew how to put himself in other people's shoes, and give them the advice that best suited them, which was often very different from the advice he'd've given himself.'

'Did he ever ask you for advice?' I sit still, unable or unwilling to be tactile, my arms glued tightly to my side like a sitting-down soldier's.

'Not really.' Now she sighs and bends her head, still so close that I can smell the pizza in her breath. 'Once or twice, I tried to offer it without being asked, but I don't think he even listened. The advice I gave him was the advice *I* thought was right for him, I never really knew what *he* thought was right.' She looks up at me, her out-of-focus smile wistful but magnificent. 'What I was trying to say before was that I'm still turning to Sam for advice even now, and I know he's not there, but he somehow still gives it to me, the same advice that he'd've given me if he were actually here, advice I couldn't've come up with by myself. And I'm not going to ask you if that makes sense, because I'm sure it doesn't, so maybe I'm the one who's crazy.'

I sigh too. 'We probably both are. On my way to meet Patrick and Claw on Friday morning, just before you asked me for a light, I was thinking that a part of me was Eden's afterlife - that she'll always be here, all the time, not just while I'm talking to her.'

'That's beautiful.'

'I'm sure it's how a lot of people feel. Grief does that. It causes us to imagine that we're not like other people, that our feelings are somehow unique. And they are, but at the same time they're not, because everyone imagines that their feelings are unique, and not just when they're grieving. That's how everything ends up being a cliché.'

'That's not true, not everything ends up being a cliché. And, anyway, there's nothing wrong with clichés if they help us get through life.'

'Said the poet like no other.'

'I told you, that was Sam.' Alex presses down on my lapels the way Eden had that Christmas morning, and touches my forehead with hers. Then she draws back and huddles up beside me again. Her arm slips around mine, and I let her take my hand.

'I was thinking that a part of me was Eden's afterlife and then I met you,' I say.

'As if there weren't enough parts already!' Alex quips, and we both laugh.

But our laughter is charged with nostalgia, and as it fizzles it becomes melancholic.

We stay quiet for a moment, rising and falling to the echo of thumping hearts and shallow breathing.

'This really isn't very sexy,' I say, and suddenly I jerk myself to life, manoeuvring myself out of the tangle. And looking down at myself while pulling apart my lapels, '*This*,' I roar. '*This* while we tell each other stories about talking to two people who are dead.'

And again we stay quiet, this time for longer. Bent forward, I'm holding my head in my hands, with Alex still beside me but apart. The bedroom's oppression has spread: the whole flat has become claustrophobic and the ghosts now are everywhere - hobnobbing ghosts of the dead and alive all voiceless in a clamour of silence.

'I think you need some time to yourself.' Alex is already on her feet. When I look up at her, she stoops down and feels my forehead with her lips, without a kiss. 'Your temperature's fine,' she says.

'I've offended you,' I force myself to murmur.

The past is a permanent ambush, lying in wait behind words, behind objects, in shadows. And I am its accomplice, an enlisted saboteur laying booby traps that blow up in my face.

Alex shakes her head. 'Is there anything you need before I go?' Her voice is cold.

'Just like that, you want to leave?'

'No, Oliver, not just like that.'

'I know I'm a mess. But I want you to be here.'

'You want me to be here but I'm not sure there's room for me. And I don't mean just here in this flat.'

Stock-still in our positions, we whisper while ghosts waft about.

There are no ghosts. There is grief and denial, and the comfort of entrenched resignation. Memories become superstitions, snuffing out the rarest possibilities.

'I know ghosts don't exist,' I say dully.

'Ghosts are not our enemies.'

I am possessed neither by Eden nor her ghost. What possesses me is fear.

Knock, knock.

Who's there?

Come out and have some fun.

'Please stay,' I say.

Alex breathes in deeply, then breathes the air out in a sigh, the whole time looking down at the distance between us on the floor.

Will she stay or will she go?

Her gaze rises in a ripple to meet mine. 'If you're sure,' she says, and after stooping down a second time, she kisses first my forehead then my nose and then my lips, while her hands knead the back of my neck. And without breaking off she folds herself beside me, three quarters of her body pressing against mine as we continue to kiss.

Is this a test?

There is no time for questions. My lapels are wide apart and my dressing gown is halfway down my back, fastening around my arms like a straitjacket, and all the time the kiss goes on. My pulse beats faster and my breathing has become shallower still, struggling not to catch as it wheezes through the tickle in my throat. Alex breathes heavily too, her body's rhythm synchronised with mine as though the same obstruction encumbers us both. She falls away from me now, and we both take rapid breaths as she pulls off her sweatshirt before briefly straddling over me and stripping me down to the stripes of my prisoner pyjamas.

'Are you cold?' she asks me almost gruffly, and when I answer with a growl she carries on, stepping over me to break out of her jeans, before we again become united in a kiss while our hands make frantic gestures with buttons and clasps half-undone.

No more questions are asked; there is only the cacophony of sex, broken by the involuntary movements that have led us to the bed.

The bed.

Our bed, mine and Eden's.

Already the rhythm is broken.

'I can't,' I am about to say, but then the doorbell rings. Disuniting, we lie side by side. 'She can't go now,' I'm thinking, 'not with someone at the door.'

'My God, you're drenched.' Leaning on her elbow Alex drags a finger to make shapes across my chest.

The doorbell rings again.

'I should get that,' I say.

'No, you should jump in the shower,' Alex says. She springs out of bed, looks around for something, *anything*, to wear, disappears and then reappears wrapped in prisoner pyjamas. 'I'll tell whoever it is that you're resting, and then I'll join you in the shower.'

'We can still make it to you yours for five o'clock.'

Alex lingers at the door for a moment. And when the doorbell rings a third time, 'We'll see,' she says.

I do need a shower. The exertions of sex, and even more so of almost attempting to thwart it halfway – more than halfway – just before the doorbell thwarted it instead, have drained me of all my reserves. I want Alex "here" but I don't know what for – I know what I *don't* want her "here" for: sex in this bed, or a shower together, which I suspect might also lead to sex, culminating in more sex in this bed. If I get into the shower now and Alex joins me, the doorbell is unlikely to save me again; I will suggest a shower together and then sex as soon as we arrive in St Cross Street, where the bed holds only memories of Alex. And the bathrooms "there" are *so* much more spacious, equipped with a proper power shower. The water barely dribbles out of mine.

Alex is back in the room, and she's shut the door behind her. 'Claw is here.'

'Claw?' I cling to the covers.

'She was letting herself in as I got to the door.'

'Ollie?' The burst of Claw's shrill voice puts paid to any doubt.

'Oh my God.' I jump out of bed and riffle through the bed sheets. 'My dressing gown, it's in the other room.'

'Forget your dressing gown, just hurry up and get in the shower.'

'Are you sure?'

'Ollie?' Another screech from the other room.

'He's still in the shower,' Alex yells back. And then to me, 'I promise to be civilised, I'll even make some coffee. Now go, before you catch your death!'

TEN

As soon as I step under the shower, which is probably a little too hot, the tickle in my throat becomes a knot, and I break into a choking cough that almost throttles me. And no one would know if it did. While it lasts, there is hardly a sound; it's as if someone's holding a pillow to my face and my mouth is full of feathers. The idea makes me retch, and I almost throw up. I bend my head back and let the water stream in and out of my mouth. The cough becomes a hiccup, and after just one sneeze it dies out. When I clear my throat, it no longer feels encumbered by a tickle.

To save time, I wash first my hair and then everywhere else with shampoo, working it up into a lather with my flannel. While I rub myself my mind begins to drift, and arousing thoughts of Alex make me hard. Then I remember Claw, and palpitations take the place of my erection.

I dry myself quickly and throw on a tracksuit I can easily change out of when we manage to get rid of Claw and can at last order a cab for St Cross Street. As I stride into the living room, I suddenly become aware of palpitations *and* an erection. I need to return to the bedroom and change.

Too late.

'Darling! Is that a gun in your pocket, or are you just happy to see me?' Already out of her coat, Claw is sprawled out on the sofa like a splodge of dirty paint, her kaftan a volcanic explosion of oranges and reds.

'Jesus, Claw.' My erection is dissolving already, and I sink into the chair across the blob.

Claw hoots with extravagant laughter. Alex is beside her making secret signals with her eyes; I know more or less what they mean.

'But seriously, you seem to have recovered remarkably quickly,' Claw yelps at me. 'When I left you, you were white as a sheet, practically the walking dead, and look at you now, all bright-eyed and rosy-cheeked! And there was me thinking *I* was the doctor.'

'Oh, but you are the doctor,' Alex says.

The laughter stops, and immediately the atmosphere is tense. There is going to be a fight, I can tell. Perched on the edge of her corner of the sofa literally baring her teeth, Alex resembles a prisoner puma preparing to pounce.

And at the opposite corner, Claw looks fully ready to be pounced on – her tone when she speaks is acerbic: 'And imagine my surprise when I came back to check on my patient and They or Them opened the door in his pyjamas! Is the dummy here too?'

'Stop it, Claw,' I say.

'Just me, I'm afraid,' Alex says.

'Ollie tells me you know Sigismund.'

'I do, very well. And William too. I suppose Oliver's told you that the four of us went clubbing together on Friday.'

Claw's extravagant laughter resumes. '*That* I would have liked to have seen.'

'It was great,' I say. 'Just what I needed.'

'Well, I'm happy for you.' Claw is serious again. 'And well done you,' she says to Alex with a short sideways nod.

'What for?' Alex asks without moving.

'For cheering this one up. Imagine if I hadn't managed to persuade him to come and see the show. I mean, really, the two of you seem so incredibly well-suited. And you've both suffered terribly, you deserve to have some fun. Who knows, it may even turn out to be more than just fun. And, wow, how amazing that I have such an intimate connection with both of you - Eden was my friend, my *closest* friend I should say, and Sam was probably my favourite patient, such a beautiful, beautiful boy.' She turns around and faces Alex directly. 'And he was *so* in love with you, I hope you know that.'

My heart almost stops. Her tone as ever sneering and superior, Claw has crossed a line by mocking our grief.

'I do, Claw, yes,' says Alex.

'Sam was brilliant but also tremendously complex,' Claw goes on. 'You really mustn't blame yourself for what happened.'

'I don't,' Alex answers, and after a moment of even more unbearable tension, 'Do you?'

The even more unbearable tension intensifies. Claw's head turns spasmodically from Alex to me, then back to Alex again. At the same time, she opens and closes her mouth, once, twice - it's as if she's watching tennis while pretending to be a goldfish. I have been on edge ever since I came into the room, fretting about what might happen next, but the image of a goldfish watching tennis makes me laugh.

'I'm glad you find it funny,' Claw barks at me.

'I don't,' I whisper back.

'Oh. I thought I heard you laugh, so I assumed you found it funny that your girlfriend was accusing me... of what I'm not sure, but certainly of *something*.' She pauses for a sigh, then craning her neck as she again faces Alex, 'But it's fine,' she goes on in a softer voice, 'it's quite common for grief to make us angry, and especially common in cases like Sam's...'

'It's not grief that's made me angry,' says Alex, her voice sounding deep and metallic.

I decide I'm angry too.

'You took my pills,' I say to Claw.

She turns to me but it's a while before she speaks; it's as if she can't decide what to make of what I've said, or why

I might have said it. 'Your pills,' she mutters eventually, still looking at a loss.

'From my bedside table.'

The kaftan slightly shifts. 'I did, yes, in order to dispose of them safely. They weren't really *your* pills, Ollie, were they?'

'But they were in my flat, hidden away in a drawer. How did you even know they were there?'

'I didn't. I opened the drawer to look for a thermometer and I saw them – the box they were in was transparent. Which reminds me...' She gets up and saunters over to her bag, which she's left on the sideboard. 'Here,' she says, handing me the empty plastic box. 'I've washed it for you. You can hide something else in it now.'

'You had no right to throw away the pills,' I say.

'I'm your friend, I have every right to care about your welfare.'

'You were worried he might do something stupid,' Alex says.

'I was, yes.' Claw is still on her feet, hovering between us like an indecisive curse. 'Ollie's been depressed, and there were an awful lot of pills in that box.'

'Sam was also depressed, but you didn't seem too worried that *he* might've done something stupid.'

Claw makes a show of shaking her head. 'So, *that's* what you're accusing me of. Not worrying enough about your husband.'

'Not worrying enough about your vulnerable patient,' says Alex.

Blowing out air, Claw looks towards the door as though mapping her imminent exit. But then, 'Fine,' she says instead, returning to her place beside Alex on the sofa. 'Sam mostly self-medicated, as you know,' she says quietly, looking neither at Alex nor at me but straight ahead. 'So, yes, of course he was vulnerable. But he was honest with me – he trusted me, which he wouldn't've been able to do if I'd given him the impression he was constantly under suspicion. There had to be a degree of mutual trust.'

My pills are apparently insignificant, and already they have been forgotten. Alex has returned us to Sam, and she and Claw seem barely aware of my presence. They fight it out between themselves, and it occurs to me as I listen to the bitterness of their exchange that I wear my ghosts more honestly than Alex, who casts around for hers in Claw's shadow.

'That's just waffle, Claw, and you know it,' she says. 'You're a General Practitioner, not a psychologist.'

'Sam described symptoms that I thought could be treated.'

'And it never once occurred to you that mixing all the drugs you were prescribing him, like the sleeping pill you left for Oliver last night, with the sorts of drugs you knew Sam was taking already was a really bad idea, potentially lethal?'

'Taking paracetamol is potentially lethal. Stepping out of the house every morning is potentially lethal. Going to sleep at night is potentially lethal.'

The pouncing puma growls: 'Except that in Sam's case there was nothing "potential" about it – he actually died.'

The room falls silent. Sam's death is no longer just part of an argument, it is suddenly real, a palpable fact that as though out of the blue has hit Alex and Claw with equal force – they both look as dazed as each other. Claw's kaftan seems to sway towards Alex in a longing to unite with my pyjamas, but then abruptly it shrinks back into its corner.

'Because he wanted to,' Claw says after some time in a whisper. Her right hand hovers for a moment in the air before she makes it into a fist and retracts it. Then with a flip of her lop-sided blondness she swivels again to face Alex. 'I know it's hard to hear but it's the truth.'

'He wanted to at that moment, and that moment might've passed if he'd had a clearer head.'

'Would you feel better if I told you that I actually prescribed him very little?'

Alex darts a narrowed glance at her but doesn't answer.

'I wanted to die too and I'm still here,' I say.

'But not because I took away your pills.'

'Which you had no right to prescribe to Eden in the first place,' says Alex.

This time the room booms with the opposite of silence. 'I've sat here patiently while you both snipe at me, one minute it's one thing, the next it's something else, and I'm sorry, but absolutely *none* of it makes sense, least of all a stranger expecting me to apologise for helping my friend. And *you*,' she lashes out at me, 'you ought to be ashamed of yourself. Or have you suddenly forgotten how Eden had to *beg* me to help, and how grateful she was when I did? You think it was easy for me? Because it wasn't, it was hard, but Eden managed to persuade me I was doing the right thing. And it *was* the right thing, whatever either of you might think.'

'It was the right thing,' I say.

For a moment Alex freezes, staring straight through me. Then turning back to Claw, 'You're right, I didn't know Eden. But I did know Sam.'

'Not as well as you might think,' says Claw under her breath.

Alex laughs, but her laughter is brittle and short. 'Is that your last resort, making crass insinuations against someone who isn't here to defend themselves, a *dead* former patient of yours? That just about sums you up, doesn't it, Claw?'

'Oh, I'm not accusing Sam of anything, I'm accusing *you* of being blind to what was staring you in the face.'

'That's enough!' I have leapt onto my feet, but the effort has made me unstable. As I totter towards nowhere in particular, I struggle to swallow and soon I begin to feel faint.

'Oliver?'

'Ollie?'

Distant voices are speaking my name. Then everything becomes a blur.

When I open my eyes, an unfamiliar whiteness blinds me, and I close them again. I hold them tightly shut for some time, as though a longer blink of darkness might conjure the whiteness away. When I open them a second time and the whiteness is still there, I squint instead, turning my head to one side. The whiteness now is different, closer but less bright.

'Oliver?' A sound, soft and caressing, not an assault. A contrast to the whiteness, welcome.

I have just woken up, but from something much deeper than normal sleep – something almost solid that is slowly dissolving, or perhaps I am dissolving within it, gradually returning to my normal state but somehow still confined in something larger and unpleasant, a hardness that refuses to subside. I experience these complex thoughts not as notions that I'm able to articulate, but as stray sensations that are purely physical - my mind lags behind my body's consciousness to an unnatural degree; for the moment I feel without knowing.

'Oliver?'

Something touches my forehead. Its warmth is like a prompt.

Where am I?

I turn my head the other way. Alex.

'Hello,' she says. There are monitors behind her, the vague sound of a bleep. My left arm is connected to a drip.

A hospital bed in a hospital room.

How?

'You're fine,' Alex says. And pointing with her eyes at the drip, 'They're giving you antibiotics, for a relatively mild chest infection that could've been pneumonia but isn't. You're also a bit anaemic, but I don't think they're too worried, they suspect it's just a lack of enough iron. Really, you're just here as a precaution.' She smiles. Two equal and beautiful curves that remind me of Eden.

I want to smile back and I try.

'Alex,' I say.

'Claw arranged it,' Alex goes on. 'They examined you downstairs and then she had them send you straight up here. She knows everyone.'

'How long?'

'Not long. Just a few hours. Patrick drove us here.'

'I don't remember.'

'It's all my fault, I should've realised how unwell you were.'

'Claw,' I say. 'She said some horrible things.'

'To be fair, so did we.'

'I suppose so,' I say.

'But then as soon as you collapsed, from one minute to the next she became a different person. She was brilliant. If she hadn't been there, I wouldn't've had a clue what to do. Patrick too, he was there in ten minutes, and carried you in his arms from the armchair to his car single-handedly. They're your friends and they obviously care about you a lot. You were right, I shouldn't've got you involved in my vendetta. It was selfish and wrong.'

I turn back onto my back. The whiteness is still blinding, and this time when I close my eyes they stay shut.

When I open them again, Claw is standing over me, speaking to another woman. 'Ah, there he is.' Blood-orange like the moon in her kaftan, she smiles and gives my right hand a squeeze. 'You gave us quite a fright *again*, young man,' she says cheerfully.

'I'm not a young man.' I feel fully conscious, and my head is again full of thoughts, not all of them coherent. Pieces are still missing.

'No, you're an old man and I'm older, so I'm positively geriatric,' Claw snaps at me good-humouredly. And to the other woman loudly, 'He's definitely better. Back to his old argumentative self, so familiar to all his longsuffering friends.'

The other woman throws her head back to give a high-pitched laugh, then she bends herself to loom above me like a cloud, almost totally eclipsing the moon and the whiteness. 'Hi, Oliver, I'm Dr Biggs.'

'Catherine is a brilliant haematologist,' says Claw from somewhere behind her. 'You couldn't be in better hands.'

'Your haemoglobin count is low, which means your body's not producing as many red blood cells as it should,' says Dr Biggs.

'You mean I'm anaemic.'

'That's right. And we need to keep you in for some tests. Your iron is only borderline-low, so we need to make sure there are no other underlying causes. But first we need to chat about your diet, and also ask you a few questions – any dizzy spells, do you take aspirin, have you noticed any blood in your poo, are you suffering from haemorrhoids, that sort of thing.'

'Does it have to be now? He's exhausted.' Alex has emerged from somewhere behind them to stand between the moon and the cloud.

'I'm pretty sure I know the answers to most of them anyway,' says Claw, the vivid oranges and reds of her kaftan reappearing beside Dr Biggs as though to throw my anaemia into sharper relief.

'Would you know if I have haemorrhoids?' I ask her.

Dr Biggs throws her head back to give another high-pitched laugh. 'No, of course it doesn't have to be now,' she says. 'We'll let you have a good night's sleep and we'll all come back to see you in the morning, how does that sound?'

'Can't Alex stay?'

'For a few more minutes, I'm sure she also needs to rest. The nurse will be here soon to prepare you for the night, and there's a bell you can ring if there's anything you need.' Dr Biggs is already at the door. 'Claw?'

'Sweet dreams,' says Claw. After kissing my hand, she touches my forehead. 'See you both tomorrow.'

'Patrick,' I say. 'Please say thank you.'

'Aw, people usually forget him, he'll be thrilled.'

'And I'm sorry about earlier in the flat.' I look from Claw to Alex, who gives me a secret nod.

'I'm sure we all are,' says Claw, smiling as she waves to us from the door.

'Good night, Claw,' says Alex.

'Isn't this *civilised*?' Claw cackles and then disappears.

'The hospital of laughing doctors,' I say.

'*I heard that*,' Claw yells from somewhere.

Constricted by wires and unfamiliar bedsheets, I turn this way and that, unable to get comfortable. My mind, restless at the best of times, after emerging from the lull of semi-consciousness has gone into overdrive.

'I hadn't really thought about it properly until now,' I say, 'but why was such a huge amount of Eden's pills left over? She must've been taking much less than what Claw was prescribing. She'd've wanted to stay as alert as she could be, but that still wouldn't explain such a big discrepancy.'

'You think she suspected that Claw was prescribing too much?' Alex pulls a chair closer and sits by the bed.

I press a button and the pillows rise up towards the whiteness. 'Maybe she knew. Maybe that's what Claw agreed to prescribe, maybe it's what Eden had to beg for.'

'A lethal dose,' Alex says.

'Or several lethal doses.'

'To give Eden the choice.'

'It's what Eden would've wanted.' When I feel my eyes welling, I blink. 'We're going around in circles,' I say. 'Claw isn't God.'

'But Eden was in pain and Claw was her friend.'

'Claw was her friend and I was her husband.'

Alex gives a sigh and takes my hand. 'Would you have liked to have been put in that position?'

'I don't know. But maybe I should've been whether I liked it or not.'

'I don't think Eden would've wanted that, do you?'

Alex is right. Eden would have suffered any amount of pain rather than burden me with the dilemma of a choice that I wouldn't have been able to make.

My gaze, half-wet, has been flitting, but now I fix it on Alex. 'I don't understand why you're suddenly defending her. I mean, who knows, maybe Sam asked for the choice and she gave it to him too.'

'Oliver, it's hardly the same.'

'Why not? Wasn't Sam in pain too? And if he and Claw both thought it would never go away...'

'Neither he nor Claw could've known that.'

'So, you're not defending her.'

'It's possible she had the conversation with Eden, and Eden managed to persuade her precisely because they were friends. And Claw knew Eden well enough to trust her. I don't think she even realised that Sam was a risk. She was too easily convinced by him that he was safe, and I still blame her for that.'

'But you don't think she's a monster anymore.'

'What Sam did was impulsive; he may have had a plan but he acted on the spur of the moment. And like you've heard me say to Claw, who knows if that moment mightn't've been different if it hadn't been clouded with even more drugs. When Sigismund told me about Eden, I convinced myself that Claw had intentionally made that moment more likely. I don't think that anymore.'

'Why?' I look right and left. 'Because I'm here?'

'We talked.'

'You talked.'

'And I admit I was surprised. She spoke about Sam as though she'd known him for years, and she might've made mistakes, but after talking to her I believe that she was genuinely trying her best to help him, same way she did her best to help Eden. We talked about other things too. You, mostly. Enough for me to realise that she wasn't the villain I'd imagined her to be, that she wouldn't've deliberately wanted to do harm.'

'And Sigismund? He got it wrong too?'

'Tomorrow,' Alex says. And getting up, she bends down to kiss my forehead then my nose and then my lips. 'It's already almost eleven.'

'When you and Claw were shouting at each other in the flat, I was terrified you'd bring it up that I'd slept with her, I thought you might've used it to call her a hypocrite for making so much of her friendship with Eden.'

Alex screws up her face. 'Really, you thought I might do that?' Her gaze as she aims it at mine is razor sharp, and makes what little blood I may have left rush to my ears. 'Well, I hope now you know better.'

'Sorry,' I say, but I say it so faintly that she might not have heard me.

I'm about to say it again when she gives one of her nods, then at last her features soften and she bends down again to give me another kiss. 'But now you need to rest.'

ELEVEN

I left hospital two days after collapsing, discharged after being given the almost-all-clear. The possibility of internal bleeding was briefly considered before being discounted – I did not suffer from haemorrhoids, and had never found blood in my poo. My anaemia turned out to be as borderline as my iron deficiency, and would be treated with supplements initially until more tests were done. At Alex's insistence, we went straight from the hospital to Clerkenwell, I took time off work, and spent the next two weeks in and out of Sam's clothes, new *and* old. They fitted me perfectly, and suited me too (if I say so myself). Stepping into someone else's shoes so entirely felt strange at the beginning, but there was something so free and unrestrained about Sam's taste that my initial self-consciousness was dispelled very quickly – I soon came to love my daily rummage through Sam's walk-in wardrobe, and grew ever bolder in my calculated mismatches. I had a feeling Sam would have approved: it was a wardrobe of contrasts in which *nothing* went with anything else, so it was natural to make a style out of going against the grain to the most extreme extent. I sometimes even had the feeling I was dressing exactly like Sam in every detail, so much so that someone who had known Sam might have reasonably come to the conclusion that I was actually disguised as him on purpose. 'Are you sure it's not weird for you, seeing me wearing Sam's clothes?' I once felt obliged to ask Alex. 'I mean, they're not exactly run-of-the mill.' She glanced up from *In Search of Lost Time* (Volume IV) and looked me up and down (I was in a corduroy purple ensemble and striking checked shirt with cravat), then returning to *Sodom and*

Gomorrah, 'They're just clothes,' she answered impassively, and I assumed that either she had always been indifferent to fashion, or she was particularly partial to Proust. The bulk of the evidence, including her own wardrobe (absolutely everything was black), pointed heavily toward the former, and (between us, at least) the subject was left to one side.

When my time off work was nearing its end, I assumed that any day now I would be going back to my flat, and I was in the bedroom gathering my few possessions (one polyester tracksuit, washed and ironed, one cotton pair of socks and a NIKE pair of trainers – Sam's shoes fitted me perfectly too), when Alex tiptoed in from the bathroom and snuck up on me, clasping my chest from behind.

'Jesus,' I said, 'you made me jump.'

'What's this? Are you missing your own clothes?'

'Oh yeah, I'm really looking forward to being Mr Bland again.'

Alex loosened her grip. 'Meaning what?'

I broke free and swung around to face her. 'Meaning I should probably be moving back to Highgate. Why, what did you think I meant?'

She sat on the bed holding on to my gaze. 'You don't like it here.'

'I've been here almost two weeks.'

'And?'

'And I'm going back to work soon.'

'And?'

'And... I'm not sure what you want me to say.'

'I want you to say that you *do* like it here and you're staying.'

'Staying for how long?' And when Alex gave a shrug, 'You mean you'd like me to move in?'

'I mean I'd like you to *want* to move in.'

'Oh. I see.' And from beside her on the bed, 'Really? Are you sure? I mean, we've not known each other that long.'

We hadn't, it was true. Everything had happened so quickly – and "everything" had not exactly been plain sailing. We had known each other two weeks, and half that time I had spent in several beds for all the wrong reasons. I had been uncertain and coughing in my bed, then anaemic in a hospital bed, then recuperating in Alex's bed, where before being uncertain and coughing in my bed I had enjoyed with her one night (or early morning) of spectacular sex, which was semi-repeated on my sofa before disintegrating in my bed. Had it not been for that first display of fireworks after *Frustration*, who knows how differently things might have turned out? Thankfully the question was entirely hypothetical, and following my recuperation, there had been several additional displays, all equally spectacular and every one of them as unforgettable as every other.

Perhaps, then, it had been just as reasonable for Alex to assume that I was staying as it had been for me to assume that I wasn't – the reasonableness of *any* assumptions after only two weeks was really quite impossible to judge, and in any case the impetus of life often moved in defiance of assumptions. All the same, there had been something about Alex's bad-temper – the haste and forcefulness of her apparent presumption – that might have rung even louder alarm bells if I hadn't been flattered.

'Yes, Oliver, I'm sure. I'd've thought it was obvious.'

Was *I* sure? Not as sure as Alex seemed to be. It *was* too soon to be taking big decisions, and moving in with Alex was huge. 'When I'm gone, you must grab life by the balls again,' Eden had instructed, and right now life was sitting next to me, offering its balls to be grabbed. If I didn't grab them now...

There was an odd light-headedness about this relatively short stretch of time that allowed things to happen as though of their own accord, more or less unchallenged, at least by me: like a punch-drunk boxer suffering blow after blow without reaction, I didn't so much go with as submitted myself to the flow like an incapable leaf drifting aimlessly downstream, willingly succumbing to the force of the current in search of life's balls.

'Well, I suppose I *could* stay. If you don't mind spending Christmas with me. Maybe New Year too, if you're lucky. Easter we'll talk about nearer the time.' With my arm around Alex, I playfully pulled her towards me, and after kissing her neck, she turned and we kissed on the lips.

But the kiss was half-hearted on Alex's part, and it soon petered out. 'This is serious,' she said.

I had already realised it was serious. No sooner had I mentioned Christmas than Eden's absence instantly transformed into its opposite again: a shining presence that eclipsed any urge to grab anybody's balls. Although I seemed unable not to vacillate between extremes, largely thanks to Alex there had been one significant change: even in my vacillating mind, the extreme of not wanting to live no longer formed part of any viable equation.

I loosened my grip and we sat side by side. 'I know,' I said.

'You *have* to be sure, or it's not going to work.'

There was nothing to be lost by trying.

Nothing to be lost except Eden.

'I'll keep the flat just in case, but yes, I'm sure.'

'No. That won't work.' She turned around abruptly and leaned into me gently, a sign of affection as if to make up for the unwavering tone of her voice. 'You can keep it for six months and that's your deadline. If you're still here in May, then you have to give it up. You know what nearly happened at your flat. If Claw hadn't arrived when she did, this precious time we've spent together just wouldn't've happened. I would've come to see you at the hospital, of course, but afterwards you would've gone back to your flat, and you'd still be there now. But you're not, things happened as they did and you're here. Here and happy, and I'm not going back to *that* hanging over our heads.'

'*That*,' I said. 'You mean Eden.'

'I mean you in that place, haunted by its ghosts.'

'You mean Eden.'

'We've agreed that a part of you will always be Eden's, the same way a part of me will always be Sam's. This isn't about Eden at all, no one's asking you to leave her behind.'

No one except Eden, who would have begged me to leave her behind. But *that* Eden was gone. The Eden I had lost, the Eden I was holding on to, her presence as I felt it, our imaginary conversations, the memories of Eden that had now become ghosts – these had all become entangled. I would need to disentangle them, and keep hold not of ghosts but of an essence.

'Then you won't mind if I bring all her photographs with me.'

'As many as you like, I don't mind at all. If it'll make you feel better, we'll even put one of them beside one of Sam.'

'Really? I think I'd like that very much,' I said.

And so the move back to my flat never happened. Christmas came and went without a tree, then the rest of the sixty days went by, and it was suddenly three years exactly without Eden. The sadness of the anniversary, which I had kept to myself, was almost unendurably painful, but like on every other day since meeting Alex the pain now felt somehow more local, an agony that never went away while elsewhere another part of me felt happy. I marked the day by not marking it in any special way, not even with a visit to Highgate, and when it passed, I was glad I had survived it.

I stayed in Clerkenwell with Alex in Sam's clothes, only visiting the flat in Highgate very rarely, to pick up the odd thing and check the post. Until it was time for the final decision, I decided it was best not to linger, and I would literally be in and out within a matter of just a few minutes. In what soon became a ritual, during every visit I would pick up a photograph of Eden, usually the one that still faced the bed from the bedside table, but after looking at it and then pressing it against my chest, I would always put it back in its place, resisting any urge to take it with me when I left. In this transitionary period, it was best not to tamper at all with the delicately balanced status quo. The deal with Alex was a six-month trial in St Cross Street away from the enticements and triggers of Highgate; if I needed an emotional crutch to endure it, then I shouldn't be there. It was not a long time, and if at the end of it I did give up the flat, the photographs of Eden would go with me.

All our friends had tried to be supportive, each in their own way, but after an initial burst of visits – Sigismund brought William and roses, Patrick chocolates and Claw, then William came alone with a cake, Joe and the Mohican with a black trouser suit, a pair of heavy platform shoes, and a black box on wheels which went straight to the storeroom in the basement - there was a long hiatus when no one came round very often; we had made no secret of our six-month plan of action, and people must have known we needed time by ourselves.

My emergency appeared to have brought peace. Accusations were put to one side, and Alex and Claw made a reasonable show of suddenly becoming friends, studiously avoiding conversations on the subject of prescriptions and drugs – even Sam was rarely mentioned, although Claw made a point of remembering him very fondly on the occasions when he was. On her first visit to St Cross Street, she had marvelled effusively at all the many examples of his exquisite taste, and had even complimented me on my new wardrobe, amazingly without a trace of sarcasm. It was a strained and nervous truce, but it was certainly better than war. And it wouldn't harm the chances of the ceasefire lasting longer that Alex and Patrick seemed to genuinely get on extremely well.

Sigismund, too, had known not to stoke any fires. When he was there, he never mentioned Claw. He was, however, free with mentioning Eden and Sam, which I suspected was deliberate, an attempt to integrate the past into the present - to move forward by a process of assimilation rather than denial.

'William keeps asking me about Eden and Sam – what they were like, what they looked like. I've shown him Eden in that tiny photo I was telling you about, the one I showed Alex before your first meeting, but Eden's half hidden behind Claw, you can barely make her out, and I don't have any of Sam. Wouldn't it be lovely if you had one on display next to a better one of Eden, mm, maybe there, on that fabulous sideboard that Sam was so fond of...'

'We will, when Oliver moves in.'

'Oh. I thought he already had.'

'When he's moved out of his flat.'

In March, I began to feel weak for no apparent reason. Urgent tests revealed my haemoglobin had dipped below 10, and my doctor suspected an auto-immune type of anaemia. Further tests, including a painful bone marrow biopsy, again proved inconclusive, ruling out one by one all the serious underlying conditions that could have caused it without actually confirming the diagnosis itself –

haematology was apparently "a quagmire of imponderables and unknowns". ('I thought that was the brain.' 'Well, it's everything really.') In the meantime, while I worried about lupus and lymphoma and a host of other terrible diseases, known and unknown, my haemoglobin gradually became almost normal again. This time my vitamin B12 count was low, but not really low enough to fully explain such a dip. The possibility of pernicious anaemia was dismissed, as was any need for a course of vitamin B12 injections. I was prescribed more supplements and was advised to "keep a watchful eye" on how I felt.

Feeling weak wasn't pleasant, but nor was it painful, and I worried more about Alex feeling worried than I did about myself. While caring for Eden, it was as if the steady progress of her illness had drained me of the capacity to worry about anything else, and I still felt that detachment when it came to my own health. I asked questions because Alex expected me to, and was glad of all the answers that reassured her. It was not that I wanted to be sick, or that I didn't care if I was sick or not. It was rather that I had become unable to entertain even the vaguest thought of sickness, perhaps because unconsciously I was terrified that sickness might take Alex from me too.

Claw did her best to appear unconcerned. The worst possibilities had been excluded, these things sometimes happened, and explanations were not always forthcoming: there were unfortunately mysteries about the human body that medicine had not yet unravelled, and our blood was such a miracle of chemistry that inevitably our knowledge of its functions and malfunctions lagged behind. ('Just try not to worry too much. If you're feeling well, it means everything's fine.' 'And if I'm not?' 'Then obviously we'll need to run more tests.') By the time they were finished with me, I had had enough of doctors, and certainly too much of their philosophy. Waffle was all very well, but was a very poor substitute for the certainty of a firm diagnosis, although admittedly it was preferable to the certainty of a terminal condition: in the end, I too had succumbed to philosophy.

And by mid-April I felt fine. Alex and I had kept to our word and had never smoked another cigarette. We ate well and exercised together, taking turns to cook and draw up routes for long walks away from busy traffic and pollution (in case dirty air was bad for my blood), often taking the tube to and from the starting point. While I was at work, Alex worked at home on her songwriting, and almost every evening I would marvel at her poetry.

The transitionary period had served its purpose well: it had cemented our relationship in an absence of doubt. In spite of all their rituals (the embracing of Eden's photograph, the out-loud conversations), even my visits to Highgate had withstood any relapse to sentimentality that might have posed a serious threat: I had learned to leave my melancholy at the door.

My mind had been made up well before the deadline: I knew where I wanted to be and the move out of my flat would be quick and forensic. At the end of May, I gave the necessary one month's notice, but I didn't need a month to pack, and everything fell into place within days. Sifting through my own possessions was easy, Claw helped me deal with Eden's clothes, and the landlord agreed I could leave most of the furniture behind. When it came down to it, there really wasn't much I was attached to; time had disassociated Eden from her things, to a larger extent than I had realised. The pieces of 1960s junk we had picked up together here and there over the years were now little more than clutter, and so were all the anonymous paintings. I would hold on to her few items of jewellery, her father's records, and a few of her favourite books, which one day I would definitely read – her Zadie Smith and Toni Morrison and Kafka, and her signed Margaret Atwood:

For Eden...

Eden had adored those three dots.

The photographs were mine, and taking Alex at her word I was not going to leave *any* of them behind, although some of them might stay in my suitcase. And there was one thing I had salvaged already. I had barely started packing when the shaded bedside lamp with the special orange glow made its way straight to the table by our bed in St Cross Street: not only could I not bear to part with it, but I hoped it might also help to soften the contours and break the harsh modernity of Alex's bedroom.

I didn't give myself much time to think – I already knew the risks of overthinking. It was not a joyful task, undoing the joyful world I had once shared with Eden. But with Eden herself no longer in it, that world had already lost its meaning. It had become an empty shell full of "things" – dangerous things that had threatened to stop me from living.

Alex offered to help, but knew not to insist - the task was not one for sharing. I did everything alone. Every afternoon after work I would make the short journey to Highgate, where two large open suitcases awaited on the bed, ready to be filled. As one item after another was removed from its customary place, and summary decisions were made about what to leave behind, the task became less difficult at first, and then almost automatic. With the bedside lamp already in St Cross Street and all the photographs of Eden packed away, even our bed, stripped down to a bare mattress in a plain wooden frame, in a room that would soon be unrecognisable, had gradually become dispossessed, the spell of its associations broken into a thousand different pieces. Like the pulling out of deep-rooted teeth, this wholesale dismantling was brutal, and it probably affected me in ways I was either not aware of or refused to acknowledge, afraid of what might happen if I did.

'I'm just tired,' I would say to Alex. And Alex would insist I should be tested to make sure that I wasn't becoming anaemic again. I wasn't, and so the excruciating process carried on at an accelerating pace, divesting me of so much more than just possessions and a flat. But still I would convince myself my gloom was just the consequence of physical exhaustion.

We were flat on our backs after sex.

'You're not sleeping well?'

'I can't keep my eyes open, but the moment we switch off the lights I'm wide awake.'

The weather was exceptionally cool for June, so I couldn't blame the heat.

'Why not take it easy for a couple of days, give yourself a break?'

'I'm nearly done, I'd rather get it out of the way.'

'It's no wonder you're exhausted. I'm not even sure you should've gone back to work, and on top of that you've done a whole month's work at the flat in one week. Then as soon as you're back here and we're in bed, I want sex!'

'That's what keeps me going.'

It kept me going but like a robot, getting on with my task without thinking. While mechanically demolishing my past, any doubts were set aside and everything was pushed to the back of my mind, all my memories, attachments, even my feelings for Eden. And this fraught accumulation became a hidden tinderbox, a ticking bomb that might explode at any time, more powerful the longer I suppressed it.

Alex had become so concerned about my anaemia that she would interpret any sign of unwellness as potentially another relapse, and so it wasn't difficult for me to camouflage my moods. She was worried enough as it was, and that was my excuse for keeping the confusion of my feelings to myself. Even if they weren't entirely clear, I had convinced myself that they were natural and they would pass.

But I also wasn't sure that Alex wouldn't have misunderstood them; she seemed to take everything personally, as though even the smallest of my attachments to the past somehow amounted to a disloyalty directed at her.

'You know the light you brought with you, the one you just switched off?'

In the dark, my heart missed a beat. 'What about it?'

'I know how fond of it you are, but maybe you could take it back?'

'You mean back to Highgate?'

'Would you mind?'

Yes, of course I would mind.

'But why, don't you like it?'

'Oliver, it doesn't belong here. It makes me feel like I felt in your flat, and I don't think I should have to.'

'Fine, I'll take it back tomorrow.'

I did. Adding to the sadness of another anniversary I had kept to myself, of a betrayal then forgiveness then a lump, I returned it to the bedside table in mine and Eden's bedroom and plugged it back in. When I turned it on, I realised that Alex was right. Highgate was where it belonged. Steeped in memories, its glow here was different, its orange so much warmer, not erasing the sadness but assuaging it at least. And on Sunday two days later it went out, switched off for one last time. The two suitcases were side by side in the hall, by the sideboard that had once been full of photographs of Eden, all packed and waiting to be wheeled to Patrick's car. Overnight, the weather had turned from exceptionally cool to unexceptionally humid and hot - the rest of summer threatened to be hell. For all its grandeur, the apartment in St Cross Street, although beautifully warm in the winter, in the summer was exposed to too much sun. There were *too* many windows, and unless they were kept shut throughout the day with heavy curtains drawn, which they couldn't be because Alex liked daylight and there were therefore no curtains to draw, by early afternoon the whole apartment was a sauna. A powerful fan in the bedroom at least kept us dry during sex.

My flat, on the other hand, was never too hot. On the hottest days, Eden and I would keep the windows shut, but even on the occasions when we hadn't, the orientation of the building was such that in summer there was never any sun coming through; if all the doors were open, air circulated freely and gave the vague impression of a breeze.

Mine and Eden's flat, mine and Eden's world.

Forgive me.

Forgive me.

Forgive me.

I promise I haven't forgotten.

Even though I know what she would answer:

You must,

You must,

You must.

Patrick was calling my phone; he was outside waiting.

I had one last look around. I went first to the bedroom. As I stood by the door breathing in familiar air, moments from the past came alive. Smells and sounds and moving images were randomly remembered, succeeding one another but more often overlapping, crowding the empty room. Walking back through the living room, another flood of vivid reminiscences played out, more rapidly now, as though in a race not to be left out. Feeling strangely vacant, I opened my front door and picked up the two suitcases. I stepped outside with what was left of my old life, put the suitcases back down and locked the door behind me.

'There you are, I was about to come looking for you.'

'Hi, Patrick.'

'You look a bit off, what's wrong? Large dose of last-minute nerves?'

'Something like that.'

'Large enough to amount to second thoughts?'

Second thoughts? Had there even been *first* thoughts, or any thoughts at all? Had there been a logical sequence? I had arrived here somehow from somewhere, but I had no idea where the starting point had been or what route I had followed. But this was not the moment to start asking searching questions.

'I don't know, I said. 'Right now, either I don't know what I'm thinking, or I'm not thinking anything.'

It was mid-afternoon, and the sun was still burning. Patrick drove an old SAAB with fierce air-conditioning that blew out arctic air. It seemed to suit my mood as we drove towards St Cross Street in the opposite direction but along the same route I had taken on foot on that fateful Saturday when the December cold had almost killed me. The short distance downhill to Tufnell Park, past the railings where I had become disembodied, had a rural feel about it that was almost exotic, but for most of the journey the view from my window was dreary. As we crossed Camden Road, the first part of York Way looked Dickensian in its semi-dereliction, incongruous in its contrast to the tall modern developments around Kings Cross. Driving past these discrepancies at speed, they appeared to me even more blatant, as though in a spliced-together newsreel whose purpose was to illustrate the extremes of inequality in order to denounce it. Around Farringdon and its many light-industrial conversions, no-nonsense bulks of brick containing fashionable showrooms and exclusive loft apartments, the air was of a solid reconstruction whose opulence lay not in ostentation but robustness. In this spartan oasis, even the brutalist Peabody blocks of social housing, prisonlike and yellow, far from jarring with its neighbours stood as trendsetting examples of a special brand of modern architecture. It was all an illusion, of course, and understatement was just a disguise, reserved for the privileged few who could afford it.

Internal theorising was all very well as a means of avoiding conversation, but as the car turned right into St Cross Street, ready to deliver me to my new life, the irony could hardly have escaped me that, no matter by what fluke, I could now count myself among the privileged few.

'It's *very* nice around here,' Patrick said. 'Clerkenwell, wow - central *and* out of the way. Chelsea, eat your heart out!'

'Weekends are very quiet, but you should see Leather Lane during the week.'

'More people work than live here, that's why. The housing is scarce, and much of it is quite distinctive, very attractive to a certain demographic. It's a *very* desirable area to live in, which means it's also very expensive, and that in turn makes it exclusive – it's a chicken and egg thing.' Patrick was ruggedly handsome and clever and gave fools short shrift, but he also had this know-all way of talking nonsense about property that Eden and I used to laugh about. It also used to amuse us how it horrified Claw, who *never* spoke about money and regarded the subject as vulgar. She would always slap him down if he dared to bring it up, even indirectly. 'Patrick, stop! You're being terribly common again.'

Patrick, a successful interior designer with a special interest in Le Corbusier's use of chrome, was my friend, and I was suddenly overcome with a flood of affection for him.

He had been as steadfast in his friendship as Claw, but whereas Claw had always made her presence felt loudly, Patrick had been our invisible friend, not in the sense that he had never been there, but on the contrary that he had always been there but without being obtrusive or making a fuss. And in less difficult times, predating Eden's illness, his wry self-deprecation and downplayed joy of life had made him fun to be around, especially on the occasions when we had seen him without Claw, whose tendency had always been to overshadow. And how had I repaid him for his friendship? I had slept with his wife and had never found the courage to own up. I could remember asking Eden if I should, but events (first sex and then a lump under her arm) had conspired to interrupt our conversation before she could give me an answer. Then her illness had happened, and Patrick had again been overshadowed.

But I had run out of excuses. Even now, so many years later, I still owed him the truth. If the past was to be left behind, first it had to be confronted.

'I've slept with Claw. It was a long time ago and it happened only once. Eden knew, I told her straight away, but I should've told you too, because you're my friend. I hope I've done the right thing by telling you now.' To make sure I kept going, I had kept my tone even and dull, like that of an announcement on a local radio station of an unexciting Sunday bazaar.

The air-conditioned air thickened with a suffocating silence made louder by the unsteady burr of the stationary car, its engine still running even though it had been parked. I felt lost – the flood of affection had as though dislodged words I should have spoken years before, or perhaps not at all, leaving me drained and feeling bereft: even at the threshold of a new beginning, everything returned me to Eden. The past, after all, was not geographic, and would follow me wherever I went, not sequestered and contained in any separate compartment but pervasive, as present in my new life as it had been in the life Alex had instructed me to end, and still making competing demands. Would I ever find a way of navigating through them?

Brrr...

Even in the air-conditioned cold I felt hot, and my body, wet with icy sweat, had erupted in goosebumps. But my self-centredness had done enough damage already. Right now, I should be attending to Patrick. I ought to say *something*, but what? Words already spoken could not be retrieved, and more words – more wrong words - risked making everything worse.

'I know you slept with Claw. But yes, you should've told me.' Patrick's voice had sunk to a baritone pitch, its roar blotting out the mechanical din.

'I'm sorry,' was all I could manage. Unable to look him in the eye, I was staring at my hands, shivering from cold or from shame.

The conversation was stilted, as though neither of us knew what to say next, or where to look – I was staring at my hands and I could tell from the sound of his voice that Patrick must be looking the other way.

'It's good that she was able to forgive you.'

'That same day,' I said.

'Right.' Now Patrick switched the engine off. 'Come on, let's get you settled in.' He unbuckled himself and went to open his door, but instead he turned around, leaning on the steering wheel to look at me lopsidedly. 'Claw and I... I don't know how to say this.'

'Patrick, you don't have to. I'm the one who owes you an explanation. Except that I don't have one. I know it happened once, but I don't know why it happened at all.'

'Because with Claw it always does.'

'Well, it shouldn't've happened with me.'

'I doubt you had a say.' Patrick gave a short laugh.

"With Claw it always does" and "I doubt you had a say". It was more or less exactly what Eden had said, causing my sadness for Patrick to be filled with my sadness for Eden. I tried to turn around so I could face him without cocking my head to one side, but my seatbelt locked and held me back.

'Careful. One more sudden movement and the airbag will inflate, SAAB were *very* safety-conscious.'

I again swung around in my seat, but this time I undid my seatbelt first. 'Did you know because you guessed, or because someone told you?'

'That SAAB were safety-conscious?'

'Patrick, please. Did you know I slept with Claw because you guessed, or because Eden told you?'

Practically hugging the steering wheel, now Patrick was shaking his head. 'Honestly, Ollie. You're raking up the past unnecessarily, and believe me, it's not a good idea.'

'I know I should've told you at the time.'

'But you didn't, and I wish you hadn't told me at all.' It was becoming hot, and Patrick started the engine again. 'I mean, what purpose has it served, telling me now? It was a selfish thing to do – selfish and pointless.' His words were harsh, and I probably deserved them to be harsher, but his tone was one of sadness, not reproach. And after making a fist that he gently punched my shoulder with, 'Still, we *are* friends, so I'm going to put you out of your misery.' He smiled and shook his head again, as though bemused by the oddness of our conversation, and his own impassivity. 'It was Claw who told me, but I didn't believe her.'

'Claw?'

'Sharing all the details of her little escapades has always been part of the fun for her.'

'Jesus, Patrick.'

'But when she told me about you, knowing she and Eden were best friends, and also knowing how in love you were with Eden, the idea seemed so preposterous that I didn't believe her. But I also didn't want it to be true, I *hated* the idea, and I wanted to be sure, so eventually I asked Eden. And when I did, that's when I realised I'd been fooling myself, that in fact I was secretly hoping it *was* true and you *had* slept with Claw, and I wanted Eden *not* to know - I wanted her to hear it first from me, and I wanted her to be so angry that when she challenged you and you told her it was true, she might even leave you. I did, I wanted all those things to happen, and you know why?' His voice was racing, catching up with itself in what seemed like a panic to join the words together and get them all out. 'Because I was in love with her and I was jealous. And if you'd slept with Claw, then surely she'd see that you didn't deserve her, and I might have a chance. Things turned out very differently, of course. Eden said she knew that it was true because you'd told her, and then she asked me how *I* felt, she asked if I was happy and we both knew what she meant – was I happy that my wife slept around? I said, yes, I was fine, Claw was Claw and marriage was hard work but we were grownups and we'd figure it out. I'm sure she'd guessed exactly what my motives were for telling her, but she was kind, and she spared me the embarrassment of even hinting she suspected.' He paused to take a breath and looked at me as though to say that if I wanted to punch him I could. Then bending his head to one side, 'Claw was Claw and Eden was Eden, and between them there was all the world of difference.' Drifting off momentarily, he puffed himself up with an intake of breath. The fist he had punched my shoulder with had stayed clenched by his side, but now unclenching it he brushed his hair aside. It was long, wet from sweat like mine, and a clump of it had dropped over his face. 'You must miss her so much,' he mumbled without looking at me.

Raking up the past didn't after all just revolve around me, and that made me more embarrassed with myself than angry with Patrick. We had hardly reached a cliff-hanger moment; I knew almost every detail of what had happened next, and I knew that it had not involved Patrick. I was the one who had slept with his wife, why on earth would I have wanted to punch him?

'I do, and it's okay if you do too,' I said, numb from the emotion of sharing my grief.

Patrick took another breath. 'Oliver, Oliver, see what happens when you rake up the past?' He pressed his lips together to breathe out. 'And I should've told you earlier too, I know,' he said. Then with a smile he turned to face me squarely. 'But now that we've both made our confessions and all *that's* out of the way, let's get those suitcases out of the boot and deliver you safely to Alex as promised.'

'Patrick, listen, if you're not happy with Claw…'

Patrick raised his hand forbiddingly. 'No, we've talked enough about Claw for one day.'

We had, but I wanted to talk about Sigismund too.

'We've never talked about what happened with Sigismund – I mean between the two of you, before he left with William.'

'What happened between me and Sigismund? Not that much. It was Claw I had a crush on.'

'Claw,' I said, my murmur fighting back another 'Jesus!'.

'I tried to hide it, of course, thinking she and Sigismund were happily married. And I did a perfect job of hiding it from Claw, but obviously a terrible job of hiding it from Sigismund. Oh well, it's all in the past now, and I'm the last one with a right to bear a grudge.'

'Bear a grudge against who?'

'Let's just say that Sigismund was very insistent. And I was weak, I gave in. Twice, as you know. Twice and we were done. And then later when he left her for William, my feelings for Claw hadn't changed, so I took her out for dinner - I think we were having dessert when I told her what'd happened with Sigismund, which she knew all about, because Sigismund had told her already.'

'Sigismund had told her already...'

'Yes, but let's try not to think about why.'

'Because it doesn't bear thinking about.'

'Because it reminds me of what *I* did.' Patrick was becoming distraught, but again he recovered himself with an intake of breath. 'In any case it made no difference. We finished our dessert, then I drove her home and she invited me in for a nightcap. And soon after that we got married.'

'Eden told me you that you'd had a thing with Sigismund, but she missed out all the details.'

'But not because she didn't know them,' Patrick said. 'You and Sigismund were friends, and none of us wanted to spoil that, not even Claw.'

'The same Claw who's been torturing you ever since.'

'Oh, I think it would be fairer to say that we've been torturing each other. It wasn't Claw who fell in love with someone else so soon after we married.'

'You mean she knew?'

'About my feelings for Eden? No, I don't think so. But she would've known my mind was somewhere else.'

'I'm not sure how true it is that Sigismund and I were friends,' I said.

But Patrick didn't hear me. 'And then of course Eden got sick, and nothing else mattered.' All his fingers tapped the steering wheel: tap-a-tap-tap. 'Hmm,' he mumbled, as though suddenly astonished by the past. Then wiping every ugly moment of it off his face, 'Now come on, out you get, time to get reacquainted with your beautiful new girlfriend and her millionaire's apartment. Oh, and we should keep this conversation to ourselves, if you don't mind.'

'Yes, of course, that goes without saying.'

TWELVE

Until recently if anyone had asked, I would have insisted that Eden had never kept secrets from me. I would have been wrong, and it troubled me that I had only discovered this recently, in the days and months after meeting Alex. It also troubled me that had it not been for Alex, Eden's secrets would probably have never come to light. Had it not been for Alex, I would not have reconnected with Sigismund. Had it not been for Alex, Patrick would not have been helping me move out of Highgate, and probably I would have lacked the final spur to own up to a secret of my own that had not been a secret after all, but in spite of that had served to uncover Patrick's secrets too. Had it not been for Alex, far more terrible things might have happened than the surfacing of irreproachable secrets whose only significance was to doubly reaffirm Eden's kindness: she had met with Sigismund during her illness in order to spare me her tears by sharing them with someone else; and before that she had been more generous to Patrick than Patrick had deserved at the time, as she had always been to everyone. She had also joined with Patrick and Claw in the effort to safeguard my friendship with Sigismund by keeping from me the unpalatable details of Sigismund's "dalliance" with Patrick. These secrets had belonged in the past, but present and past had banded together to bring them to light, and this recurring lack of separation augured badly for the future. In another paradox that I found it hard to get my head around, Alex, without whom a future had looked so unlikely, was somehow also implicated in a past she had never been part of. Eden, Claw, Sigismund, Alex. Then Sigismund again and then Patrick, once more leading back to Eden. And now, wheeling one suitcase each, Patrick and I were about to walk the short enormous distance to Alex, uniting her and Eden in a loop.

If there had been these two or three secrets, might there not have been more? Somewhere in the back of my mind, locked up but unforgotten, there lurked the possibility of the worst secret of all: that the leftover stash had not been accidental, that it had been assembled on purpose just like Alex had said, to serve as Eden's last resort. And what tormented me was not the secrecy, or the possible conspiracy with Claw; it was rather all the unspeakable horrors that I could suddenly imagine haunting Eden in the weeks before she died, and from which she had excluded me out of love.

But it might not have been like that. Through cold calculation, Eden might well have simply wished to safeguard every possible option; it was certainly true that all her life she had been prone to practicalities far more than to unspeakable horrors.

It was impossible to know the truth when the past had contained so many secrets. The present had been poisoned with doubt.

'Is that it, two suitcases?' Alex, on the other hand, was beaming.

She held the door open for us - two men who a few minutes earlier had cemented their friendship in an air-conditioned SAAB by exchanging confessions that might well have had the opposite effect. The heavy loads that both of us had carried on our shoulders for years had been lifted, but whereas Patrick seemed more buoyant, the effect on me was that I felt completely adrift, trapped in no man's land between two worlds: while being greeted at my new home by Alex, the first thing I wanted to do was to unpack all the photographs of Eden.

The wheels on my suitcases were worn, and made a rasping sound as they revolved across the uneven wooden floor.

'This room feels so remarkably spacious!' As on every other occasion when he'd visited the apartment, Patrick was in awe.

Alex laughed. 'Well, it is a large room, so it's hardly surprising.'

'But it's not just a matter of size,' Patrick insisted, 'the air in here is somehow lighter, so thin that it takes your breath away. It reminds me so much of the air in the Alps.' And after taking consecutive deep breaths, 'It sounds ridiculous, I know, but it's true.'

'In winter, maybe,' I said, 'but in this heat it feels more like a sauna.'

'But an outdoor one, somewhere in the mountains.'

I almost clucked my tongue. 'Through here,' I said, heading for the bedroom.

'Are you unpacking now?' Alex asked.

'Why?'

'Pick out the photograph of Eden you'd like on the sideboard, to go beside Sam's.'

'Really?' I turned around to take a look.

'I haven't put it out yet, I thought we'd do it together.'

'Thank you,' I said, and already my mood had lightened. Once again, Alex had anticipated my unease, and had greeted me not just with words and a smile but also with an effort to bridge the chasmic distance between my two worlds.

Secrets were not secrets unless they were unknown, and unknown secrets were not secrets all; existing only as possibilities that might or might not prove to be fact, they amounted to empty conjectures in limbo. Secrets that had been revealed did not imply a domino of secrets that had not, and innocent secrets implied nothing at all. This was not a logical deduction but rather a decision made rational by absolute knowledge. The perfect was the beautiful, the good the most beautiful, and the object of beauty was love. This Platonic distortion badly remembered from school, encapsulated the impossibility of Eden's coexistence with evil, or with secrets deriving from anything other than beautiful goodness and love.

As I carefully unpacked one by one all the photographs of Eden, I gave out a joyful cry. In my hands was the photograph of Eden that had stood on the bedside table, and in my heart was Eden herself; far from laying any claim to possession, with the throb of every beat she cheered me on.

In the living room, Patrick and Alex waited by the sideboard.

'I chose this one,' I said.

'I thought you might,' said Alex. 'And this is Sam.'

When she turned the framed photograph around, I flinched. 'Oh,' I said.

'Looks a bit like you, Ollie,' said Patrick.

'Not really,' Alex said, setting Sam's photograph down.

'He had a beard,' I said, still clutching Eden's.

'Sometimes,' said Alex. 'Is that why you looked so surprised?'

'Yes. I mean no. Did I look surprised?'

I *had* been surprised, but was it because of the beard? Or was it because, even with a beard, Sam had looked *too* much like me?

'Well, beard or no beard I think it's uncanny,' said Patrick, bending down to look at Sam's photograph more closely.

'I don't see it,' said Alex.

'I mean, sure, they're not *identical*, but come on, there's certainly more than a passing resemblance. The more I...' Patrick cut himself short. 'But if no one else can see it, I'm probably imagining it.'

'Eden,' Alex said impatiently.

The moment I placed Eden's photograph beside that of Sam, I caught myself wincing again. It was like looking at my wife and an imposter. Patrick wasn't imagining anything, and I could see what Patrick could see because it was there. Why was Alex pretending not to see what to us was so blindingly obvious? The likeness was remarkable; had she deliberately chosen a photograph of Sam with a beard to disguise its full extent? Was it the reason I had not seen any photographs of Sam until now? Was it the reason I was here, just as I had suspected when Alex tried to dress me in Sam's clothes for *Frustration*? Perhaps it really was the reason she had wanted to meet me in the first place, and everything else had been subterfuge.

I couldn't hold back any longer. 'You even had me wearing his clothes,' I said. 'Is that why I'm here? To remind you of Sam?'

'But you don't remind me of Sam, you're nothing like him. I've told you all this already. And by now you should know why you're here.'

'Should I?' Did I? I knew the bare facts: I was about to move back to Highgate when Alex decided that either I would stay with her in Clerkenwell, with a deadline of six months for completely moving out of my flat, or that would be the end of our relationship. She may not have expressed herself so bluntly, but it was still an ultimatum and those had been my only two choices. And here I was now, with no flat to go back to, dressed in Sam's clothes and discovering that I was practically his double.

'When we first met, didn't you say my smile reminded you of Eden's?'

It was true that we'd had this conversation already. 'Yes,' I said, 'but apart from the smile, you look completely different. And I've never tried to dress you in Eden's clothes.'

Alex gave a backward nod. 'I see, so you're not here because of my smile.'

'No, and I told you that the first day we met.'

'You don't look *that* alike,' Patrick cut in, picking up Sam's photograph to have another look. 'You do both have the same mysterious gaze, but otherwise you're roughly the same shape and you're both very handsome, that's all.'

'No one's eyes remind you of Sam's,' I said to Alex, 'but Patrick thinks we have the same mysterious gaze.'

'Sam's eyes were brown like mine, yours are green,' Alex answered. 'And in photographs he always looked different.'

'It's not really my business,' said Patrick, 'but maybe the photographs were not such a brilliant idea.' And after a few awkward seconds of silence: 'Honestly, Ollie, don't you think you might be taking this a little too far? I mean, Alex has a point, she and Eden, they're not too dissimilar either.' Putting down Sam's photograph, he now picked up Eden's. 'You're right, they have almost identical smiles, and that's what I remember most about Eden, her smile, so I'm not surprised it was the first thing you noticed. But at the same time, I agree with you, they're so completely different that any similarities become almost invisible. When we saw his photograph just now, I think you and I both focussed on the similarities because we didn't know Sam, and that's all we could see, which made us think that we saw more than what was there.'

'I suppose now that you've pointed it out, there is a vague resemblance,' said Alex. 'Maybe subconsciously the similarity was part of the initial attraction, but Patrick's right, to me Sam was so much more than what he looked like. And so are you, by the way, with clothes or without.'

'And you did say that my smile reminded you of Sam's.'

'Because it did.'

'The smile of someone who wasn't quite done yet.'

It was true that what Patrick said made sense, and Alex had at least acknowledged that there was some resemblance. But really the resemblance was striking, and went far beyond the similarity of our smiles - had it honestly not registered until just now, when it was pointed out to her by Patrick? And why hadn't Sigismund mentioned it? It was impossible that neither of them had noticed it. Had they colluded with each other to stay silent? Perhaps the resemblance had embarrassed them both - Sigismund because it might have embarrassed Alex, who in turn might have been worried that it might embarrass me. Ulterior motives were not always ill-intentioned...

Alex took advantage of the lull: 'Now can we please feed poor Patrick? We've not even offered him a glass of water.'

Sandwiches had been prepared – halloumi with tomato and cucumber, and avocado with beetroot houmous. Alex would serve them with iced coffee.

'Not for me, thank you,' Patrick said politely. 'It's quite late, I really should be heading back. And I'm sure you guys could do with some time to yourselves on your big day.'

'We've made you feel uncomfortable,' I said.

Patrick laughed, and I knew he was laughing as much about our tête-à-tête in the car as the argument about the photographs and my resemblance to Sam. 'I'm married to Claw, remember?' he said, and already he was at the door.

When he was gone, I helped Alex set the table and we sat down to eat. My eyes kept drifting to the photographs, which in my mind had already come to symbolise the enormity of a day when nothing had changed and yet everything had changed. As we drove away from Highgate and arrived in St Cross Street, I knew what I had given up, but what exactly had I gained?

'These chairs are giving me a bad back,' I said. 'We should have some cushions made at least.' And when Alex made no comment, 'Or aren't we allowed to make any changes?'

'I think cushions would be ugly without making any difference,' Alex answered dryly.

I very nearly picked another fight, but I stopped myself. Patrick was right, this was our big day, and I knew very well that Alex was what I had gained – which meant I had gained quite a lot.

'I like the halloumi,' I said. 'I've never had it with cucumber before, they go together well.' And when again she made no comment, 'What's wrong, you're still annoyed about the photographs?'

Alex rolled her eyes. 'I don't think it was me who was annoyed about the photographs.'

'I've just moved out of my flat and you're already rolling your eyes at me,' I almost snapped at her. 'I suppose I expected Sam to look different,' I said instead, keeping very calm and holding on to the idea of our big day. 'After They Them I expected something else.'

'You expected Sam to look like the dummy.'

'No, Alex, that's not what I meant.'

Alex wiped her mouth with her napkin and sat back in the sheerness of her chair, staring straight at me. 'Go on,' she said.

'They Them has connotations. You must've known that.'

'Connotations like what?'

Alex was already irritated, but I didn't want to stop. Big day or not, Sam was staring at me from the sideboard as though as curious about me as I was about him – not knowing everything about him was making me wonder how much I might not know about Alex.

I pushed my plate aside and piled my hands one on top of the other in front of me. 'You were They and Sam was Them, and the show was about you and Sam. That's what you've told me. But you must've known that to most people They Them would mean something else. I even remember thinking that you might've been a They, but then Joe confirmed that you were definitely a She, and that Sam, who he said was the original Them, was probably a He. And I know that the show wasn't about that, it was about the warmth of the interaction between They and Them - *The price of love is life and death* – but then if Them was supposed to be Sam, why was the dummy so androgynous, with a pencil moustache *and* wearing lipstick?'

Alex took a moment. Then, 'Hmm,' she began, her voice now low and more relaxed. 'Well, "androgynous" has nothing to do with They Them, so it was obviously a mistake if that was everyone's impression of the dummy. Sam did sometimes have a moustache, and we both occasionally wore bright red lipstick. But whatever Sam was, and he was many things, he definitely wasn't androgynous – is that even a word anyone uses anymore?'

'Them was supposed to be Sam, and Them was a Them, not a He.' I tried not to sound antagonistic.

'The dummy was a Them, you're right, but so was They. I'm pretty sure we've talked about all this already, but I don't mind explaining it again: Yes, Sam was the original

Them, but Them isn't Sam. Only Sam was Sam. And possibly partly because he was hard to define, he and I shared this incredible closeness that sometimes blurred the line of who was who, and that was what They Them was about.'

'And Sam and I share a resemblance that maybe also blurs the line of who is who. For you, I mean.'

'Oh, Oliver, not that again,' said Alex. But then she reached across the table and cupped my hands with hers. 'You may or may not look like him, wearing or not wearing his clothes, but you know that's not the reason you're here. You're here because I asked you for a light, and after that there wasn't a choice.'

'But we don't share that same kind of closeness.'

'No, we share a different kind of closeness. Isn't that a good thing?' Alex squeezed my hands one last time and then let go of them. 'But Patrick was probably right, the photographs were not a good idea. You've officially moved in. We should be celebrating, not arguing about the meaning of They Them.' Already she had swung out of the chair and was making her way to the sideboard.

'Don't,' I said. 'Please.'

'Are you sure? I'm happy to put Sam back in the drawer.'

'And leave Eden alone? I don't think she'd like that.'

Alex ran a finger across the top of the two wooden frames, first that with Eden's photograph inside and then the slightly smaller one with Sam's. 'They do look happy together,' she said.

As life became settled in St Cross Street, the dynamics of conflicting friendships soon came under strain. Claw visited often; Patrick more often still. At first Sigismund and William visited together, but Sigismund would always snap at William, and William stopped coming, only rarely popping in to deliver a cake.

Very quickly Sigismund had shed his initial self-restraint, and would now talk incessantly about Claw, almost egging himself on to lose his temper. And if anybody tried to change the subject, he would fly into an even wilder rage. He was visibly put out, and the real target of his outrage was obviously Alex - her partial pardoning of Claw, barely falling short of a complete exoneration and apparently developing into a friendship, appeared to have offended him deeply. It was as if it had awakened secret demons.

'Maybe things aren't going right with the baby,' I said to Alex after one of his visits.

'No, Oliver, this has nothing to do with the baby. There was *never* going to be any baby. It's always been the same: Sigismund gets overexcited, but as soon as practicalities get in the way, he gets bored.'

There was never going to be any baby – Alex had said it so casually, as if it meant nothing. Did it not cross her mind that perhaps it meant something to William?

How settled had life in St Cross Street *really* become? I had not yet figured out precisely the meaning of a change that I knew was monumental. But perhaps that was a good thing. If losses were easier to measure than gains, what I had definitely *not* lost was Eden, and what more could I have hoped for than Alex? We had already been happy, and at the very least the move had made our happiness less tense. My health was good, I was glad to have gone back to work, I enjoyed our long walks every weekend, and our friends were keeping us busy. And even more importantly, sex was still great, although secretly I had the feeling that it might have been greater in the warm orange glow of the bedside lamp that Alex had forced me to take back to Highgate.

It was now the middle of September, and early on a Sunday afternoon, after calling to make sure we were alone, in other words that Claw wasn't there, Sigismund arrived looking sheepish. On the pretext that he wasn't staying long (but yes, he had time for a quick Gin and Tonic), he declined the red sofa and the three of us sat uncomfortably in the electric chairs gulping down early booze (I had opted for a glass of wine and Alex for a bottle of beer).

'William thinks I should apologise,' Sigismund said, staring down into his drink.

'To us or to William?' Alex asked.

Sigismund looked up. 'I've already apologised to William. I got home on Friday night to find him packing his bags.'

'Has he left you?' Alex asked.

Now Sigismund shrugged. 'Maybe it's for the best if he does.'

'I thought you said you only rowed when you were here,' I said.

'But because we always rowed, he stopped coming, and then we started rowing at home. He thinks I've been behaving like a child. I mean, *he*'s the one who told me Claw came onto him.'

'Claw is Claw, and will always be Claw,' I said, remembering my conversation with Patrick. 'She comes on to everyone.'

'Claw is Claw, she comes on to everyone, and I'm pretty sure she's also still being reckless with drugs.' William might be threatening to leave him, but when it came to Claw, Sigismund was still like a dog with a bone.

'Maybe,' I said, taking one more sip of my wine. 'All *I* know for sure is that she did what she could to help Eden, and Eden was grateful.'

'I agree that she was reckless with prescribing drugs in the past, but whether she's still doing it or not, I also agree with Oliver that she did her best for Eden.'

'But, Alex, I've never doubted Claw's dedication to Eden,' said Sigismund bitterly. 'And it does explain why Oliver should still feel an attachment to her, out of loyalty and a misplaced sense of duty – even *I* feel it sometimes, that and the guilt of having left her for a man after cheating with Patrick, which she's very adept at playing on to get what she wants – and she does get what she wants, or we wouldn't still be in touch and she wouldn't still be married to Patrick. We all go back, is the point I'm trying to make - Ollie and Claw and I, to the time we all shared with Eden. But you, suddenly best friends with her? That I don't understand, I'm sorry.'

'That's not the only reason I'm still friends with her,' I said.

'And who said we're best friends? *I* never did, and I doubt Claw did either,' said Alex.

Sigismund was glaring daggers at us. 'I'm sorry,' he seethed, 'but I think you're both being blind. The woman is a narcissist, with sub-zero capacity for empathy.' Then swinging in his chair to face me, 'Sure, she can go through the motions of caring for her friends when they're sick, but did she stop for a minute to think how rotten it would make you feel and what problems it might cause for you before she seduced you? No, of course she didn't, but even if she had, I doubt it would've made any difference. And did it bother her one bit how Eden might feel if you told her, which she must've known you probably would, or how Patrick would feel if he found out? I'm pretty sure it didn't.'

So, Alex hadn't really "guessed" that Claw had got me into bed – almost certainly she knew because Sigismund had told her.

'I wouldn't say that Claw seduced me, exactly,' I said.

'But she did exactly get you into bed,' Sigismund riposted.

'And Patrick did find out,' I said, 'she actually told him herself.'

Alex gasped, but the outburst I expected from Sigismund didn't materialise. I had broken my promise to Patrick in order to goad him, but Sigismund hadn't been goaded.

'I should've told him at the time, but I didn't have the guts,' I went on, as though suddenly in the grip of a spiralling confessional. 'But then last June when he was helping me move in with all my stuff, I kind of blurted it out. And he said he already knew because Claw had told him. Apparently, she always tells him everything; she makes a point of it.'

The only reaction again came from Alex. 'Why *are* you still friends with her?' she asked me. 'If Patrick was telling the truth, then Sigismund's right, Claw's beyond the pale.'

'He was definitely telling the truth. And I feel really bad, because I've told you things I promised him I'd keep to myself.'

'You feel really bad but you still told us,' Sigismund said angrily.

But I was on a roll. 'Claw told Patrick and then Patrick told Eden.'

'What?' Alex clutched her drink with both hands so tightly that her veins became swollen. 'I don't understand, why would Patrick do that?'

'You feel really bad but you're telling us more.'

'Sigismund, stop it,' Alex said, lifting up her beer and bringing it back down with a bang. 'We've all broken confidences, every one of us, so please, let's not suddenly be getting all moral. If we're going to sit around this table judging other people, we *should* know all the facts, otherwise we might be judging them unfairly.'

'There's no such thing as all the facts,' muttered Sigismund into his empty glass. 'There are facts we even hide from ourselves, and they're just as much facts as what Oliver told Patrick or Patrick told Eden.'

I erased Sigismund's nonsense with a wave of my hand. 'Because he had a crush on her,' I said, answering Alex's question. 'He told her I'd had sex with Claw hoping she would leave me.'

It was too late to leave anything out, and there was nothing to be gained by holding back. The confrontation might do all of us good, clear the air once and for all. And it should also help to put things in perspective, remind us all how utterly trivial everything else was compared to losing Eden and Sam.

'Was that really necessary?' Sigismund was staring at the table shaking his head. 'Did you have to spill it *all* out – every single secret Patrick trusted you with? Why?'

'Because I did sleep with Claw, and Patrick was right, Eden deserved better. I shouldn't've got away with it as lightly as I did.'

'All roads always return us to Eden for comparison,' Sigismund said, bending forward to lean on his elbows. 'And we all fall short. We're flawed and she was perfect.' Then slapping the table almost soundlessly, he fell back in his chair, his whole body attached to the wood.

'Unbelievable,' I said, and I almost threw my drink at him; so much for putting things in perspective. Then turning sharply to Alex, 'You know who else Patrick had a crush on, before he had a crush on Eden? Claw.'

'I assumed that's why they married,' Alex said. 'I assumed that when it ended with Sigismund, he must've felt something for Claw.'

'"When it ended with Sigismund, he must've felt something for Claw." Hmm... no, that's not *quite* how it happened,' I said. 'Patrick's feelings didn't switch from Sigismund to Claw; it was Claw he wanted from the start. It had *always* been Claw. It had *only* been Claw. But Claw was apparently oblivious...'

'And even though I wasn't as oblivious as Claw, I didn't take his feelings seriously and I managed to seduce him,' Sigismund said.

'You mean you managed to get him into bed,' I said. 'Because according to Patrick he wasn't *really* seduced.'

Sigismund gave a wounded look. 'No. He wasn't,' he said meekly.

'But you still didn't stop,' I said.

'After the second time, he told me that he still wanted Claw. And then I did stop.'

I raised my hands theatrically. 'Can anyone else see the irony here?'

'Yes, Ollie, we get it, I'm a hypocrite.'

Alex leaned across the table towards him. 'Is that why you left her for William, because you couldn't have Patrick?'

'I don't know... Maybe that's one of the things I've been hiding from myself. But what I do know is that I shouldn't've told her.'

Now Alex drew back. 'Told her what?' Her voice was dull and deep, her tone almost indifferent.

'About me and Patrick...' Sigismund paused to rap the table with his knuckle, once, then a second time. 'I slept with Patrick knowing Patrick wanted Claw, and then I told her.'

Watching Sigismund closely in the few frozen seconds that followed, I couldn't help wondering if his sudden flash of honesty might not have been pre-emptive - a tactical confession to something he suspected I already knew.

'That's almost unforgivable,' Alex murmured in the same impassive tone.

'It was an awful thing to do,' Sigismund acknowledged to the table. 'And all that time later when I heard she'd told Patrick about you...' His gaze fell on me softly.

I held it less gently. 'Patrick told you,' I said.

'We kept in touch for a while,' said Sigismund. 'And yes, he told me that you'd slept with Claw and Claw had told him. He also told me he'd told Eden, hoping it might give him a chance. He's always been too honest, but his flaw wasn't that. It was trying to come between you and Eden. Nothing was the same after he told me.'

'He told me too,' I said, 'and we're better friends now than before.'

'When you slept with his wife, he was in love with yours, so at least the confession was mutual,' Sigismund said. 'The only one who still doesn't know about Patrick and Eden is Claw.'

'And we should keep it that way,' I said, 'especially as there was no Patrick and Eden.'

Alex softened her voice. 'Wouldn't it be great if you and Patrick were friends again? All these things, they happened such a long time ago.'

But they *had* happened. And after hearing about all of them, was that what Alex thought was most important, whether Sigismund and Patrick could be friends again? And in any case, shouldn't it be more up to Patrick than Sigismund?

Sigismund paused to take air through his nose, and after puffing it out, 'No, I don't think so. Too much water under the bridge. Life's too short.'

Life *was* too short, as some of us ought to know better than others. But in spite of that, the trivialities had once again prevailed - and *I* was the one who had insisted on bringing them all to the forefront. Why was it suddenly so important to expose every hypocrisy and uncover every wrong? Had I gone too far, mistaking cruelty for catharsis? Had it made me feel better that Sigismund was so incapable of any other perspective than his own, or that Alex was so indifferent to his faults? Had my world revolved around my grief for too long, detaching me completely from the real world? Why did I suddenly *want* to be angry with Alex?

'Oh, come on now, Sigismund.' Alex pushed her chair back and stood up. 'I think you can do better than hide behind clichés.'

'You want me to leave?'

'No, of course I don't want you to leave.' She kissed the top of his head. 'I'm getting us another drink.'

We hadn't quite run out of permutations, and I couldn't resist.

'Was anyone else in love with Eden?' I asked Sigismund.

'Mm?' Sigismund screwed up his face. 'Anyone else like who?' And then, 'Oh. You mean was *I* in love with Eden. No, Ollie, I wasn't.'

Alex was back with the drinks. 'Gin and Tonics for everyone, we've run out of beers and there's very little wine left.'

I took out the slice of lemon from my drink and squeezed its juice into my mouth before putting it back in. 'And nothing's ever happened between you two?'

'I just told you,' Sigismund said testily. 'Eden only ever had eyes for you, you know that.'

'No, I meant you two,' I said, my eyes wandering from Sigismund to Alex and then back to Sigismund.

'It's a fair enough question,' Alex said, 'but does it really matter what the answer is? If we did go down that road, where exactly would we stop? Let's just say we all have a history and leave it at that. The past is the past, and we should all be moving on from it. Isn't that why you're here?'

'It is,' I said, even though I wasn't really sure that it was, 'but moving on from the past doesn't mean not needing to know it. You said yourself we should know all the facts, because otherwise we might be judging each other unfairly. Sometimes we can learn a lot from the past.'

Alex clasped one hand around her throat, as if to explain the sudden gruffness of her voice: 'What? That we're none of us saints? That things that happened in the past could happen again? That we should all feel under constant threat?'

Yes! Because we all really *were* under constant threat. How could she not know that? But still I wasn't sure what I was doing, or why I was doing it. I knew that if it hadn't been for Sigismund, I would not be cross-examining Alex; I would know I had no right to, and in any case I wouldn't want to. What was it about Sigismund that made him so important? And the answer was so obvious it had almost escaped me: I had seen his reflection in Alex, and that was what made him important. I was not after all refusing to move on from the past; I was resisting moving on from it to Alex.

'No,' Sigismund said, his eyes widened as he fixed them on mine. 'Nothing ever did. But it did happen with Sam a few times. And William doesn't know, so...'

'Sam.' After whispering the name at Alex, who looked back at me woodenly, 'You told me Sam was keeping his distance,' I said.

'He was, at the beginning.'

'Things just happened,' said Sigismund. 'They happened unexpectedly and they ended very quickly. Nobody got hurt.'

'Nobody got hurt and everyone lived happily ever after. Except they didn't, did they?'

'Ollie, that's unkind,' Sigismund said.

'Oh, is it? Well, at least you're still alive,' I shot back.

'Stop!' Alex again pushed her chair back and got up, then she walked to the sideboard, picked up the two photographs that had stood there since June, brought them back and set them down beside each other at the end of the table, Eden and Sam facing me and Sigismund, and also her when she returned to her seat. 'There they are,' she said, 'Eden on the left and Sam on the right. And here are the three of us, doing a great job of learning from the past. I thought we'd settled all this nonsense, I thought we'd agreed to leave Sam and Eden alone. There, with each other on the sideboard.'

'I never asked about Sam,' I said, 'it was Sigismund who told me, and I really wish he hadn't.'

'I'm not like Eden and you're not like Sam, not better, not worse, just different. And that means *we*'re different too, as a couple, which means the past is nothing to go by. Sigismund did nothing wrong, and you've no right to judge him.'

And William? What rights did *he* have? Had Alex thought of him at all before so readily absolving Sigismund of any wrongdoing? 'Nobody got hurt,' Sigismund had said, as though everyone had done William a favour by withholding the truth. How many *more* times had

Sigismund cheated? How many more lies had he told? What other, more recent transgressions had he managed to conceal by the grotesque and cynical invention of a surrogate?

What was it about Sigismund that made Alex so blind? Or had the blindness been entirely mine? "All these things, they happened such a long time ago." How easily Alex had swept them aside, "these things" that to me had seemed so enormous, and how easily she had assumed the right to offer friendship on Patrick's behalf.

And after one exoneration there had followed another: Sigismund had done nothing wrong and I had no right to judge him for the "things" that had "just happened" between him and Sam. How easily she had felt able to distance herself from a past that to some degree at least must define her, in the way my past defined me, in the way *everyone's* past was a part of who they were, to a larger or smaller extent.

'I remember how outraged you were that I'd gone to bed with Claw,' I said to Alex, 'so I don't know what any of that means - why everything's so different when it comes to you and Sigismund and Sam. Does it mean that you and Sam had an open relationship? When Claw said you shared a very open lifestyle, that's not what I imagined she meant.'

'What is it that you're trying to find out? If I had sex with other people while I was married to Sam? I did, yes, we were both free to do what we wanted.'

'And was that what you wanted? To have sex with other people?'

'Ollie, stop,' said Sigismund.

'It's not what I want now,' Alex answered.

'But it might be what you want in the future? And please don't say the future is the future.'

'Why not? That's exactly what it is.'

'And what about William? Has anyone stopped for a moment to think about him? Maybe you and Sam had an open relationship, but it's obvious that William and Sigismund haven't, so how can you say that Sigismund's done nothing wrong?'

The words had been flying in a furious back and forth, and when Alex fell forward, her arm stretched out across the table, pointing a finger at me, automatically I leaned forward too, readying myself for whatever came next. But as our gazes locked, silently she gathered up her finger and straightened in her chair. Then bending her head to one side to give a crooked nod, 'You're right,' she said distantly. 'We've all made mistakes we regret.'

'I shouldn't be here for this,' Sigismund said, but as he made to get up by leaning forward, the doorbell rang.

'Stay,' Alex said, her arm already in Sigismund's way. 'Oliver?'

A pause echoed the coldness in her voice.

'Oliver?'

When I heard my name repeated, that same gust of coldness almost came as a relief.

'Yes, stay,' I said. Avoiding eye-contact with Alex, I had fixed my gaze instead on the distance between Sigismund's neck and the back of his chair, and retrieving it to vaguely let it wander, I attempted to make it less hard. And when I spoke again, my tone was almost cordial: 'But there's something I've been meaning to ask you.' Picking up Sam's photograph, I pointed it at Sigismund. 'Don't you think we look alike?'

'I'm getting the door,' said Alex.

'Patrick thought we did,' I said.

'I don't know, I hadn't really thought about it,' said Sigismund. 'I'm not attracted to you, Ollie, if that's what you're asking.'

'It's Patrick,' Alex called out from the door. 'He's coming up.'

THIRTEEN

I am beginning to suspect that the move to Clerkenwell was a mistake. Or perhaps the mistake was leaving Highgate. Either way, my nerves ever since have been frayed, and my behaviour has become unpredictable. After embarrassing myself in front of Patrick on the day of the move, I have lost control again, this time lashing out at Sigismund, unfairly according to Alex. Instead of leaving the past to one side, I have constantly been digging into it, tearing through the uneasy equilibrium of the present to pick at the scabs of old wounds. Why? What part of my new life is causing me to slide into this self-destructive mode? Or is it possible that on the contrary an instinct for self-preservation is what's driving my thoughts and my actions? Have I or have I not seen Sigismund's reflection in Alex? Do I already have a different destination in mind?

What would Eden say if she were here?

If Eden were here, she would be horrified.

If Eden were here, we would be together somewhere else.

Eden. Whose kindness has become entwined with secrets that have led to unforgivable suspicions and then to an unhealthy obsession with Sam, which has caused me to become mistrustful of everyone else. Including Alex, whose patience is as easily regained as it is lost.

Hours have been spent around the square wooden table, with me as the accuser and one electric chair after another serving as the dock in a courtroom. People come and go, and the only surprise is that they always come back, to the same claustrophobic tableau.

Beside me at the moment is Sigismund, and on the table in front of us the photographs of Eden and Sam, Eden smiling and Sam looking stern, as though bashful in the presence of Eden for resembling me so much – and he does, however much Sigismund and Alex may pretend not to have noticed. And it may not be a deliberate pretence, I do understand that; I too, after all, am jealously possessive of Eden's uniqueness. Perhaps Patrick was right; perhaps the photographs were a mistake. The truth is that I have developed an affinity with Sam that I cannot ascribe to anything except our resemblance, while at the same time being aware it goes much deeper: I feel what I know Eden too would have felt, and feel it for precisely that reason.

Sigismund, who a few minutes earlier somehow managed to keep a straight face while railing against Claw for being a narcissist. And whose answer just now, when I asked him politely if he could see the resemblance between me and Sam, was that he doesn't find me attractive, obviously unable to conceive of any other plausible reason for my question except one that revolves around himself.

When it comes to Sigismund, why is Alex so forgiving?

When it comes to the past, why is Alex so keen to forget?

And yet Alex was right that I was wrong to judge her previous life, she was right that the future isn't always shaped by the past, and above all she was right that we have all made mistakes we regret. So why has the past been yelling at me first from the sideboard and then from the end of the table that I ignore all its warnings at my peril?

Patrick is on his way up, I can hear the lift clanging its way upwards, and Alex is waiting for him at the door. At the table, Sigismund is staring at the photographs of Eden and Sam as though they're yelling something at him too.

'Eden,' he remembers absently. Then with a jerk he shifts his gaze by a fraction and he frowns. 'You do look like Sam,' he says, speaking normally now, 'you look like him *a lot*, and I'm wondering how I could've missed it. Hmm.' And turning from Sam's photograph to me, 'Does it bother you? I suppose it must do.'

'Sometimes. If I think too much about it.'

'Then don't,' Sigismund says simply.

I think too much about everything, and not thinking too much about anything would certainly make life much easier, but would it make it better? It occurs to me that Sigismund is not a very good advertisement for his philosophy.

'Hi, Patrick, come in.'

Patrick has arrived and Alex shuts the door.

'I'm being a nuisance, I know, always turning up like this, unannounced and uninvited...'

'You seem upset. Has something happened?'

'What's happened is what should've happened years ago... Ah, but I can see you have guests...'

'Only *one* guest,' Alex says, 'but a very special one.'

Sigismund and I both stand up.

'Oh my God,' says Patrick.

'Surprise!' says Sigismund.

'Sigismund!' While still yelling out his name, Patrick throws himself at Sigismund.

'Patrick,' mutters Sigismund, while the palms of both his hands hover over Patrick's shoulders without landing.

But Patrick won't let go. 'How long has it been?' he asks Sigismund's neck.

'Too long,' Alex answers when Sigismund doesn't.

'Ollie's looking at us like he thinks the world's gone mad,' Patrick says. 'And I'm not surprised, he's heard me say the silliest awful things.' And falling back from the embrace, 'Which of course I didn't mean, but you know what Claw is like.'

'*I* do, yes,' Sigismund says.

'We all do, Sigismund,' says Alex.

'We're none of us perfect,' Patrick says musingly.

'Yes, we've already established that,' Alex agrees with a smile.

'But that's not the point,' Patrick goes on.

'Sit,' Alex orders us. 'I'll make some more drinks.'

'Nothing alcoholic for me,' Patrick says. Then returning to Sigismund, 'How's William?'

'I'm sure he's fine,' says Sigismund. 'In spite of Claw being what she's like.'

Patrick chuckles to himself. 'I did almost call you. But then the story was that you'd run off with someone else.'

Sigismund hesitates, raising both hands before bringing them together in a silent clap. 'As you say, we're none of us perfect.'

Patrick nods. 'I think none of us around this table would be casting the first stone.'

'Or any stone,' I say.

'But I *have* thrown a black stone behind me,' says Patrick. 'It's an old Greek saying, it means I'm never going back.'

'Going back where?' I ask.

'I don't like it if the stone has to be black,' says Sigismund. 'It just plays up to racist stereotypes.'

'Sigismund's right.' Alex has arrived with the drinks. A tray of Gin and Tonics and a glass of fizzy water for Patrick, all with ice and lemon.

'Forget the stone,' Patrick says. 'I've left Claw.'

It's been drizzling all day, but the rain has now become heavy, and the room has darkened with the sky. The windows are being lashed with such force that the noise is of liquid made solid as it impacts the glass; one wave after another is being driven to its target by the wind. For a few long moments the whole building seems to rattle in a fierce electric storm, as though the air has been charged with the voltage of concurrent executions in four separate electric chairs. Then a single ray of sunshine hits the table lighting up the photographs of Eden and Sam, and a fraction of a second later the rain has come to a stop and now the room is in a hush.

The silence is broken by my laughter. One stone has led to another, Patrick has left Claw, a storm has hit, and suddenly the mood has become apocalyptic. There is no escaping the past, even in my new life with Alex. All the different links to it keep coming together in ridiculous ways, locking us in its embrace, in the grip of all its terrors - even Eden and Sam seem to be laughing at us in the sudden glut of light.

'Come on, no one's died,' I say, when no one else laughs. 'What are they all thinking?' I wonder.

'I should've done it a long time ago,' Patrick goes on, picking up where he left off as though restarted by my prompt.

'And is there someone else?' Sigismund asks.

Patricks bends his head. 'Joe, from the Cutting-Edge Arts Centre.'

'Joe? But I thought he was with Babe, the Mohican girl,' I say.

'Babe thought so too,' Patrick says. 'Apparently she's very upset.'

'How old is he?' asks Sigismund.

'I've no idea,' Patrick says.

'Probably the same age as William,' I say.

'Oh dear, I think I may have given you the wrong idea,' Patrick says, raising his hand to his mouth as though to stifle a laugh. 'To be clear, I've not run off with anyone and nor has Claw, so Joe's age isn't really that important. Let's just say that he was young enough for Claw to have sex with, which doesn't mean she has the slightest inclination to adopt him – "just fun" is how she would describe it, and I'm sure Joe would agree. So, anyway, she slept with him last night, and when she told me this morning, I decided that was it, I'd had enough, I just couldn't see the point of our marriage anymore, and I packed my things and said goodbye and then I left. Two suitcases, like Ollie.' Then turning to Sigismund, 'Remember how you told her you'd slept with me? Sorry, it's a long time ago now and I'm not trying to be mean, but I honestly think that's what started all the telling. Tell, tell, tell, we've all of us done nothing but tell ever since. Well, not nothing exactly.' A moment's silence follows, then Patrick gives a melancholy sigh. 'Why *did* you tell Claw that you'd slept with me?'

Sigismund's face becomes red; in a cartoon he would also have steam coming out of his ears. 'Are you seriously asking me that now, after all these years?'

Patrick gives a nod, but then keeping his voice very calm, with perhaps just a hint of a slightly ironic smile, 'Actually no, I think I prefer not to know.'

As though on cue, once again the room has darkened and the windows are being lashed. The building rattles in the excess electricity of four more executions, and this time there is no ray of sunshine. The rain doesn't stop, but slowly it becomes less violent. Another storm has hit, and no one is laughing.

'Joe, though,' I say, just to say something.

'Joe's neither here nor there, and he certainly isn't to blame,' Patrick says. 'I saw Claw eyeing him up when we went to see They Them, but then she's always eyeing everyone up – well, everyone she finds attractive, so practically every man under forty – and the boy seemed so wrapped up in being yang to Babe and his boyfriend – separately, not together – that it never crossed my mind he'd even consider being yang to a woman twice his age. But Claw kept going back, for a Japanese magic show, for a Samuel Beckett monologue, then almost every night for an all-nude staging of *Othello*, and her yin got the better of him in the end. Babe was off sick, and after a few drinks at the bar, they went upstairs. The rest, as they say, is history forever repeating itself, and tomorrow it would've been someone else.'

'She's quite the magician herself, when she puts her mind to it,' says Sigismund. 'There aren't too many men she can't conjure out of their pants. They're not even aware that it's happening until it's too late.'

'Rings a bell,' I can't resist saying.

'Ditto,' says Patrick. 'Except I *was* aware, and my mistake was still wanting to get out of mine even after God knows how many other mugs got out of and then back into theirs.'

Hilarity again, and this time I actually find it hilarious.

Alex, on the other hand, doesn't. 'That's right,' she snarls, 'we're all witches, casting evil spells to get you all out of your pants, because you're all so irresistible, you poor, defenceless lambs. And to think that five minutes ago we were debating the colour of stones...'

Five minutes ago, I might have agreed with her. A few months ago, she might have disagreed with herself – hadn't she proclaimed in full view of Bertrand Russell that proprietary people like Claw always took what they wanted, and also somehow managed not to get all the blame?

I look again at the photograph of Eden, and the sadness I feel makes me happy. Cutting through all the talk of lost love and betrayals, through the smallness of secrets and lies and gratuitous disclosure, it reminds me of my good fortune and gives me the will to imagine tomorrow.

'I don't understand why you're defending her,' says Sigismund to Alex.

'She's not,' Patrick, says. 'She's just pointing out that the three of us are all hypocrites. And we are, she's right. I mean, who *hasn't* slept with Claw?'

'William,' I say. 'Apparently, not *everyone* has sex with her once.'

'I slept with Claw while I was married to her,' Sigismund says.

'But you also slept with me,' says Patrick.

Time for some more telling. 'With you and then with Sam while he was going out with William,' I say.

Patrick's face becomes rigid. 'Sigismund slept with Sam?'

'At least I didn't stab my friend in the back to try and go after his wife,' Sigismund grunts at the table.

'His friend who slept with his wife and didn't tell him,' I say. 'And if anyone forced Patrick out of *his* pants...'

'I see,' Sigismund says, and turning first to me and then to Alex, 'So, *you*'re defending Patrick, *you*'re defending Claw, and of course I'm the villain.' And raising his hands in the air, 'Fine, strap me in and pull the switch, I'm not going to put up any resistance.'

'You were always such a drama queen,' Patrick bends to mutter into Sigismund's ear. Then reverting to his vertical position, 'Alex is right. Claw is Claw, but she isn't a witch.'

Once more as though on cue, there is thunder in the distance and the table is suddenly flooded with sunshine.

'We've wasted too much time discussing Claw,' Alex says briskly, as though Sam hasn't even been mentioned. 'Patrick, Oliver will help you bring your suitcases up from the car. We've got plenty of space and we'd love you to stay for as long as you like.'

'All those times you and Claw used to bicker,' I say, 'I thought you were playing – all the times you were pretending to be outraged by Sigismund, or teasing her about the poisoned Narcissus. I thought the two of you were putting on a show to cheer me up.'

'We were, in a way.'

'Even Eden thought you were happy, or at least she pretended she did.'

'We *were* happy some of the time.'

'I suppose I was the poisoned Narcissus,' says Sigismund.

'No, that was William,' Patrick says, and when he catches my eye, we both smile.

'Right then,' I say. 'Let's go bring those suitcases up.'

'Oh. No. Sorry. That's so sweet of you both, but I'm driving on to Brighton tonight, to stay with friends. Well, one friend in particular.'

'One friend in particular, so there *is* someone else,' says Sigismund, but Patrick ignores him.

'And I might've found a job there as well. I'm taking next week off to decide.'

'So, where did you meet this particular friend that you're spending tonight and the whole of next week with?' Sigismund asks.

'At a Design Fair in Manchester. And yes, they're also a designer.'

'Oh, *they*!' Sigismund scoffs.

'They are, as it happens,' says Patrick.

'You kept that very quiet,' I say.

Sigismund arches his eyebrows. 'It's for real, then. You're meeting an actual they/them.'

'I'm meeting Carl, but sometimes Carl is Carol.'

'But you're only meeting Carl,' says Sigismund, not letting up.

'Tonight yes, and I'm staying with them too.'

'And where will Carol be?'

'Sigismund, stop it,' I say, while Alex stays silent.

Patrick is unfazed. 'I'm meeting Carol on Monday. I'm hoping they might offer me a job.'

'So, it's Carl at home and Carol at work,' says Sigismund. 'Which one was it in Manchester?'

'Both. But I only met Carl.'

'It's fashionable, isn't it, this whole they/them thing.'

'I wouldn't know,' answers Patrick, refusing to be rattled by Sigismund's sarcasm.

'No? Wasn't that what attracted you?'

There is no pause in which to be deafened by Alex's silence.

'No, Sigismund, I'm pretty sure it was Carl I was attracted to. And if you saw them, you'd know why.'

Breathing through his nose, Sigismund looks ready to spit out more unpleasantness; it almost seethes at the edge of his lips, but then he makes a long sucking noise, as though to hoover it up before it has a chance to gush out. And his voice is a mushy shade of hushed when he speaks:

'William's leaving me. I don't want you to go.'

FOURTEEN

It's December again, and I am on a pilgrimage. They Them, the unforgettable performance by a poet like no other, was on a Friday. This year isn't a leap year, so if I had come to Russell Square on the same date as last year, I would have come tomorrow, but tomorrow is a Saturday. The crowd is always different on a Saturday. At midday there would have been no milling army of heavy coats dancing to the clockwork choreography of drudgery and everyday routine. If I had come tomorrow, my mood would have been different too, because tomorrow is Alex's birthday and exactly three years since Sam ended his life. For these reasons I am marking the anniversary on another Friday, one day short of one full year.

Marking, not celebrating.

The elevator stops. It makes hardly any noise – freshly oiled? The metal door towards the exit slides open. A mass of heavy coats slithers through – this time not so solidly black. The colour is mostly from hats, so many of them this year.

It's as if a freezing nation has had enough of mourning.

A shuffle of feet, invisible in the congestion: from a cauldron of damp, steamy breaths, bodies are expelled like a fart. At the barriers plastic tickets touch out, flaps swinging open, then shut.

A man into his phone: *I forgot my umbrella.*

From hats and from umbrellas: tartan, paisley, lurid pink - colourful too but not open. The day is overcast but not yet wet; only damp.

Outside, the colours more intense even in the absence of sunshine, lit up by the electricity that gleams out of windows. An early Christmas tree at the foot of Brunswick Centre, flashing multicoloured lights. Over the blues and reds and yellows reflected in yesterday's puddles, the crowd becomes dispersed, disunited. "One" broken into several, each another "one".

And here I am again.

Fogbound in the mist of my breath, warming my hands with its moisture.

A smoker for a day, standing in a doorway contemplating life, ready for a final attempt.

I imagine the scene from above: defiant human dots embracing life, hunting, gathering, occasionally mating. Vaping fruity flavours, clinging on to life in clouds of steam. A recalcitrant few, poisoning ourselves with tar and nicotine. Now, later, all of us grieving, for some of us the object still unknown. The price of life is love and death.

The man into his phone: *I'm not coming back.*

Broken by the addition, either broken or unbroken by another subtraction – one equals nothing or one. The end or a beginning.

The future now unknown,

I am done with doing sums.

I caress the old Dunhill between forefinger and thumb as I extract it from my left trouser pocket. I flick it open. A strong reek of petrol, reminiscent of the past; a flame feeble and blue.

I light a cigarette.

Standing alone in a doorway,

A smoker again for one day.

I take my phone out to look at the time. One more puff, then I stub my cigarette out on the pavement. I pick up the butt off the kerb and throw it in the nearest bin. When I arrive at the *Moonlight Café* in Marchmont Street,

Claw is sitting at the same corner table at the back. She waves at me without standing up. I wave back.

At the table I bend down to kiss her. I kiss her cheek; she kisses the air - loudly: Mm-wah!

'And the other,' she says, turning her face. She wears little make-up, just a touch of mascara, copper-green eyeshadow, and light purple lipstick; all very subtle.

I bend down again to kiss her other cheek; she kisses the air - loudly: Mm-wah!

Her smell is no longer familiar.

'You've been smoking again, I thought you'd given up,' she says.

'I'm smoking today. No more from tomorrow.'

'Make sure you don't, it's a filthy habit and it doesn't kill you quickly,' says Claw. And with that out of the way, 'Well, here we are again. What a year!'

'A long one,' I say.

'They're all as long as each other, Ollie, and none of them are long enough. Time passes far too quickly.'

The *Moonlight Café* also has a Christmas tree this year, a skeletal pine sparsely decorated with antique-looking baubles and red lights shaped like lanterns – a tasteful concession to the festive season that goes almost unnoticed. The clientele looks bookish, too snobbish to ever admit they might share even a smidgeon of my penchant for tinsel. At Christmas time there's no place for tastefulness and minimalist nonsense, as far I'm concerned. 'Kitsch *is* baby Jesus,' as Eden used to say.

'Not quickly enough,' I say to Claw, after asking the waiter for a double espresso.

'We're not here to be miserable, are we? I've left them short-handed at the practice to take the day off just for you.' And putting down her cup to look at me frowningly,

'You said it's been a year since They Them, is that why we're here?'

'I'm not sure why we're here, to be honest.'

'But it's not because you're having second thoughts.'

'No, Claw, it's not.'

'Thank God for that! I know I'm not exactly impartial, but Alex wasn't right for you.'

'She wasn't. But she did save my life.'

Claw lifts a finger to her mouth. 'I'd say we *all* saved your life, even Sigismund.' I bend my head to say I know what she means. 'But not because we stopped you from taking all those pills,' she goes on, 'which would've either made you sick or sent you to sleep and given you the mother of all migraines the day after, and a migraine from hell the day after that, when you woke up in some godforsaken psychiatric ward strapped to your bed.'

'Sam somehow managed.'

'Because Sam knew what to take. Nothing I prescribed him could've killed him.'

'But mixing it with all that other stuff...'

'All that other stuff, exactly – *that's* what killed him. But it's no wonder I got all the blame, with all the garbage Sigismund was feeding Alex. Serves me right for trying to be civil even after everything he did. I hate to say it, but Patrick was right, I *should've* hung up on him.'

'Alex said you made a pass at him, the day you met him for the tickets.'

Claw roars with laughter. 'Is that what he told her, that *I* made a pass at *him*? I literally had to push him off that day, he couldn't keep his hands to himself. And I know he didn't *really* want sex, why would anyone want sex with me if they were gay and they had William, who I *was* a bit flirtatious with, I admit. No, what he wanted was revenge – Patrick chose me over him, *in spite* of being gay, or *almost* gay, or whatever he's decided he is; in fact he never wanted Sigismund at all.'

'Yes, Patrick told me.'

'Well, he told me too, the night he took me out to propose. When I told him I knew he'd slept with Sigismund, because Sigismund had already told me, that's when I first heard that he'd always wanted me, not Sigismund, and that Sigismund had practically forced him into bed, not just once but twice. And Sigismund being Sigismund even after all of *that*, all these years later and with William on the verge of leaving him, he tried it on with me while I was married to Patrick, to prove he was as good as Patrick *and* to get his own back. Well, it didn't work.'

The telling has so stop, so I keep my mouth shut.

'One double espresso,' says the waiter with a faint Italian accent.

'Thank you, Giulio.'

'Pleasure is all mine, Signora Claw.'

'Did he just wink at you?' I ask after he's gone.

'He might have. Why, are you shocked?'

I shrug. 'I was going to say he seems a bit young, but then Joe's even younger.'

'I have the run of the house now.'

'So?'

'It means I can accommodate. Older men's lives are so dull they think paying for a hotel room is the ultimate in decadence - for a lot of them it's actually part of the turn-on. Whereas young men like Giulio have very little money and live in tiny flats with ten other people – in other words they couldn't afford a hotel room and their own place is out of the question. As was mine, while Patrick was coming and going.'

'You had boundaries.'

'We did, and I respected them.'

'Not always,' I say.

'Well, you were hardly a stranger.'

'But you still told Patrick. And then you told me he must never find out.'

Claw gives a sigh. 'Because you two were friends, and I didn't want you feeling self-conscious. And before you say it, yes, Ollie, I know that what happened between us was wrong, I know it should never have happened.' She gives another sigh. 'I do miss Patrick terribly, you know. And the sex was brilliant, so he can't've been *completely* gay. I mean, to marry one gay man was bad enough, but *two*?' With a blink she cuts her reverie short. 'Now, please, can we leave the past alone and talk about today and why we're here? Is there something on at the Centre that you'd like us to watch? Or are we exorcising ghosts?'

'I just thought we'd have a drink there before lunch. I've spoken with Joe, and Babe won't be around until this evening.'

'Oh good, so Joe will be joining us,' says Claw, caressing her cup with her lips. Then she goes through her bag for her purse and takes out ten pounds. 'I always leave a generous tip,' she leans forward to whisper, 'but not *too* generous, or the whole thing becomes too transactional.'

'You're talking about money,' I say.

'No, I'm talking about etiquette,' says Claw.

Claw was a conundrum. I liked her, in fact I liked her very much, but I wouldn't trust her as far as I could throw her. She was not the just accuser she pretended to be. She never forgot and only rarely forgave, which made her vindictive. A master of innuendo, she preferred to imply things than to say them, and was excellent at giving the impression that the worst parts had perhaps been left unsaid. But she *had* been a good friend to Eden, and more recently a good friend to me too.

Since our reunion on the night after They Them, my opinion of Sigismund had taken a nosedive. I still couldn't be sure if it was Sigismund who had enlisted Alex or the other way around – most probably they had enlisted each other – but whoever had done the enlisting, involving me in their vendetta against Claw by attempting to manipulate my grief had shown unforgivable selfishness at best and at worst a ruthlessness that bordered on evil. After my illness, Alex had at least conceded that Claw was not the monster she had first imagined her to be, whereas Sigismund had doggedly insisted right up until the end that Claw *was* a monster who habitually poisoned her patients with reckless prescribing. If anyone was a monster it was Sigismund – a sordid user of people and a two-faced, back-stabbing hypocrite with a chip on his shoulder so huge that it would crush whoever slighted him or got in his way. I was glad that William too must have seen what I had seen, and hadn't wasted too much time before making his escape. It didn't much matter whether Claw was being fair or unfair about Sigismund, because I had drawn my own conclusions.

The worst about Patrick had come from Patrick himself, but in spite of it I liked him – in fact I liked him more. Since our heart-to-heart in the SAAB, when it all came out and Patrick had invited me to hate him, our friendship had grown exponentially. My confession had led to Patrick unburdening himself of his, and by making peace with each other we had finally made peace with ourselves. This in turn had spurred Patrick into action in his marriage to Claw, giving him the courage to end it. And courage had been needed, because in her relationships with men I had no doubt that Claw was a bully. I liked her, but there were many things about her I disliked.

I suspected that Sigismund had given as good as he had got, and in that sense his marriage to Claw had been equal. In different ways, Sigismund and Claw had both mistreated Patrick, and also in different ways they had both supported Eden to the end, even if in Sigismund's case he had done so behind my back. No, that was unfair. The secret had been kept from me by Eden, not by Sigismund, and its primary purpose had been to protect me, shielding me from her anxiety about my future, although I could see now why Eden might have also needed an occasional escape from my suffocating love, made more stifling and oppressive by its urgency. What would Eden think of Sigismund now? The question was easy to answer, but for that reason begged another, and then another and another after that: How could we both have misjudged him so badly? Had he perhaps become a different Sigismund than he had been in the years when our friendship with him had been closest? Was he not the same Sigismund who, to Eden's full knowledge, had so shamelessly preyed on poor Patrick? A circle of seemingly unanswerable questions that I would not allow to haunt me, certain that the unfathomable nature and depth of Eden's kindness could have easily answered them all: my mistake was to have answered the original question on Eden's behalf.

However different he might or might not have become since even before he had left her, in Sigismund Claw had met her match. There had been no such equality between her and Patrick. Their playful repartees, which I had misinterpreted as love, had been a shallow surface, and beneath the happy polish of that fragile veneer there had lurked an abyss of abuse – snubs, insults, compulsive unfaithfulness, and most perverse of all the never-ending cruelties of gratuitous disclosure. How easy it was to hide behind the truth and use honesty as a weapon. How easy and at the same time how transparent: more than anyone else, whether consciously or unconsciously Claw had been harming herself.

With William lost, no sooner had Patrick packed his suitcases and driven to St Cross Street on his way to a new life in Brighton than Sigismund's claws were tearing at him.

'William's leaving me. I don't want you to go.'

The order of words had been revealing. (Something's happening to) Me. I (don't want something). You (should do what I want). Patrick would have fared no better with Sigismund, and might well have fared far worse. The transparency in Sigismund's case went the other way. No, it would be too generous to say that he cared more about himself than about anyone else: he *only* cared about himself.

'I'm going.'

I was glad to have witnessed that split-second moment when Patrick might have been flattered, mistaking egocentrism for love. Patrick had not been misled, neither flattered nor fooled. He had answered immediately, and that was the moment when I finally lost all my fear.

'Can you wait fifteen minutes?' I asked him.

'I'm not changing my mind.'

'Nor am I, but I need fifteen minutes to pack.'

'Sure,' Patrick said.

'Are you going somewhere?' Alex asked flatly.

'I'm going with Patrick.'

'To Brighton?'

'For a couple of nights, while I try and figure out where I'm going after that.'

No one asked any more questions. I stood up from the table and picked up the photograph of Eden as I made my way through to the bedroom. I changed out of Sam's clothes and into something of my own, packed the one empty suitcase with the few possessions I had bothered to unpack, returned the photograph to its place with all the others in the suitcase I had barely touched since moving to St Cross Street from Highgate, and in less than fifteen minutes I was back. I had not expected Alex to interrupt me, and she hadn't. I was grateful for that. Grateful that I hadn't been delayed, and more grateful still that Alex had known better than to ask for explanations, because like me she must have known that there were none: sometimes the end could be as abrupt as the beginning.

When my suitcases were at the door and Patrick had already called the lift, my eyes fell on the photograph of Sam, and I heard myself ask if I could take it. 'For Eden,' I said. And Alex answered that I could.

'I'm glad you're coming with me,' Patrick said in the car. 'I'd like you to meet Carl.'

'I'd like that too, if Carl doesn't mind.'

'You're my best friend, and they've already met William who isn't, so why would they mind?'

'William?'

'We've kept in touch. I like him.'

'I like him too,' I said.

'And he isn't just leaving, he's practically already left. But it seemed kinder to pretend not to know.'

'Mhm,' I said, nodding to myself. Then leaning forward gently so my seatbelt wouldn't lock, 'I also like Claw, even though I know she's horrible.'

Patrick laughed. 'You're *her* best friend as well, so that's good.' He turned to look at me briefly. 'I *thought* I liked Alex, but then I decided I didn't.' Then returning to the road, 'As for Sigismund, I'm honestly not sure why I threw myself at him like that, but I knew within a couple of minutes that he hadn't really changed and I wasn't very happy to see him. Oh, and for the record, I've never disliked Claw. It was myself I was beginning to dislike. Does that make sense?'

We were still passing a lorry when I answered that it did. Eventually it would make even more sense, more sense than either of us could have imagined at that hair-raising moment on the M23.

Eden and I had been putting money aside for a place of our own, maybe starting a family too, and I would spend it while deciding what to do with the rest of my life. After another minor episode in August, my anaemia had turned out to be chronic – and that was the closest to a diagnosis I would get. I was responding well to treatment, which had not yet had to include blood transfusions. But the threat of serious illness had made the details of the rest of my life seem more urgent. Today I had moved out of St Cross Street. Had Alex and I ever amounted to more than two strangers brought together by a cigarette and grieving? Had we ever *really* been together? Whether we had or we had not, we were not together now, and would not be together in the future. Tomorrow I would give up my job, and tomorrow I would also find out that Highgate was still empty, or half full with all the things I had been forced to leave behind. There had been just one short-term tenant, a Korean actor in London for three months, and she had left the place virtually untouched, still cluttered with anonymous paintings and 1960s pieces of junk. When we spoke on the phone, the landlord said he was delighted I was moving back in. And after spending longer than a couple of days by the sea - one night in a hotel and then almost two weeks with Patrick and Carl and occasionally Carol, including a weekend with William and flapjacks - I was back in my bed, basking in the special orange gleam of the shaded bedside lamp, looking up at Sam and Eden's photographs while intentionally failing to imagine all the promises and threats of a future I was glad was unknown.

And Alex? She was no more a monster than Claw was. Although like everyone else she had flaws - how could she have learned so little from a past in which she had allowed Sam to fall into Sigismund's clutches? - there was a great deal I would always feel grateful to her for, not least for my decision that I wanted to live. But the end had not come as suddenly as I had thought at the time. My feelings had been drifting, waning, fading for some time, probably since even before I moved in, but by increments so small that they had seemed to me incapable of ever adding up to a subtraction – until that fateful afternoon when they had snowballed, culminating in the moment when they actually added up to just that, the moment I asked Patrick to wait for fifteen minutes. The end had not after all been as abrupt as the beginning.

It was the cleanest break. No need for explanations, no blame, no regrets. *'No words. None of that indie shit,'* as Eden used to call out to the DJ every time we went to a rave.

FIFTEEN

The sun appears to be lower in winter, in a hurry as it traverses the sky without giving off any heat. It's a matter of perspective, and there is nothing more real or more true than perspective. Everything is as it appears, not as science claims it to be. If it feels as though the sun is less hot, then it follows that the sun must be less hot. The earth, or where on it one happens to be, seems as irrelevant as which heavenly body revolves at what speed around which: in *our* universe, everything revolves around us. We even turn the clocks back and forth, deciding if the mornings should be lighter or that daylight should last long into the night. This collective self-centredness inclines each one of us to imagine that our own rightful place is not only at the centre of our own lives but of *everything*. And while we *make* the world go around with our ambition, we *break* it with our warped sense of our own self-importance.

Not all of us fall prey to this delusion. I feel myself blessed by the smallness of my ambition, and the corresponding smallness of the world – the tiny microcosm - I aspire to belong to.

In December the night begins at four in the afternoon, and at just after two I can still make out the sun, majestic in its vastness even as its glow barely penetrates the thin patch of cloud that travels in front of it towards the east but at a much faster speed – unless that too is an illusion.

'You're chuckling to yourself,' says Claw.

'Mhm. I was just thinking…'

'You were looking at the sky.'

'I was thinking how stupid we are. And before that, I was thinking how horrible *you* are.'

We have left the *Moonlight Café* and are stretching our legs in Russell Square before making our way to the Cutting-Edge Arts Centre. The bitter cold has not put people off. Some walk along the paths in small groups, others sit on benches with steaming take-away hot drinks, chatting loudly with visible breaths that appear to be hotter than their coffees and teas, the smokers almost always alone, standing with an arm around their waist while the other is bent at the elbow, holding cigarettes aloft with extended fingers, a few taking only the occasional puff, as though more enslaved to the ritual than in need of nicotine. They are perhaps already considering the leap to flavoured steam.

'My, we're not mincing our words today, are we?'

'But I like you.'

'Why?'

Claw's pace is steady and brisk – underneath her heavy coat, dark grey with broad maroon checks, she's wearing a fisherman's turtleneck jumper, a baggy denim skirt, and a gorgeous pair of retro ankle boots. It's as if she's dressed down for a day in the country but hasn't quite managed not to be smart. I had mentioned coffee, a visit to the Centre and then lunch – which she has obviously assumed will not be somewhere fancy. Normally she would have relished an excuse for dressing up, and for my sake must have made an effort not to. That is one of her redeeming qualities, in fact. That she can sense when an effort is needed.

'Because you're not really horrible. I think being mean to other people is your way of being mean to yourself.'

'Huh. I'm almost flattered that you think I'm so complex.'

It strikes me how green everything is. Some trees have shed their leaves but many haven't, and there are so many bushes – there used to be more, a whole jungle of them, but Camden Council had most of them cut down in the noughties, railing and gating the square to stop men using it at night for sex. I grew up in the estates north of Euston, and often used to come here after school, and although I remember the greater abundance, the relative sparseness has not made the greenness less vivid. And in winter the rain and the cold seem to bring darker colours to life, making them brighter, somehow luminescent even when the sky is overcast. Or perhaps my good mood is playing tricks on me.

'You're chuckling again. Dare I ask what you were thinking about this time?'

'I was thinking how all this green seems much greener in winter.' I take Claw by the arm and I bring us to a standstill at the edge of the pathway. 'This is nice,' I say, 'walking like this, together. We've never done it before, and we've known each other years.'

'I used to walk with Eden in Hampstead. We'd get lost in the Heath, but then we'd always find our way and have tea in Kenwood House.'

'I never knew.'

'No. That was *ours*.'

I nod, and we start walking again.

'Hmm, I wonder,' says Claw. 'Maybe I'm horrible but you can't help liking me, so you try and find excuses for me.'

I laugh. 'That's possible too, I suppose.'

Now it's Claw who brings us to a standstill. 'I've always made light of all the sex, pretending to myself it means nothing. And I've been doing it for so long that I'm not sure I would know how to stop.' She hesitates, her face suddenly ancient with lines. 'I hate myself for how I treated Patrick. I never really thought I deserved him, so maybe you're right

– I was trying to make him leave even though I didn't want him to.'

A man into his phone: *I'm coming home now.*

'You should never have been with him in the first place, with either of them. Patrick has a crush on you, has sex with Sigismund instead even though he still wants you, then after telling you about the sex with Patrick, Sigismund runs off with someone else and you end up marrying Patrick after all. It's like you've all been playing a game.'

'And what's this? Is today not a game?'

The man into his phone: *I am, I'm coming come now.*

'Well, if it is, at least it's an enjoyable one.' It is, almost idyllic, and the perfect setting for sharing with Claw the one piece of the game that the men have conspired to keep secret.

Should I or shouldn't I…

I think I should.

One last piece of telling.

'Then Patrick falls in love with Eden, and so he tells her I've slept with you hoping she'll leave me, but fortunately I've told her already.'

'Leave you? She adored you.'

'Claw, did you hear what I just said?'

'You thought I didn't know, but Eden and I told each other *everything*. It was before you and I happened – in fact, I've often wondered if that was why you and I happened - and at the time it was just a suspicion, which Eden and I both laughed off as something silly that would fizzle out and die. Eden blamed me, of course, and she was right. "If you're not careful, you'll lose him," she said. "And Patrick's too precious to lose." She made me swear not to embarrass him by letting him know we'd discussed it, and I did, I gave her my word that I wouldn't. I gave her my word and I kept it, even after he'd spoken to Eden, which was after...' Her voice falters, but when she looks at me, she tries to smile. 'She could never take me seriously, you know. Always tried her best to find excuses for me, just like you - I must be either very bad or very sad for everyone I love to keep having to do that...' She gives one of her laughs but cuts it short. 'We lost her, Ollie. Compared to that, all this nonsense seems so hideously trivial.' Claw's voice has lost its strength, and her gaze falls away. But she recovers it quickly, and aims it at me gently. 'Now come on, Joe must be wondering where we are. And I do see what you mean about the greenness of the green.'

We walk around the park one last time and take the north-east exit. We walk at a more leisurely pace, and Claw becomes unusually quiet. I would have imagined her becoming defensive, but she's surprised me, not just acquiescing in my theories but reinforcing them. If there is a grain of truth in my extenuating theory, then perhaps she is mulling over the question that goes back to the root cause: why would she want to be mean to herself?

She lets out a long sigh and then she speaks. 'I say it's all nonsense but we both know it isn't. I've said it before - what happened between us should never have happened, and I know it was my fault. But as if that wasn't bad enough - and let's not be skirting around, we've been doing it for too long – the next thing I did wasn't just bad, it was *hateful*. I told Patrick, knowing full well by that stage that he did have a huge crush on Eden, so even if you hadn't told her, at the back of my mind I must've known Patrick would...'

'And that's probably the reason you told him.'

'But, Ollie, don't you think that makes me not just worse but a thousand times worse...'

I knock my side against hers to interrupt her. 'No, Claw, it doesn't.' Then I reach with my hand across her other shoulder and give it a shake. '*Think* about it.'

'I should've thought about it then – all of it. But I swear I didn't know she'd found a lump.'

'I know. She wanted to be sure before she worried you.'

'And when she had the diagnosis and she told me, in the same breath she also told me about Patrick – that sheepishly he'd told her I'd confessed to him that you and I'd had sex, that she'd answered it was true, but then had somehow found a way, like only Eden could, to shrug the whole thing off very gently. I was too shaken and shocked to be furious, with Patrick or with myself, which was probably the intention. All I could think of was that Eden had cancer.'

'You and I had sex, then I had sex with Eden after telling her, and that same day was when she showed me the lump.'

'That same day…' Claw repeats the words slowly, her voice again fading as her gaze falls to the ground.

'But I don't think Patrick knows that when he spoke to her, Eden already knew she was probably sick. And there's no good reason he should ever find out, I think you'd agree there's been far too much telling already.'

Giving out a heavy breath, Claw leans her head against my shoulder. 'Eden's kindness… I think it's rubbed off on you. Well, some of it anyway.' She tries to laugh, but her laughter is lost in the effort of holding back tears.

'Did Eden make you promise not to tell me all the details about Sigismund and Patrick?' And pulling her closer without waiting for an answer, 'Maybe some of it's rubbed off on all of us,' I say.

I keep my arm around her as we walk the last few yards to what used to be *The Slaughterhouse Inn.*

I am fully expecting Joe to be awkward, possibly even hostile. After being lured into bed by the expert machinations of a woman twice his age, he must harbour *some* degree of regret, surely. And in the young, the leap from regret to resentment is a short one: blame is a form of retrospective self-defence. He was friendly enough on the phone, even when I said I was coming with Claw, but putting on an act on the phone isn't hard, and is not a reliable gauge of how he might react when he comes face to face with his seductress.

He is lying in wait at the entrance, still short-haired but not so preppy, his bulges ever-bulging while he beams his winning smile.

'Hey, have a look who it isn't if it isn't who it is!' He gives me a hug, then pulls back. 'Not just any old not anyone – *the* not anyone, returning to the scene of his crime.' Now he turns to Claw, eyeing her up like an eagle. 'And look who he's brought with him, the gorgeous main woman herself!' A tighter hug and then two kisses. Then to me, 'You said on the phone it's been a year since They Them, so I assumed the visit was supposed to be romantic, to see where it all started kind of thing. But Dog told me last night that you and Alex aren't together anymore.'

'That's right, we're not,' I say. 'And this is not supposed to be romantic.'

'That's good,' says Joe, 'because apparently she's seeing someone else.'

'That doesn't surprise me,' says Claw.

'We're not here to talk about Alex,' I say. 'Now can we please go through and get this over with?'

We follow Joe from the brightly lit entrance through

the same red velvet curtain to the bar. A dingy darkness falls on us suddenly, and as the eyes adjust, the room fills up with dissipated grey. A few inadequate spotlights make fuzzy circles on the floor, while others climb the bar and smash against the glint of coloured glass.

I do not suggest we stop for a drink.

There are very few people around, and in the absence of noise and a crowd the whole place feels dismal. As we walk past the small empty stage on our way upstairs, the memory of They Them does not come alive. Even though I still remember vividly every moment of that Friday afternoon a year ago, while retracing my steps I do not in any meaningful sense feel like I've been here before. Instead, it's as if I'm on a guided tour of the reconstructed pages of a novel I had once been enthralled by, discovering with every step how totally it has failed to be recaptured. And I realise that this was precisely the purpose of this artificial visit: to *not* feel anything at all.

'This is where our table was,' says Claw. 'Ah, happy days.'

'Yes,' I say, because some of them were: happiness is both as real and as deceptive as the heat from the sun.

'So, where's the husband today?' Joe asks Claw.

While we scale the floral oranges and yellows of the carpeted staircase, I can't bear to look at any of the photographs. More recent ones may have replaced some of the older ones, and in one there may be a table by the stage.

'Gone for good, I'm afraid,' Claw answers cheerfully. 'Shacked up with a Carl and working for a Carol, except they're actually one and the same.'

'For real?' The surprise has stopped Joe in his tracks, with one foot on the landing and the other on the stairs.

'Yes, Joe, for real,' says Claw. 'An original and genuine

they/them, not the travesty of Alex with that dummy.'

'That's tough, no?'

'It should've happened long ago,' Claw says distantly. 'Patrick can't help being who he is, and I can't help not being a saint, as you both know.'

Joe grins smugly. 'That's why you're so fit for your age. Not being a saint keeps you young.'

When he opens the third door to the left without knocking, I breathe heavily as I take it all in: the blue divan is still in its corner, clutter and props still litter the floor, the large dressing table and its mirror with a halo of lightbulbs are in their place against the wall, but the Art Deco armchair is gone. The room feels more and at the same time less real than it felt the first time I was here. More real because without Alex it is just a room, nothing else, and therefore I am able to observe its every detail undistracted. Less real because this time I can't even imagine why last time I had thought it so unreal, which makes it little more than a fleeting impression – a dead page from a novel I have never read before.

'The divan is still there,' Claw says, casting Joe a meaningful glance.

'You *both* look really good for your age,' he answers speculatively.

'Right, I think I've seen enough,' I say. And to Claw, 'We can skip lunch if you like, leave it for another day.'

Claw is already spreading out on the divan. 'Are you sure? It's your day, if you want me, I'm all yours.'

Joe gives a little cackle. 'Why not make it *everyone's* day?' His glazed-over gaze is insistent, darting back and forth between me and Claw. 'I've got poppers,' he remembers.

'Sorry, but that's not the kind of day I had in mind,' I say. 'But you two go ahead and have fun, I'll find my own way back downstairs.'

'Are you sure?' Joe and Claw ask together.

I smile to say I'm sure. And the moment I step out of the room, I am glad to be alone. My smile is already less forced as I rush down the stairs, becomes a grin as I march through the empty auditorium past the bar, and culminates in laughter the moment I spill out into the street.

A man into his phone: *Maybe tomorrow.*

Today, tomorrow, Eden's presence will always be everywhere, filling every absence. But I no longer feel incomplete. I no longer crave for the end.

I feel happy. The day, all whose different parts must have lasted so long that already it has begun to get dark, has not been unsuccessful after all. The lights on the Brunswick Centre Christmas tree still flash on and off, shedding off magnificent colours that electrify the street. Trailed by artificial shadows, people loll, dawdle, mill about, a few hurrying into and out of the station in a race to escape the approaching rush hour. As I zigzag my way through them, I feel at one with the collective movements of their dance, even as the freezing cold sharpens under my skin.

'Ollie, wait!'

I stop and turn around, just in time for Claw to fall into my arms. She holds me tightly, and I hold her tightly too.

'Thank you,' she whispers. 'If it hadn't been for you…' And as our bodies separate, 'I just wanted you to know I'm doing my best.' When I smile, she smiles too. 'But you're with Eden now,' she says.

'Yes,' I say.

She blows me a kiss as she walks off, *not* in the direction of the Cutting-Edge Arts Centre.

Picking up my step as I turn into Lambs Conduit Street, any hint of more recent nostalgia washes over me completely. I walk alone in the way I have always walked alone - deaf to all its sounds, I soak up the lights of the city as fanatically as ever. Brighter as night-time begins to kick in, all the same their phantasmagoria this evening is more muted than the Jackson Pollock incoherence of last year's irregular heartbeat. I am happy *and* calm, but there is one thing I still can't resist: I will have a ritual cigarette in Red Lion Square Gardens, the pocket of green I had hidden in with Alex, on the bench we had shared near the bust of Bertrand Russell. And there my pilgrimage will end, after waving goodbye to the man who I hope will allow me to linger alone in the gardens after dusk, for the time it takes to smoke one final cigarette.

Without Alex.

Without ghosts.

Without promises or pleas for forgiveness.

No longer counting days or working out equations and calculating sums.

Leaving poetry behind.

After a long day of remembering, tonight I will go to bed late. Looking up at Sam and Eden's photographs before switching off the dim orange light of the bedside lamp, I will wish them both goodnight.

That was the only question Patrick had asked me – why? Why, at the last minute, had I decided that I wanted Sam's photograph too? 'I know you said you wanted it for Eden, but was that really true?'

I had answered that it was, and Patrick had taken his eyes off the road for a moment to give me a smile.

But tonight, while lying in the dark fully awake, I will realise I had wanted it not only for Eden but also for Sam.

For Eden and Sam.

In the unknown of the future, this way neither of them will ever be alone.

By the same author

The Dead of August

"A sophisticated, comic novel that brilliantly captures the triumph and folly of art, media, and publishing."
***Kirkus Reviews* (starred review)**

Named to *Kirkus Reviews'* Best Books of 2015

Bowl of Fruit (1907)

"BOWL OF FRUIT (1907) is an incredible read, with well-crafted characters and a plot that is refreshingly original."
***IndieReader* (5-star review)**

POLK, HARPER & WHO

"As with other Cacoyannis novels, the language, the cleverness, the juxtaposition of heartbreak and humor and the presence of truly hilariously drawn characters is at least half the pleasure of reading the book."
Casey Dorman - Lost Coast Review

The Madness of Grief

"A well- written, richly complicated, and deeply engaging coming-of-age tale."
***Kirkus Reviews* (starred review)**

"A rollicking good read in which profound truths about the human psyche, about memory and betrayal, about love and forgiveness, emerge with such finesse that the reader is carried along hardly aware of the complexity and depth of the novel."
Publishers Weekly's BookLife Prize 2021 - Quarter Finalist

Named to *Kirkus Reviews'* Best Books of 2018

Finger of an Angel

"An erudite, richly layered, and unsettling psychological tale."
Kirkus Reviews

"introspective, bleak, and quite often beautiful... a real pleasure to read"
Publishers Weekly's BookLife Prize 2022

The Coldness of Objects

"For the author, love is the antidote to a complicit society rendered indifferent to authoritarian rule... Cacoyannis has written a thoroughly gripping novel, using the rhetoric of a real-life pandemic to fashion a chilling vision of an abnormal 'new-normal' to come... intriguing, timely, and terrifying"
Kirkus Reviews (starred review)

"a small jewel, filled with exquisite language, intimate human characters and poignant drama... deep, beautiful and unforgettable"
Casey Dorman - Lost Coast Review

"a chilling perspective on authoritarian rule, surveillance society, and life without civil liberties... striking in its timely focus on the fissures that can lead to societal collapse and on the frightening normalization of the inhumane"
Publishers Weekly's BookLife Prize 2022

Named to *Kirkus Reviews'* Best Books of 2021

REIMAGINING BEN

"In this lightly absurdist comedy, fraternal twin brothers find their lives upended by a narcissistic writer and exacerbated by their unresolved rivalry... A humorous and entertaining character study of two brothers besieged by the preposterous."
Kirkus Reviews

"reminiscent of the work of Samuel Beckett, with a sprinkling of Seinfeld... disorienting... frenetic... unsettling... dizzying... unique in its sensibility and in the highly unusual events and interactions explored"
Publishers Weekly's The BookLife Prize 2023

Printed in Great Britain
by Amazon